STUART FIELD

BLIND SPOT

A NOVEL OF SCIENTIFIC ESPIONAGE

A DANGEROUS TECHNOLOGICAL
ADVANCE THAT COULD BE FRIGHTENINGLY CLOSE

Outskirts Press, Inc.
Denver, Colorado

Blind Spot
A novel of Scientific Espionage - A dangerous technological advance that could be frighteningly close
All Rights Reserved
Copyright © 2007 Stuart Held
V 1.0

Cover Image © 2007 JupiterImages Corporation
All Rights Reserved. Used With Permission.

Outskirts Press
http://www.outskirtspress.com

ISBN-10: 1-4327-0008-1
ISBN-13: 978-1-4327-0008-9

Library of Congress Control Number: 2006936951

Outskirts Press and the "OP" logo are trademarks belonging to Outskirts Press, Inc.

Printed in the United States of America

DEDICATION

After writing my first book, BEHIND THE YELLOW FILTER, I wavered in my resolve to write a sequel or even continue to write. My family, in particular my wife, Nina, never wavered nor told me anything but to continue writing. My children said, I owed it to them and the grandchildren. "They have to know who their grandfather was, and this is the best memory they will have of you."

I dedicate BLIND SPOT to my wife, Nina, children – Marc, Rebecca and Andrew - and my grandchildren
Hunter, Victoria, Madison and Samantha.

Thank you to my pre-publishing readers:

Muriel Antokal, Anthony Capetola, Lynn Hansen,
John Softness, Chris & Michael Swirnoff and James Vena

A NOTE OF THANKS

Jack Klein is probably the only person I know who can edit something I have written and still keep the story in my voice. Jack is a friend of many years, an Old Asia Hand, who is now retired. I thank him for editing BLIND SPOT.

PREFACE

The decade of the 1960's was the most joyous and heart wrenching the author can remember. It was the Beat Generation. It was Camelot. It was the first landing on the moon.

It was also a time of civil rights unrest, of the Viet Nam War, the Berlin Wall and the Bay of Pigs. It was a decade of assassinations, John F. Kennedy, Robert Kennedy, Martin Luther King, Jr. and Malcolm X.

One of the most exciting events of the 1960's was the space race. Russia and the United States worked feverishly to be the first to orbit the earth. Russian cosmonaut Iurii Gagarin accomplished the feat April 13, 1961. Alan B. Shepard, Jr., one of the original Mercury astronauts, made it into space 22 days later on May 5, 1961. President Kennedy in a speech to congress May 25, 1961 predicted, "We will land on the moon at the end of the decade." We did exactly that May 25, 1969, though Kennedy never lived to see it happen.

The space race brought many advances in consumer and military products. Velcro, measuring devices and pointers, just to name a few. Major advances at the time occurred in the field of LASERS – Light Amplification Stimulated by Emission of Radiation. The military has used this technology in the development of weapon targeting systems.

In this book the writer develops a Personal Tactical High Energy Laser – PTHEL – which blinds the enemy. It is a weapon that we believe does not now exist. We are certain however, that it has been researched. Laser weapons the size of a large military vehicle have been developed. But, no such weapon has been developed that is lightweight or accurate enough for use by one or two men that we are aware of.

Three communist world powers – USSR, East Germany and China – become interested in developing a PTHEL weapon. They form a company called REC, Ltd. to pool their resources to make the building of the weapon possible. Robert Schein, a CIA agent working under the cover of a photographic distributor – TAG Photographic Inc. gets involved in trying to thwart the venture. He also becomes personally involved because of a kidnapping of a close friend, a scientist forced to work on the weapon. This is an action packed story of a technological advance that could be frighteningly close.

The author is a 40-year veteran of the photographic wholesale distribution industry and has worked on a number of military projects. He has also traveled extensively in the countries Schein visits.

This book is a work of fiction. Most names, characters, and incidents, except for certain incidental references and photographic products, are of the author's imagination and do not refer to or portray any actual person.

TABLE OF CONTENTS

CHAPTER 1
ABDUCTION

It was a clear, cold wintry day in February with the feeling that winter was here to stay forever. Fortunately there was no snow today and the day started out for Howard Lovering as it did every day in Bedford, Massachusetts. Lovering was an exacting person who always had everything in its place and in its order.

Dr. Howard Lovering was the chief physicist at the David W. Mann Company. Mann manufactured highly secret photographic equipment for the blossoming electronic industry.

In the late 1950's early 1960's microminiaturized integrated circuits was just beginning to come into their own. The first Texas Instrument calculator was manufactured in 1962; it cost $2,500.

Precision machine shops that were able to work to very tight specifications were called upon to build the precise equipment required. David W. Mann was the leading company in this area and brought their abilities a step further; they developed a state-of-the-art specialized, accurate, step-and-repeat camera that became one of the most popular in the industry. This equipment, with its advanced electronic controls, uses Nikon Ultra Micro

Nikkor Lenses and a very high tech illumination system that Mann developed in-house.

Lovering got into his car, backed out of his driveway onto the street and made a left turn to start his trip to the office. His routine fifteen-minute drive would bring him to the office at 8:45 AM. He turned on his radio to get the news and settled in for his short ride.

Suddenly from across the street a black four-door Ford with a removable police light on its roof made a u-turn and appeared alongside of Lovering's car. The driver motioned for him to pull over. As Lovering did, another black Ford pulled up behind his car. Two Asian men, in dark suits, with pistols drawn approached Lovering's car and signaled for him to get out. Lovering complied - as soon as he got out, one of the men grabbed him by the elbows, turned him around and pushed him against his car. The other man put on a pair of steel handcuffs.

A couple of neighbors, who were walking their dogs, watched the scene in complete surprise. They thought the police were making an arrest for some sort of traffic infraction. They did not approach the cars nor did they shout out or say anything. They just stood and stared.

Lovering is a gentle, soft-spoken man - actually a genius - who had never been in this type of situation. He didn't know what to say or was too shocked to react. He was roughly pulled to the front car and shoved into the back seat. As soon as the door closed the car took off. The second car followed.
The neighbors continued their walk thinking what they saw was their police department in action. They thought nothing further of it the rest of the day.

The abduction of Howard Lovering took all of four minutes. It was a clean take with no outside interference. The driver of the car holding Lovering was smiling to himself saying that his karma was good today.

Lovering asked in a nervous voice – "What did I do? Where are you taking me? Why is this happening?" The man alongside of the driver said, "All will be explained shortly, please do not struggle and try to relax and enjoy the ride." Lovering was having none of it and for the first time in many years started to shout, "Get me out of here – stop the car immediately – bring me to a police …" He was stopped in mid-sentence when the man beside him produced a pistol and said, "Please do not make me hit you or take any further action. Sit quietly – do not struggle."

Lovering was too stunned to speak any further. He decided to try to figure out where his captors were taking him. He saw a couple of road signs and one was an airport sign. He figured they were taking him to the airport – but why he asked himself. The car was heading for the Schuylkill Tunnel – They *are* taking me to Logan, he thought. As they rode through the tunnel the man in the front seat quickly turned toward Lovering and before he realized it he was jabbed with a hypodermic needle in his right thigh and the plunger was squeezed. Lovering almost immediately closed his eyes and passed out. The man sitting beside Lovering unlocked the handcuffs and put them in his pocket.

The two black cars pulled up to a private jet plane on the far side of the airport. One man from the second car and two men from the first car pulled Lovering out. With Lovering's arms wrapped around the shoulders of two men, he was carried up the stairs into the plane while the third man stood guard. As soon as Lovering disappeared from view the guard gave a signal for the two cars to leave.

About five minutes later the pilot of the plane was given

permission to start his engines from the Logan control tower. With the plane door closed and everything in order the pilot then asked for permission to taxi and line up for takeoff – the tower granted his request and he was given his estimated takeoff time at 0945 hours. The plane was rumbling down the runway with wheels up at 0947.

CHAPTER 2
CAPE CANAVERAL

The press site was jammed with visitors from all over the world, VIPs, photographers, newscasters, friends and relatives of NASA. Everyone was anxious and standing as the countdown for Mercury 7 continued. We were thirty-minutes from liftoff. The caution that NASA exhibited in this launch was very conservative and everyone was crossing his or her fingers that today would be the day. There already had been ten postponements of the launch.

John Glenn was on top of this Atlas Rocket in his Mercury 7 capsule. Glenn's calm voice echoed throughout the press site with everyone trying to listen to every word from Mission Control.

A Life magazine photographer, Joe Sherschel, came running up to me and said his motor drive wasn't working and could I help? Mr. Segawa, one of the Nikon 'F' camera designers, was acting as a technician and we ran over with our tool kit to see what could be done. If need be I had an extra 250 exposure film back ready to replace the photographer's camera. Segawa, as calm as a cucumber, reached up to the camera that was attached on a tall tripod with a 1000 mm Nikkor lens. He unscrewed four screws from the camera back. Looking at the button control unit, he touched a few things with his screwdriver, put the cover back on and said to the photographer, "You can continue now." Another crisis averted, I said to myself. It was now fifteen minutes to launch.

TAG Photographic is the distributor of Nikon in the United States and we were at the John Glenn/NASA launch assisting photographers by lending them equipment and servicing camera problems. I am Robert Schein, vice president of marketing and new product design. TAG Photographic was very popular among the photographers because we were lending them equipment to use for their assignment - free-of-charge. This gave us entry into NASA and to the inner circle of the Life magazine photographic staff. Chief Photographer Bill Summits and I became very friendly and he made sure that whenever there was something going on, we were invited.

The tension at the Press Site was getting a little thicker as Mission Control said "Ten minutes to launch." One of the Mercury capsule checks was not coming in to the satisfaction of Mission Control and they said, "There is a hold at ten minutes." People started to get antsy.

A minute or two later, Mission Control continued the countdown and people started to breath easier. Everyone was guardedly excited. The countdown could still stop, like last time when Mission Control went to nine seconds and then there was a hold for two hours because all of the cameras had to be reloaded. At ten seconds the automatic motor drive cameras started up and when Mission Control stopped for about two minutes at nine seconds the cameras were out of film.

It became a particularly important issue for NASA because the cameras closest to the Atlas were important recording instruments and had to be reloaded. They had to record the lift-off in case there was a problem or an explosion.

With Life magazine's help I was part of the reload team that brought me very close to the Atlas. When I took a moment to look up - it was a scary sight. This is a huge rocket when you are so close. I was about a hundred yards away. If you were afraid of heights then this is not the place to be. Wow! – I thought. The countdown was now five minutes and still counting.

The world was watching, the excitement was incredible and then it started, ten – nine – eight – seven – six – five - four – smoke started to blossom from the bottom of the rocket – three – two – one – "We have ignition and lift-off!" The bottom of the Atlas looked like it was engulfed in smoke and flames as it very slowly started to rise. The sound hit us, deep and guttural, as it roared into the sky. People were crying and yelling Go – Go Baby Go! It was a small dot now and Mission Control said, "The first-stage separation has been successful." Then, soon there after, the same report came for the second stage. John Glen was now in orbit.

I grabbed Segawa by the arm and said – "Come on let's get out of here." He looked at me puzzled. We jumped into our car and fought through heavy traffic, made a dash to the Holiday Inn in Canaveral. We went to the central area of the Holiday Inn just off the swimming pool and walked into one of the bedrooms that were converted into an operations center for Life and National Geographic magazines. There on television we watched in awe and listened to mission control as Glenn started his three orbits of the earth.

This was a historic moment – February 20, 1962 - and I wanted to experience every bit of it that was possible. I ran back to my room to call my wife, Debbie, so we could share it, and I saw that the message light on my phone was flashing. I called the desk and the operator said that I was to call my office immediately. Curious, I called and Doreen Parks, our administration assistant, got on the phone and said, "Mr. Albert needs you back in the office ASAP. You are booked out of Orlando in three hours so get going." I asked, "What's going on?" Doreen said, "We have been in conference with the FBI all morning – just get going." So much for history, I thought.

I ran back to tell Segawa that I was leaving. As we stood talking in the Life magazine operations center, I noticed a camera lying on the table that I had never seen before. I called over Bill Summits and he said, "Oh that is a new 35mm self-contained underwater camera called the Calypso. It was loaned to us by Jacques Cousteau." I said, "This camera is really something else. Is there a chance I can borrow it and show it to some people?" Bill said, "Sure, I have three of them – here." He handed me the camera, no questions asked.

I was on my way to Orlando when John Glenn successfully landed in the ocean, was picked up by helicopter and taken to a nearby aircraft carrier - the USS Randolph.

CHAPTER 3
RETURNING TO THE OFFICE AND A BRIEFING

I got home to Glen Cove, Long Island, very late in the evening and was too charged up to go directly to bed. The house was asleep and it was nice and quiet. I made a peanut butter and jelly sandwich and with a glass of milk I read the newspaper for about a half an hour before I thought I might be able to close my eyes and sleep.

I climbed the stairs to the bedroom and undressed, dropping my clothes on the floor and slipped into bed where my wife was fast asleep. I stroked her bottom and she cuddled up to me and I finally was able to relax and close out the world and go to sleep.

The alarm went off at 6:00 AM and the house was immediately awake and jumping. It was a school day, and Marc and Rebecca, two of my three children, were moving about getting ready. After Debbie showered, I must have stood under the flowing water for thirty minutes. Refreshed, I dressed with the idea of making the 7:30 AM Long Island Rail Road train to New York City.

I ran down the stairs – said hello to everyone who didn't seem to notice me or have any reaction that I had been away and now home except from Andrew our 10 month old. He at least smiled when I said hello. Debbie came over to me with a cup of coffee and said, "I hope you will be staying home for a while." I replied, "I was called back to the office so I am not sure what is in store for us."

Marc called out, "Dad, did you see John Glenn's rocket go into space?" "Well" I said, "I am being spoken to. How shocking. – Yes Marc, I was there and I even got a chance to talk to John Glenn a couple of days ago." "Cool" was his intuitive reply. I then said to Debbie, "I will call from the office – gotta run, 'bye." Kissed everyone and flew out the door.

My train arrived in Penn Station about a quarter to nine and I was in a rush to get to the office. I decided to walk downtown on Seventh Avenue instead of walking through 32nd Street to get to my office on Fifth Avenue and 23rd Street. I was afraid that I might run into some of our photographic dealers and would have to stand and talk to them for a while. 32nd Street, in the eyes of the photographic industry, was the camera capital of the world. Willoughby's, Olden, FotoShop, Minifilm, Penn Camera, Spiratone, etc. all did business within a two-block area.

It was a cold and windy day. After spending a week in the Florida sun the wind took my breath away. The wind-chill must have been below zero. I was walking fast to not only get to the office but to generate as much heat as possible.

I gratefully arrived in the lobby of my office building breathing heavily as I waited for the elevator. I was tapped on my shoulder and there beside me was my boss, Luke Albert. "Just like Florida?" he mockingly asked, "Welcome back." We rode up to the fifth floor and on the way he said, "Please be in my office at 10:30. I will explain what we are up against then."

As we walked into the office, Doreen met us. She gave a file folder to Albert and said, "Welcome back" to me. Albert indicated to Doreen that we would be meeting at 10:30 and we started walking down a long corridor to our offices. His was straight ahead and mine was the last office on the left before you reached his. I hung up my hat and coat on the back of my office door and walked over to my desk trying to evaluate what was on it before I sat down to attack it. You couldn't see the top of the desk with all the papers strewn over it. I said, "This is going to take some doing." I sat down and started getting to the bottom of the avalanche.

At about 10:30 and two cups of coffee later I knocked on Albert's door and walked in. I can't help it but every time I walk into his office I feel as though I am walking into a mausoleum. The office had dark walnut walls, large mahogany desk and dark furniture, plus a huge conference table that could easily seat twenty people. Albert was on the phone and motioned me to the conference table.

As I sat down a few of our foreign operatives came into the room. I was surprised to see Bob Claypool from Tokyo. We hugged and said we would get together later. Werner Merz from West Germany and Harry Collins from Great Britain also were part of the group. It was like old home week seeing everyone. Doreen stepped into the office and we all sat around, making small talk, while waiting for Albert to get off the phone.

TAG Photographic is one of the leading photographic wholesale distributors in the United States. In another realm TAG is recognized as The Company, the Central Intelligence Agency. The CIA operates outside of the United States. The Federal Bureau of Investigation operates within the U.S. boundaries. The CIA gets domestic access through companies it owns in various industries. These companies provide cover so their operatives can work within the United States. The FBI has always objected to this but has been unable to stop the practice.

Luke Albert and I have been the face of TAG Photographic in the camera industry for ten years. TAG distributes the Nikon, Mamiya, Fuji and now the Sigma photo equipment products. We are very proud of our business accomplishments. We have had some incredible success with the Nikon and Mamiya camera products in the marketplace.

During these years we have also satisfied our parent organization, the CIA. Over the years our operatives have accomplished some difficult negotiations that included agreements with various government agencies in Japan, West Germany and Hong Kong. TAG's success not only has financed the entire TAG operation, its profits have produced an extra fund for the CIA to work with. This method of funding allows the CIA to have undefined budgets that the taxpayer does not have to be made aware of because taxpayer money is not used.

Albert got off the telephone, walked over to the conference table and said, "Good morning. I thank you all for getting here today on short notice so that we can conduct this briefing. Before we bring in our guests I want to fill you in on what has happened. Dr. Howard B. Lovering, a physicist who works for David W. Mann Company, is missing. We believe he has been abducted by a group of people from Asia." My mouth dropped. I am good friends with Howard and have been involved with him for four years. We have traveled to Japan together to visit Nikon and have shared dinner in each other's home. I was stunned.

Albert continued, "The David W. Mann Company is a large customer of TAG and uses the Nikon Ultra-Micro Nikkor high resolution lenses. The lenses are used in the Mann step-and-repeat camera that is used in the manufacture of integrated circuits. To properly operate these difficult high-resolution lenses you must have an efficient and bright illumination system. Lovering has designed an extraordinary system that is highly secret and if tampered with, to try to see what makes it tick, it falls apart in your hands. If you purchase one of the Mann Photo Repeaters – cost of about $300,000 each – and try to look at the illumination system, you will not learn the secret that made it so successful. Since Robert has been involved with Mann from the beginning I am asking him to give us a quick briefing of the photographic part of the electronics industry and the Mann equipment."

That took me by surprise. I stood up and said, "We all are pretty much aware that our lives eventually will be taken over by microminiaturized circuitry. Vacuum tubes and printed circuit boards as we know them will give way to the integrated circuit industry. I also suspect that the photographic process that is now responsible for helping to manufacture these tiny circuits, within five to ten years will become obsolete, as machines will start making machines."

I continued, "An electronics design engineer can't be expected to work on the head of a pin to make a drawing for a circuit. He works on a drawing board, about 40" X 50," and eventually the drawing is transferred to a Rubylith material. The Rubylith is placed on a sturdy large graphic arts type camera and reduced in one shot, fifty to one or one hundred to one times onto a 2" square high-resolution glass plate. The plate is then reproduced six to eight times by a contact printer. The plates are placed on top of a David Mann Photo Repeater and the image is reduced ten times more through our Ultra Micro Nikkor lenses.

"Lovering's secret is the illumination system. When light goes through a lens, because of the shape of the elements in the lens there is a fall-off of light as you go from the center to the edge. This is called cosine fall-off. Somehow Lovering has been able to force enough light evenly through the lens to get the highest resolution out of the lens across the entire image surface. It is a remarkable light source. From there the small image – some lines about a micron (1μ) in size or smaller - goes to the production floor to be made into microminiaturized circuits." With that I sat down ready to answer any questions. There were none.

Albert then said to Doreen, "Please show our guests in." The two 'guests' were FBI agents by the names of Elkin and Tomkow. Introductions were made and we all sat around the conference table waiting for them to start. When they were ready agent Elkin spoke up.

"Three days ago the Bedford Police Department received a call from a resident who was complaining that a car was partially blocking her driveway with the engine running. The police responded and tried to locate the owner, Howard Lovering. There didn't appear to be any foul play until one of the neighbors who watched the morning's activities retold what he saw. Bedford police realized this was a kidnapping and called in the FBI.

"We are aware that TAG Photographic is one of the largest vendors to the David W. Mann Company, where Lovering works. You supply them with special lenses." Albert said, "That is correct." Elkin continued, "We are coming to you for assistance. We believe that Howard Lovering was abducted about 8:30 in the morning three days ago. He related what the neighbors saw and described the two black Ford Crown Victorias.

"By looking at the map and talking to the local police we made an assumption that the vehicles were going to end up at the airport. We checked the Schuylkill tunnel cameras in Boston and saw two Ford Crown Victorias, one right after the other, pass through at about 9:00 AM. Logan Municipal Airport, five minutes from the tunnel, was the obvious destination.

"Upon checking the private planes that left Logan around 9:30 AM – there was only one private jet plane we weren't able get a handle on. Their flight plan was to take them to Toronto, Canada. Upon checking into the ownership we found that the aircraft is leased and the lessee was Chang Industries out of Hong Kong." Albert and I looked at each other trying not to show our surprise. Madame Chang, also known as the Dragon Lady, owns Chang Industries.

Elkin went on, "We are checking with Interpol and have already checked with the Royal Canadian Mounted Police. There is no record of the plane arriving in Toronto. The plane has seemed to disappear. That is just about all we have." Elkin sat down and waited for a reply from Albert. Luke Albert sat there a moment looking up at the ceiling,

"I'm not sure why they abducted Lovering," he finally said, "If they wanted his technology all they had to do was purchase it. It would have been a lot cheaper, with less stress, than abducting him. They wanted Lovering for something else.

Gentlemen, our group will help the FBI in any way we can. We will do some sniffing around for you out of the country and report as we go along. We expect that you will do so as well and report whatever you learn." Elkin and Tomkow nodded, "Everything from TAG will be coordinated through Mr. Schein. He will visit with our operatives in Europe and Asia. Claypool, Merz and Collins will go back to their respective posts and see what they can find out before Robert gets there.

"Mr. Elkin, I assume that you and Mr. Tomkow will carry the

ball for the FBI – correct?" They nodded again and Tomkow said, "That is what the Director requested." "Fine, let's plan on having another meeting within two days. I will tell you of our progress – if any. The longer the abducted person is missing the harder it will be to get back – alive." With that the meeting broke up and the FBI agents left the room.

Albert said, "It becomes interesting when the FBI asks for our help. I am sure they are befuddled and maybe a little embarrassed that they are visiting us. As I said earlier, I think someone is looking at Lovering for some other reason then just an illumination system for the Mann Photo Repeater. Our job is to find out what it is and where he is so that we can bring him home. I am open for suggestions - people?"

I started, "The Chang involvement is interesting. When I last visited with Hyacinth Chang (fourth daughter of Madame Chang), a few years back, she showed me some new manufacturing equipment and photographic machinery but I would have to say it was harmless stuff. I didn't see anything that was a weapon or something to be concerned about that might be turned into a weapon. I think the Changs are due for a visit."

Harry Collins in his British accent said, "I wonder where their plane ended up, from that part of Canada they could go over the cap to Europe or Asia. I wonder where they were headed." Albert said, "You picked your poison, Harry. We need to find out where they landed. Why don't you follow this up with your contacts in MI-5, Scotland Yard and the RCMP?

"Bob, get back to Tokyo and see what part of the trail you might be able to pick up in Japan from the Chang involvement. Chang Industries is a major sub-contractor for lenses and camera parts for many of the camera manufacturing factories. "Werner, Philips in Frankfurt and Braun in Düsseldorf have

16

been at the David Mann doorstep for a couple of months. Let's see if they got frustrated and decided to take the situation into their own hands. Everyone is to report to Doreen daily unless you are onto something that does not allow you to. However, I don't want days to go by from not hearing from you. That will get us nervous and we will start sending out people after you.

"Robert will check in with Doreen and try to put all of the information together. He will leave for Hong Kong in two days. All right people, this seems to be a very organized group and they seem to have no fear about carrying weapons. So make your arrangement for any kind of difficulty. Thank you." The meeting ended and as we were walking out I said to Bob "I guess I will be visiting you in a few days. I am feeling I will end up back in Tokyo." Bob said, "I look forward to it." We all shook hands and said "We will be seeing each other shortly – have a safe trip."

Albert called out for me to return to his office. I closed the door and advanced to one of the side chairs in the front of his desk. "Robert, this can be a messy situation. I think you better scoot up to Mann, nose around, take a look at where Lovering was abducted and talk to his family to find out what has been going on that might be a difficulty if anything." I said, "That was where I was headed. I thought it would be good to get a birds-eye view of what happened before I started to do any serious traveling." All Albert said was "Good." I left his office to find Doreen to start making my plans.

I called home to tell Debbie that I was gearing up for yet another trip overseas. I suggested we go out to dinner tonight so that we could visit with each other for a quiet couple of hours. She said she would get a sitter for the kids. She then said, "Let's go somewhere nice and have them watch over us for the evening so we don't have to make any decisions." "Good idea," I said. "Let's go to Zangi's; we are always treated royally there." Deb said she would make a reservation.

That evening, Nicole Zangi outdid himself. He took wonderful care of us. We had a tasty Northern Italian, style meal of pasta with a light sauce, red snapper and asparagus. The wine was a chardonnay and it was delicious. We finished the entire bottle while having a platter of cheeses. It was a quiet table overlooking Forest Avenue in Glen Cove. The street scenery wasn't a great view but as usual I couldn't take my eyes off of my wife. She was in a black tight fitting dress with a single strand pearl necklace I had brought back from Japan. She looked beautiful. She laughed when she caught me staring at her. I was very proud of her and I told her so.

The evening will go down in our memories as one of the best nights ever. When we got home I drove the sitter to her house and then made it back to our house. Debbie was in a sheer nightgown sprawled on our bed waiting for me to come into the room. I ripped off my clothing and stroked then kissed her from her toes to her face. She was very responsive and then she stroked me and rolled onto me toying with me. She slowed me down by whispering in my ear saying, "We have to be very quiet, we don't want to wake the kids." Just at that point, I didn't think she could contain herself, because she broke the rule of silence before I could say anything. I kept on saying shhh, shhh and continued stroking her breasts. We held each other for a good half hour before we cuddled up and went to sleep. It certainly was a night to remember.

CHAPTER 4
ON TO BEDFORD

I got out of the house early and sped in my Pontiac Tempest to LaGuardia Airport to get the Eastern Air Lines hourly shuttle to Boston. I arrived in time to get the 8:00 AM plane. I was hoping to finish everything in one day and not have to stay overnight in Boston.

An hour and twenty minutes later we arrived in Logan. My rented car ticket from Avis (We Try Harder) was waiting for me at the counter. I got on the Avis bus and found my Oldsmobile vehicle in spot #166. The ride to Bedford was about three quarters of an hour.

At about 11:30 I pulled into the David W. Mann parking lot. I could see Burt Wheeler, Mann president, through his corner office window and caught his eye and he waved. The receptionist buzzed me in. Burt met me halfway to his office and we started walking back. He said, "We are so upset about Howard and any danger he might be in. I am beside myself. I have known him for years and I just don't know what to do. I talk to Helen (Howard's wife) every day but I feel so helpless. I don't know what to say to her." "Burt, this is obviously not a normal situation and I am sure whatever you say is more then what she is getting from the police or the FBI. Hang in there." Neither Burt nor Howard knows of my dual life as an agent for the CIA. They just know me as their supplier of Nikon products. So, I started my visit just asking the questions a person would ask if he had just read the newspapers.

Burt Wheeler started in David Mann's machine shop as a kid of 17 just out of high school. He has been with Mann for 35 years and after attaining his mechanical engineering degree in night school, he was advanced rapidly and is now the president of Mann. There is probably no one more knowledgeable with what Mann manufactures then Burt Wheeler. Even today he lives on the production floor looking over people's shoulders working the steel. That truly is his first love. He is a so - so paperwork guy who is smart enough to have hired a top-level office administrator, Naomi Pivnick. She literally runs the show for him.

Mann's sales manager is Bill Toby; he does an adequate job moving out the big Photo Repeaters. Bill is a lightweight technically; he is backed up well by the Mann staff. I guess Toby's success is that he can sling the crap with just about anyone and is a good glad hander. Both Bill and Naomi joined us in Burt's office.

Burt said, "I've been answering all sorts of questions about Howard, who David Mann is doing business with, suppliers, etc. The FBI is scrounging whatever information they can from us. I hope it is helping." I said, "That is how we heard about it. The FBI contacted TAG because we were on your suppliers list. Have you guys had any negative negotiations lately?" Burt asked, "Like what – give me an example."

"If someone wanted to purchase a part or an incomplete Photo Repeater or maybe just an illumination system? How does that sound?" "I would have been negative if that occurred," said Burt. "The way we are beating our competition is through Howard's illumination system. I'm no fool. I know eventually they will catch on but in the meantime we have an edge and we've got it to ourselves. Why should I sell it or give it away now? In a few months or in a year we might be open to that but that is a big maybe."

I asked, "Did you get any related requests about illumination systems not involving the electronics industry?" Much to my surprise Burt responded, "As a matter of fact, yes. I read a couple of proposals that were interesting but far away from what we are now doing. I felt that kind of an effort would conflict or take our attention away from what we are currently doing. I didn't think it was for us." "Do you still have these proposals?" "Sure, Naomi can find them in the files and give a copy to you before you leave." "Great, maybe the Nikon factory can put a bid together." Burt laughed and said, "Always being the salesman, Robert, good move. What do you say, Toby? Are you looking for additional business for us?" "Always," Toby shot back.

I reviewed our normal business with the three of them trying to set their purchase orders up for the next six-month period. I explained, "The Ultra Micro Nikkor lenses required about three months' minimum lead-time. The special glass and grinding of the elements that goes into these lenses is a very tedious process. When that is completed, each lens goes through a quality control test that has a very high failure rate. It is very expensive to do this work. When I visit the factory, in a couple of weeks, I will be fighting off a price increase. I suggest you order enough lenses to take you through the entire year. That way I can reason with them to stabilize the pricing for the year."

Burt asked, "How much do you expect the price to go up?" "A minimum of 10 – 15 %". Burt whistled, "At $1,400 per lens that is an awfully high increase." My reply was, "I don't think the factory ever expected this high a rate of rejection. The Mann illumination system is very unforgiving. I don't think the factory has a choice." Burt continued, "Bill, how do the TI and Hewlett Packard orders look?" "In the bag,"

"All right, Robert, we will commit to 150 lenses in the next six months and another 100 lenses for the fall period. That will be a total of 250 lenses at $1,400 each, or $350,000. I will need some terms for this size order. We do not get paid completely for each finished unit until the Photo Repeater has been delivered and has proven to meet specifications thirty days later. I need another thirty days after delivery from TAG." "I don't see a problem with that and I will talk to Luke Albert right after lunch and set it up."

Burt and I then left for lunch. On the way I asked, "Can you drive by where Howard was kidnapped?" Burt smiled and said, "Are you now going to be a sleuth and solve the crime like Perry Mason." I said, "You never know." We had a chuckle over that and about fifteen minutes later Burt drove us slowly by the area and I took it all in. As we passed by I noticed one tree still had police tape on it that had been used to rope off the area while the police were investigating. It was an unremarkable street. Just like anywhere, USA. Howard would have been totally unsuspecting, totally off-guard.

When we got back from lunch Naomi had an envelope waiting for me at the front desk. I put it into my briefcase and as I have done a dozen times before, Burt escorted me through the factory to see the activity and get a feel of the business that was going on. As a mechanical engineer I always felt a pang of excitement walking the production floor. I enjoyed watching people working the automatic milling machines and lathes. One of the Mann secrets was how metal moved on metal, smoothly and effortlessly, separated by a slither of oil. It was poetry in motion. Well, maybe not poetry to everyone, but for me it was beautiful to watch.

Finally we went into the air-conditioned "QC" – quality control – room where there were three systems in final checkout. The illumination systems were being aligned to the Nikkor lenses. This took a number of hours and without Howard around maybe a bit longer. Burt was visibly upset when his mind obviously drifted back to Howard. He really missed his employee and close friend.

Burt walked me to the door of the building and thanked me for coming. I thanked him for the order. He said if he heard anything about Howard he would get word to me through my office. I said, "Thank you, Burt, I think I will visit Helen for a few minutes." "I am sure she would appreciate that," he said "Tell her I will be over on my way home." I nodded, got into my car and drove off.

Helen Lovering and Howard have been married for about 38 years, with no children, and have led a pleasant life - until now. I am sure Helen is frantic with fear for Howard. I got out of the car and as soon as Helen saw me she hugged me and started to cry. My heart went out to her. Some friends were in the house as well as a contingent from the local FBI office ready to listen in on any questionable telephone calls and take care of her general safety, checking her mail, escorting her to the supermarket and so on.

Everyone was in earshot while we passed simple niceties. I know that Howard is an avid gardener and said, "How about a walk in the garden to see what Howard is planning to do this spring?" Helen said, "Fine" and got a sweater. The wintertime isn't the best time to visit the garden but it was a way to get her out of the house so that I could ask her a couple of questions.

I started out with – "Now that we can talk with no one listening how are you really doing?" "I'm a total wreck and scared to death" she replied. "I can understand that, hang in there; I am sure the FBI is doing everything possible to find him." Helen said, "Why haven't they put the word out to the press? We have not received one telephone call – Why? I just don't know where to turn."

"Helen, I know some very influential people around the world. I promise you I will ask them to get involved to see what we can come up with. All we will be doing is backing up the FBI. How does that sound?" "Anything will be wonderful, Robert. We must find him. Our lives are so dependant upon each other. I don't know what I would do without him." "I know, but let's not get ahead of ourselves," was all I could say.

"Helen, was Howard working on anything that might be of interest to someone other than David Mann?" "I don't think so," she said. "But you know how Howard is always doodling and writing in his journal. He was fascinated with some sort of laser project that he thought Mann might work on but it never came about." "Hmm, Helen do you have his journal?" "Yes." "Can you slip his journal into my coat or briefcase without anyone noticing it? I have a lot of people in Tokyo who might make something out of what he was working on and – you never know - that might offer a lead." She nodded.

Armed with the Mann proposals and Howard's journal I drove to the airport hoping to get on the 5:00 PM EAL Shuttle. This would give me a chance to get home at a reasonable time to visit with the family. I wanted to be able to spend some time with the kids before I went gallivanting around the globe again.

CHAPTER 5

A VISIT TO THE OFFICE TO BRING LUKE ALBERT UP TO DATE

After a fun night at home, a lot of laughs playing backgammon with everyone, I got to bed before midnight. I was dead to the world within five minutes. I am sure my wife was wondering what happened to that guy who kept her up most of last night. In the morning I packed, Debbie drove me to the train; I took a cab from Penn Station to the office and got in about 10:00 AM.

My flight was at 6:00 PM aboard Pan American 011 to Hong Kong with a stop in Fairbanks, Alaska. As usual when a photo distributor sends people overseas, my ticket was first class. Pan Am was using the now popular Boeing 707 jets. I kind of missed the old four prop, slower Strato-Cruiser. That was true luxury in flight, with its two floors, one for eating, drinking and talking and an upstairs for sleeping. It was a first-class airship with impeccable service that made the trip to Asia like flying in a dream cloud. Doreen informed me that she had ordered a car to take me to the airport at 4:00.

Luke Albert is my mentor and the person who hired me almost twelve years ago. Albert was a field operative who had an exciting, successful career and eventually ran into some serious problems that put him behind a desk. Luke started TAG for the CIA. He made personal arrangements with the factories we represented that have served him like a security blanket with the CIA.

Without Albert there might not be a TAG Photographic. The factories involved all loved him and trusted him. Albert was considering retiring. He was constantly in pain from old wounds suffered in the Army as a Ranger during World War II. He was in Japan most of the war hiding out in the forests and rice fields reporting troop and ship movements from his listening post.

He was almost dead when found in the forest of Hakone by a Russian Jew, Alex Triguboff and his Japanese wife, Miyako. Ultimately, Albert and the Triguboffs became lifelong friends and currently Triguboff runs the Far East office of TAG Photographic in the Marunouchi District in Tokyo. In Japan, importing and exporting a product requires a broker. Triguboff has been that broker since the start-up of TAG. Alex Triguboff is aware of the CIA connection to TAG but is not a participant in that part of the business.

I remember when I first met Albert I thought he moved like a cat; he had piercing dark brown eyes that seemed to be looking inside of you. Albert has been a second father to me. He has taken me under his wing and has trained me to be able to back him up in our dealings with the factories. We have become good friends these past years and I think the world of him.

I knocked on his door and entered his office, then found a seat on one of the side chairs in front of his desk. He looked up from signing letters and asked, "Well, Robby, do we have anything to go on yet?" "I think so," I replied. "I have two proposals that Mann was looking at that might be a clue. I also have Lovering's most recent journal, which I believe ties into possible solutions for Mann to bid on the proposals.

"Mann ultimately passed on the projects because they did not want to water down their marketing efforts for Photo Repeater sales. I think it was a good choice on their part but you have to keep on looking at the next move. I think this might have been something pretty big for the Mann Company had they gone through with it.

"I saw two proposals that were similar to one another. They were looking at concentrating a laser beam to a small diameter and being able to throw it a great distance. One trading company fronting a proposal was Mashpriborintorg; a Soviet government supported trading company. The other was Mei Cao Lin Trading, which I believe is supported by the Chinese government. I was surprised to see that Mei Cao Lin's address was located in the same office building that is owned by Chang Industries." Albert said, "An obscure point might also tie them in because Madame Chang's first name is Lin." "I never knew her first name; I always called her Madame Chang." "And you will continue to do so," said Albert. I understood and nodded.

"Finally, from what I could decipher from Lovering's journal was that he was playing around with some drawing of a reflector system that would be sensitive to the Infra-red part of the wavelength. Thus, I believe he was already toying with the idea of accomplishing the task of the proposal. It certainly would be an interesting bit of experimentation for a scientist. That is what I have gotten so far."

Albert had disturbing news. "Werner Merz has reported in and said that a notable scientist, Dr. Walter Voss from Philips was missing. His specialty is working with halogen lamps. I don't know if that works with lasers but he was abducted two days after Lovering in the exact same method, including two black Mercedes." "In a strange way it does make sense. Halogen lamps have to be focused and usually have lenses involved to concentrate their light output. Yup, I am convinced this is all connected."

"Have we heard from Harry Collins yet?" "I'm afraid not." Albert said, "He had to make a dogleg to Canada first then back to England. I'm sure he is in the hunt, but hasn't reported in. I expect he will contact us by the weekend. At least I hope so."

We then reviewed my planned factory visits – orders, problems, etc., – which was covered fairly quickly. I reached into my bag and pulled out the Calypso camera Life magazine lent me. Albert's eyes became wide. He said, "After Glenn's orbital I saw a picture of him in the newspaper using a handheld camera underwater while relaxing in the Bahamas. I was curious what the camera was. I imagine this is it?" "Yes, Bill Summits loaned me the camera to show it to a couple of people. I think the factory will be interested in this – do you agree?" "Absolutely," said Albert, "This is a good find. Let me know what they say."

As I was leaving, he stopped me. "Robert (Oh, oh – something formal, no "Robby") I want you to be very careful in China. I don't trust the Dragon Lady and I want you to get to Tokyo fairly swiftly. Because of this new twist with Mashpriborintorg Trading we might want you to swing through Moscow. I will set up everything and will let you know. Doreen will make the arrangements if it works out that way." "That's fine." We shook hands and I left Albert's office. I took two steps out of his door, made a right turn into my office, closed the door behind me and said out loud, "Whew, what the hell have I gotten into this time?"

The day seemed to fly by. Before I knew it Doreen was in my office organizing my paperwork, information, tickets, cash advance and red diplomatic passport. I said, "How come I rate a red passport?" Doreen simply said, "Mr. Albert arranged it

BLIND SPOT

because you might be jumping around to many countries and we do not necessarily want anyone to check your luggage."

She next gave me my .45 caliber pistol and shoulder holster with a box of shells. I then put my left foot on my chair, un-strapped my, snub nosed .38 caliber and its ankle holster and handed them to her. I said to Doreen, "The hardest thing I have had to do on this job was convince my wife that I must carry one of these things. She wasn't too happy about that." "That is what you say every time I give you a pistol. Let's move on. You have to live with this if you want to stay alive and that is all there is to it." She was right but I still can hear Debbie and the argument we had about carrying a pistol. Wow, that was one beauty of an argument!

Soon I was in my hired car on my way to Idewild International Airport. The driver had taken me to the airport before, so I was in good hands. I closed my eyes trying see what was ahead of me. We got to the airport in about three quarters of an hour and I checked in on Pan Am's first class flight 011 to Hong Kong.

CHAPTER 6
HONG KONG

After about sixteen hours with a refueling stop in Fairbanks, we started our approach into Hong Kong International Airport. It was about 8:00 PM and the lights were on throughout the City giving it a mystical glow. I always thought this was a beautiful fascinating place to visit – at least from the air.

I found a baggage handler and he took my bags to a forest green Rolls Royce which is the signature vehicle of the Peninsula Hotel in Kowloon. The Peninsula has operated a small fleet of the green Rolls Royces since before World War II. I checked in and was shown, by a manager and bellhop, into a spacious suite overlooking the Repulse Bay.

As I unpacked my bags the phone rang and it was Hyacinth Chang. Hyacinth and I got to know each other about ten years ago when her identical twin sister, Juniper Chang, was murdered by the Yakuza (Japanese Mafia) during a negotiation I was involved with in Japan. Juniper was drop-dead gorgeous and so is Hyacinth.

"Welcome to Hong Kong; it's been a long time since you were here." "A couple of years." "Too long," she said. "How about meeting me in The Bar, just off of the lobby, at about 10? We can catch up and see what we can schedule."

It always amazed me how this happens in Asia. I never told her when I was coming in other than to see if she was going to be in Hong Kong and if she would find some time for me starting next week. Here it is Saturday and she already knows when I arrived, where I am staying, and just about the right time to call my room. Incredible I thought. I said "Sure, I will be in the lobby at 10." We hung up and I went about my unpacking and thought I would freshen up after my long flight.

At 9:55 I took the elevator to the main lobby. The Peninsula's lobby is huge. It is the place to have afternoon high tea if you are anywhere near the hotel. It is the place to be seen and the place to see celebrities. As I was looking around Hyacinth Chang was walking through the glass lobby doors. The doorman upon seeing her took off his cap, made a slight bow and held the doors open for her.

Hyacinth looked magnificent. She was wearing a tight black Suzie Wong-style dress with a high slit up the seam. Her jet-black hair was in a bun set off by a white camellia. Her jewelry was, as usual, understated: simple-gold-and diamond necklace with gold and diamond bangles on her wrist. As I said of her sister, the same held true of Hyacinth. She is probably the most beautiful woman I ever got to interact with in business. As soon as she saw me she smiled and walked in my direction. Every male eye in the lobby was on her. Even the women were carefully watching her.

She stuck out her gloved hand and I kissed it. She smiled and much to my surprise moved closer and kissed me on my cheek. The first thing I could think of was how big this is going over with all of the people in the lobby. If I have done nothing else this trip this has got to be a high point. I put my arm around her waist and we walked to The Bar, a noted spot for a quiet drink in Kowloon.

We were shown to a table in an empty corner of the room. A waiter came by and Hyacinth ordered a Courvoisier and I ordered my usual Chivas Regal scotch, over ice. I have learned over the years that in Asia you take your time and do not start any conversation concerning business. You try to show interest in your visitor – with this particular person that was not hard to do – after a while you get around to discussing business.

I asked how her mother, Madame Chang, was and if all was in good health. "My mother has been ill with a serious stomach complication and had to be operated on to clear a blockage in her large intestine. She received quite a few blood transfusions but appears to be doing well now. She hasn't been in the office for about two weeks. It has been a hectic time." "I am sorry to hear that she has not been in good health. Is she, by any chance, accepting visitors?" "Not really," said Hyacinth.

Shifting gears we chatted about what we had been doing these past few years. She asked to see pictures of my children, which I just happened to have. I made sure I put them in my pocket before coming downstairs. She looked at them and made pleasant comments as though she were a visiting aunt. I teased her, saying, "You are not married yet, what are you waiting for?" "I guess I am still 'sowing my oats' as you say in your country."

Now that was an interesting picture, I thought. I imagined Hyacinth, out and about jumping into bed with whoever pleases her. She must have noticed the blank look on my face because she immediately defended herself saying, "I'm only 32, I have plenty of time to settle down." "You are absolutely right," I conceded. She nodded and gave me a very sly intimate smile. I said to myself, hold it Robert – cool down. Take this conversation somewhere else.

I figured it was time to start business. "How many planes are in the Chang Industries fleet?" She looked at me and thought then said, "Four planes; one long range jet, one short range jet and two twin engine Cessnas. Why do you ask?" I ignored her question and asked, "Do you sub-lease or loan them to other organizations?" "We loan them out for a fee if we are not using them." Again she asked, "Why?" Again I ignored her question and asked, "Is Mei Cao Lin Trading Company owned by Chang Industries?" This time Hyacinth became wary – she sat up straight on the edge of her chair. She said, "Mei Cao Lin is not a part of Chang Industries. I can say that for certain since I am a member of the board of directors of Chang Industries."

I could see that Hyacinth was becoming very guarded and tense. "Mei Cao Lin Trading happens to have the same address as Chang Industries. I came to visit them and was curious." Hyacinth said, "They lease space in our building. We must have forty or fifty companies leasing space in our building; we do not own them, we would be extraordinarily diversified if we did. They do business in many industries which we have little or no interest."

I said to myself; let's go for the whole enchilada. "Hyacinth, does your Mother have an interest or ownership in Mei Cao Lin Trading?" It was as if I touched her with a hot wire. She got very straight and very agitated and said, "I have no idea. My Mother has many interests in many businesses that are not part of Chang Industries. In fact, she owns stock in AT&T, IBM and Eastman Kodak - does that make her the owner and decision maker? I would say not. Why do you ask?" she now demanded.

"Lin is part of the company's name," she quickly interrupted, "Lin is a very common name in China. What difference does that make?" "Well for one, it is one of your Mother's forenames." That caught her off guard. "Very few people know that Lin is one of her forenames," she said. "That is not hard to find out" I said. "I guess not'" she replied slightly defeated. I gather Hyacinth is used to getting her way and she was not happy this was not going her way.

She thought a moment and said, "What do you want with these people?" "I only want to ask them a few questions and learn about whom they represent - nothing special." She chose her words carefully and said, "I will try to see if my domestic sales manager can arrange an appointment for you." I thanked her, "That would be very kind."

"How many days are you staying in Hong Kong, Robert?" "Well, I have to visit Mr. Yoshida's new Hong Kong factory for the Sigma Lens Company, then I was going to visit with one or two other people besides your company - then go on to Japan. I would say about two or three days." "That's a quick visit," she said. "Can you make it one more day?" "Sure." "Good, I will make a dinner reservation at the Repulse Bay Hotel and we will watch the sun go down and the moon come up." The Repulse Bay Hotel is a beautiful spot on a quiet beach with a long history. "That will be fine. In the meantime, I will visit you in your office at 11 tomorrow if that is OK with you." "That will be fine," she said and stood up.

I signaled to the waiter and he brought the check which I signed. I walked Hyacinth to her waiting driver and Mercedes 500. Just as she was about to get into the back seat she turned to me, pulled me close and kissed me on the lips. I was shocked. I couldn't put two words together to say anything - much less object. I was dazzled – her aroma and taste were delicious.

She asked, "Shall I send my car for you tomorrow?" "No, no thank you, I would like to take the Star ferry across and look at the bay to get the feel of Hong Kong." "Very bourgeois," she said with a smile. "As you wish," she added and drove off.

CHAPTER 7
BEING A TOURIST AND A BUSINESSMAN

It was early Sunday morning and after a refreshing breakfast of fruits and cold cereal from the buffet I took a leisurely walk down Nathan Road; a twisting road to the Star Ferry docks by the old clock tower. I got on the next ferry, they run about every five minutes, paid the extra twenty cents or so to go to the second deck and found a spot near the railing amidships as the ferry did its ten minute ride across the Harbor.

Hong Kong's harbor is a traffic collision waiting to happen - even on Sunday morning. International shipping, sampans, junks, pleasure boats, motor launches and ferries seem to all come to the same point at the same time and somehow seem to survive without crashing into one another. They all survive to make the next pass or just get out of the way of a ferry coming up quickly on them. It's an exciting ride and gets your heart beating.

When we reached the Hong Kong side I walked a few blocks to visit a little jewelry shop that Hyacinth introduced me to a few years back. I wanted to bring back some ivory or jade pendants for my wife and daughter. The negotiation in China was always pleasant and fun. Unlike Japan, you never accepted the seller's first offer. It was always too high.

However, your counter offer should not insult the seller. In the end I am not sure who the winner is but if you are both happy then it is a successful sale. I purchased two beautiful large jade pendants that I was sure my girls would like.

I then did some window-shopping amid the crowds in the noisy streets in the hyper-active metropolis. Hong Kong is very invigorating. All along I was making my way to the Chang Industries office building. I made it to the lobby of a modern glass building with 16 floors. Eights and combinations of the number eight represent good luck in China. I took the elevator to 16 and got off onto the plush carpeted waiting area of Chang Industries.

It was Sunday so there was no one at reception. I waited a minute or so and someone came to the area. I knew that would happen because of the surveillance cameras I spied in the ceiling. A building uniformed woman asked whom my appointment was with and I replied Hyacinth Chang. She turned and indicated for me to follow.

Hyacinth has a modern corner office with a magnificent view of the harbor. The furniture was all light beech-wood with dark black and gold touches. Everything went together and was very inviting. The fresh flowers that were displayed were beautiful. They were on the coffee table and a display was on the conference table. The chairs were soft suede. The comfort could be a little disarming.

Hyacinth would return in a few minutes, I was told. I was asked if I wanted anything to drink – coffee, tea or a soft drink. "A cup of black coffee would be fine." I sat down in one of the four plush suede chairs near the coffee table and made myself comfortable. My coffee arrived with a small plate of cookies. I was relaxing when a determined Hyacinth Chang returned to her office. She held up her hand walked to her desk, picked up the phone and said something in Chinese. Then she hung up and walked over to me. I got up and kissed her offered hand and we both sat around the coffee table. A few minutes later a young girl came in and put a cold drink that looked like bubbly mineral water next to Hyacinth and left.

Hyacinth started, "You can meet with Mei Cao Lin tomorrow at 10 AM. My domestic sales manager made the arrangements. You will be meeting with the executive vice president, Mr. Cao." "Hyacinth, thank you very much for doing the footwork for me; it makes everything easier."

I then asked, "Did Chang Industries loan or lease a plane to Mei Cao Lin recently?" She said "No." It was an unequivocal negative response. She obviously didn't want to discuss it further. I changed the subject and asked how "Al Bernard and his company were doing?" (Bernard is the representative of Chang Industries Photo Division in the United States) She was very blunt, "He is older, a little wiser and he still serves his purpose for us. Why do you ask? Are you interested in representing us?" "Definitely not," I bristled, "In no way do we wish to interfere with Bernard's activities or his relationship with your company."

Hyacinth smiled, "Then can I assume we are finished with our business discussion." "Not exactly, do you have any contact with people who are involved with the sales, preparation, and building or purchasing of equipment involving lasers?" She shook her head no but replied, "We might be involved in one or two of our companies with lasers but I can't recall them at the moment. I think you will find that Mei Cao Lin is somehow involved with that type of equipment." "Thank you now let's get some brunch. I am starved."

As we started for the door Hyacinth tripped, I caught her in stride and she grabbed me around the chest. We were standing close to and she said, "Excuse me that was clumsy." I asked if she was all right and she replied, "Yes." In the meantime I realized she was checking to see if I was carrying my pistol. She did it in an interesting, polite and intimate way. She was as light as a feather and her aroma was delicious, I thought.

We decided to go to the Gloucester House a few blocks away from her office. The Gloucester House is the size of a football field on the second floor of an office building. Its specialty is dim sum. There must have been a hundred tables with hundreds of girls walking around, with specialty dim sum dishes that they were pushing. From a distance they looked like the girls who sell cigarettes in a nightclub. However, they were not dressed in short skirts, but in blue dress uniforms with a white apron. You could probably have a different dim sum specialty from each of the girls. It got my gastric juices flowing.

The restaurant was noisy and there were many family groups. We were shown to a table where diners were well into their meal. We ignored them, they ignored us. After there were about twelve bowls in front of us we were finished. One of the waitresses came over and looked at each bowl -- prices were determined by the size or color of the bowls. When I paid the bill I was amazed that it only came to about US $10.

We then went for a long walk. We got to the Mandarin Hotel went to the left side and up a hill to the tram that would take us up to Victoria Peak to get the full view of Hong Kong. I must admit, the view alongside of me was just as magnificent. I couldn't take my eyes off of Hyacinth. She was beautiful and she knew that I was staring at her.

After Victoria Peak we headed back across the harbor to my hotel for afternoon tea. The Peninsula was always crowded for tea – especially on a Sunday. We were seated on a soft couch in the middle of the lobby. There were people seated all over and around us. I am sure everyone was watching Hyacinth. Hyacinth was next to me, close. Tea was served on the coffee table in front of us. I ordered black coffee and she ordered Darjeeling tea. Along with the service came a platter of un-crusted small sandwiches and an assortment of small finger cakes.

We were having a casual conversation until she asked "Have you been to Canada lately." "No, not for some time." She continued, "Chang Industries has opened a new housing development project in Vancouver. I have spent some time there these last few months. Canada is a beautiful country."

"Tell me about the development, it sounds interesting." "Well, Calgary is planning on the winter Olympics in 1976 and Canada is spending a lot of money on infrastructure. We decided that Vancouver would be a wonderful spot for an exclusive development with all kinds of concierge services and yet not be too far away Calgary. You should go and take a look – it is truly a magnificent location and the facilities will be first-rate when they are finished."

"Does it have its own airport?" "It certainly has. The runway is large enough to handle jet planes. I think this will sell out at a quick rate and my company will do very well with it. You should buy one of the apartments, Robert." "I think they might be a little too rich for my blood." "We can give you a special deal and make some favorable arrangements for you. Don't say no so quickly, think about it." "I will think about it but I can assure you this is out of our league." She coyly looked at me and said, "Not necessarily."

As we were finishing our tea she said, "This has been one of the most relaxing afternoons I have spent in a long time. I don't want it to end. Will you have dinner with me tonight?"

"Without question, I don't want to see this day end either. It has been fun." "Good, I will pick you up at 9 and we will go to the Jumbo Kingdom floating restaurant in Aberdeen. I will make all the arrangements. See you later." We got up and walked to the hotel entrance where she turned and planted a kiss on my cheek and walked out to her car. God, what a walk I thought. I have to stop mentally undressing this woman – though she is something to behold. Whoa, Robert, what the hell are you thinking? You are an older happily married man – what the hell is the matter with you. "Right" I said out loud and walked to the elevator without looking back.

CHAPTER 8
THREE IS COMPANY

Howard Lovering woke up slowly. He had cobwebs in his head and was completely disoriented. Finally he opened his eyes and it was light. He was in a fine bed with silk sheets. He quickly sat up and realized that he was in a strange place.

Lovering was the guest of his captors in a luxury apartment in a new building complex about fifty miles north of Vancouver. He was dressed in a blue jumpsuit, had been recently bathed and shaven. He recognized the scent of Old Spice cologne. There was also an addition of two bracelets, one on each wrist. They appeared to be perfect circles. They were very light and if he hadn't stroked his arm he might not have noticed them. "What are these?" he thought.

Lovering swung his legs out of bed and tried to stand up. It was an effort but he finally came to a standing position. He shouted out, "Is there anyone here?" There was no answer. He stumbled to the window where the blinds were drawn. When he opened them the bright sunlight came into the room and unveiled an opulent setting. The room was furnished in heavy Ming Chinese furniture with strong touches of red and gold. Everything looked weighty and plush. "Where the hell am I?" he asked out loud to no one in particular.

The view out the window was magnificent: snow-covered mountains with a hard terrain. He could see he was in a new building complex and was in a finished wing. There were three or four more buildings under construction.

He went into the next room and found a sitting room with the same heavy Chinese motif. He saw a door but found it was locked. He pounded on the door but no one answered. He decided to sit down on the couch and try to figure out what happened. He put his elbows on his knees and his head in his hands. "I have got to think this through. I remember, we were in a car in Boston and I was jabbed with a hypodermic needle. I must have been drugged," he thought. "The terrible thing is, I do not know what has happened since. It is a complete blank. I imagine someone – when they are ready – will come for me and maybe explain what is going on. I'm in a plush room, with an outside terrain that I do not recognize and I seem to be in good health. I guess I just have to wait it out."

What Lovering didn't know was that the next two rooms were occupied with captives who were going through the same uncomfortable experience. A Dr. Walter Voss occupied the rooms immediately to the right of Lovering's. To the right of Voss' rooms was a Dr. Alasdair Little. Little was an electronics wiz-kid who worked for the J. Arthur Rank Company in Great Britain. Voss worked for the Phillips Company and headed up the lamp division.

The three doctors – all scientists – were recognized specialists in their fields. These were high profile men who could not be out of sight for long without raising alarm. People will start seriously trying to locate them if they do not contact their offices.

Their captors knew that and knew they would have to act quickly. They were organizing a meeting of the scientists to try to call off or slow down the people who might be searching for the famous three men.

Just as Lovering was deciding that all he could do was wait it out there was a knock at his door. Startled, he got up to see if he could open the door. As he approached the door with his hand out an electrical charge pricked his wrists and both wrists came together – inside wrist to inside wrist – and the bracelets clicked together. His wrists were bound together by a strong magnetic field and he couldn't pull them apart.

The door opened and two young women dressed in kimonos came into the room. They were smiling and said "Good morning, Mr. Rovering. Did you sleep well?" Without waiting for an answer they turned Lovering around and started guiding him out the door by holding on to his elbows. As he got out the door he was turned to his left and saw that there were two men being led just ahead of him. He recognized Walter Voss and called out "Voss – do you have any idea what is going on? Voss yelled back "Who is that?" "Lovering – Howard Lovering." "Howard, thank God someone I know – I have no idea what is going on?"

No one was stopped from talking. The women had a purposeful stride and kept everyone moving. They were walked in to a banquet room where there was a screen in the middle of the room and a number of chairs on each side of the screen. The screen was about six feet tall and half the width of the room. The three men were directed to sit on one side of the screen. As they sat, each was flanked by their female escorts. Suddenly, their bracelets lost their magnetic charge and the captives found they could separate their wrists.

Alasdair Little, in his thick British accent, asked, "Who might you gentlemen be?" Voss replied in a slight German accent who he was, then Lovering in his Boston accent replied in kind. One of the escorts silenced them with a loud SHHHhhh. The lights were dimmed and the men could hear footsteps then chairs moving on the other side of the screen.

An English speaking voice from the other side of the room said, "Good morning gentlemen. I'm sure you have a number of questions to ask. Before we give you the floor let me try to fill in the gaps so we can put you at ease and perhaps answer some of your questions.

"You were all flown to a secret location. We apologize for our rather dramatic way of bringing you together. For your inconvenience we will wire one million US dollars to your personal accounts to whatever bank in whatever country you desire. You have earned this money for just being here. The transfers will be made at the conclusion of this meeting.

"We have an exciting and important project for the three of you to collaborate on with our group of scientists. We have tried to get your companies interested by presenting unsolicited requests for proposals and have been summarily turned down. We understand why your companies might turn the project down but unfortunately the product we are seeking to manufacture still must be developed. The project is too important to us to wait for a breakthrough that might not happen in our lifetime.

"You three gentlemen are the leaders in specialties that are required to develop this product. We ask that you give freely of your time and knowledge during the next sixty days. If you are successful you will be rewarded beyond your dreams. If you discover a path that can be followed to continue the project each of you will be given nine million dollars. Imagine, just for participating and finding a path you will have received a total of ten million dollars.

"If nothing is developed we will present you with an additional million dollars just for trying. All you have to do to start the cash flowing is for each of you to contact his company and take a sixty-day leave of absence. Your calls, as you can expect, will be monitored. Our location and project are not to be discussed. You will also be given the opportunity to talk to your families with the same conditions. Are there any questions?"

Alasdair Little spoke up first. "I think I can speak for all of us that we resent the methods you have used to bring us here. As far as I am concerned you can stuff the whole thing. How dare you restrain me and force me to think only about what you are interested in. I am already a wealthy man and I do not need any help from your kind."

The voice from the other side of the curtain asked, "Do I assume that Dr. Little is also speaking for Dr. Lovering and Dr. Voss?" Voss and Lovering replied, "Yes." A muffled conversation started on the opposite side of the screen which none of the three scientists could understand.

Finally, the English speaking voice said, "We would suggest you go back to your rooms and reconsider what we have discussed." Little interrupted and said, "Stick it up your arse – balderdash – if we are to work with your people then why do we have magnetic handcuffs on our wrists? Ridiculous – we want out of here."

The voice very calmly said, "You saw how easy it was for us to bring you here. It will be just as easy to move you around the globe if necessary. I also warn you that it will be just as easy to bring your families here and show them to you. I would think of the ramifications to each of you personally before you turn us down. Our people are watching your families as we speak."

Lovering snapped his fingers to get the attention of Little. He then put a forefinger to his mouth, indicating for him to be quiet. Lovering said, "Will you allow the three of us to sit together in one room to discuss this?" "Of course," was the voice's reply. Lovering continued, "Then we would like twenty-four hours to reconsider your offer. In the meantime we also would like to be together to discuss the proposal."

The voice said, "You may meet together in one hour for one hour. Then you will be separated to consider what we have set before you. We hope that reality and understanding will win you over. Thank you, gentleman, we will leave first then you will be escorted back to your rooms. Your joint meeting will take place at five o'clock in Dr. Lovering's room. Good day, gentlemen."

With that there was some shuffling of chairs, then steps and finally the lights were brought up to full power. As the three men got out of their chairs they each felt an electronic pinch and their hands were drawn together and the magnetic field was set to full power. They were walked back to their rooms and as soon as their doors were closed their wrists were released.

CHAPTER 9
ABERDEEN

At 9 PM Hyacinth drove up to the door of the Peninsula Hotel in a steel grey XK two-seater Jaguar with right-hand drive. She took the keys out and flipped them to me as she got out so she could walk around the car and sit in the passenger seat. "You drive," she said, "It will be more fun that way." I'm not used to driving on the 'wrong side of the road' so I guessed it would be an interesting challenge.

The drive from Kowloon to Aberdeen is about three quarters of an hour. When we got out into the countryside I was able to let the car air out. I was topping 100 miles per hour and it was a gas. The top was open and the weather was beautiful. I have to admit, besides the view; the sight beside me was pretty spectacular as well. She was dressed in tight-fitting canary yellow slacks, a black silk blouse that was open to her cleavage, a yellow cap and a yellow silk scarf that was flowing in the wind.

As we drove into Aberdeen harbor the traffic picked up and we slowed down to almost a crawl. We parked and walked to the dock to get a sampan to take us to Jumbo. The restaurants offered motor launches, but, the sampan was slower and provided close up views of the boat people preparing dinner for their families. The boat city had just about everything that was available ashore. Some boat people never set foot on dry land.

We arrived at Jumbo Kingdom floating restaurant, which is the size of a football field. We climbed the stairs to the top deck and were seated amidships by the window on the starboard side. The sun was down, the view of the harbors twinkling lights was beautiful and romantic.

We ordered drinks, Chivas for me and a Gibson Martini for Hyacinth. We talked for a while and I was surprised how open she was about the new facility her company was building outside Vancouver. She was either trying to sell me a condo or was telling me that the project is something I should pay attention to because of recent events. I couldn't figure out if she was talking in code and was trying to help me or was just being enthusiastic about the project.

We ordered dinner of baby squid in an exotic sauce plus Chinese duck skin wrapped in thin pancakes. Additionally, we had baby bok choy and a very light fried rice dish that had a perfumed aroma. The dinner and our shared selections were delicious. Throughout the meal we drank an Australian white wine. I thought this wine needed more time to mature. It was a young wine and Australia was actively pushing their wine products throughout Asia. I could have passed on this one.

At about 1 AM we took the restaurant's motor launch back to shore and Hyacinth drove us back to my hotel. We talked a little but in general it was a fast trip. When we arrived she leaned over kissed me on my check and said, "I will see you after your meeting with Mei Cao Lin later today and then we will go to Repulse Bay – have a good sleep. Oh, don't forget your swimming trunks." I got out of the car and watched her drive away. I had a strange feeling, very uneasy, that she was trying to tell me something but was not ready to let it out.

I went to my room and placed a call to my office and immediately got Doreen. She said, "There have been additional developments in the case. Harry Collins has reported that a brilliant electrical engineer of the J. Arthur Rank Company, Dr. Alasdair Little, has been reported missing. Upon checking further, Collins found that he was abducted in the same manner as our two other missing persons.

"Obviously, the three scientists are being held together. The laser proposals you brought to our attention have been reviewed by a number of knowledgeable people. The three captured scientists make up a possible team to further develop the next step in lasers. We are not sure in what direction this development might go but one possibility is that it could result in some kind of weapon. Collins is working closely with Scotland Yard and MI-5 to see if it can be determined how they got Dr. Little out of the country though we do not know for sure if he has been taken out of the country."

I interrupted and said, "I would bet the house on it. He is out of the country and he is with Lovering and Voss. Doreen, please look into a new building development, about fifty-miles north of Vancouver that is being built by Chang Industries. I have a strange feeling about that place and I would like to know more about it." "Will do," she shot back. "Has Luke been able to make anything out of this yet?" "No but he is spending a lot of time with the FBI agents. They have certainly overstayed their welcome." Doreen is very protective when it comes to Luke Albert. She is concerned about him and probably doesn't approve of all of the time the FBI is taking.

"By the way" she said, "Collins was unable to find out where the Chang Industries plane landed in Canada. He said he has a suspicion that it was somewhere near Vancouver. But, he was unaware of any possible landing site." I interrupted, "A new runway, that is not yet government approved, is being built by a private company about 50 miles north of Vancouver. I believe it is tied in with the information I have asked you to research." "That is very interesting. I will immediately inform Collins and Albert about this development," she said. "Have a wonderful day and let me know when you get the information I am looking for – bye," and hung up the phone.

CHAPTER 10
AN AGREEMENT OF THE THREE

At five sharp there was a rap on Lovering's door and it was opened. Little and Voss entered with their wrists held together by the magnetic field bracelets. One of the women escorts emphasized, "one hour," and closed the door. The magnetic fields were released.

The scientists immediately started whispering, certain that they were being bugged. Lovering walked over to the radio and turned it on in hopes to create some background noise. The three of them stood near the window, figuring they should not make it easy for them to listen.

Little started but, Lovering put up his hand. "I am not prepared to bring my wife into this," he said. "I will agree to whatever they want us to do if it gets us home." Voss chimed in "That is a big if." The three stood silently thinking over their prospects. Little spoke, "Gentlemen, we are not sure of the project – what if we are designing something that is a horrendous weapon of some sort? I am not sure we are prepared to do that."

Lovering said, "If we do design something that might be outlandish we might be able to put our heads together and figure out some method to neutralize it. I think we should capitulate and let them think we are willing to design whatever it is they want. After all, my colleagues, how many times in your life have you been given a project without the mention of how much it is going to cost?" They all smiled. Lovering said, "If we are as smart as they say we are we should be able to control the development and be able to sabotage or find a counter measure to it if necessary. In the meantime, there is no need to put our families in any kind of danger. Are we agreed?" The two others nodded.

Now that they had a plan and felt like they were all on the same team they moved to the couches and started a conversation like the scientists they were. "Where do you think we are?" asked Voss. "I haven't a clue," said Little. Lovering said, "From what I was able to determine from the trucks and signs on the trucks doing the contracting work on the other buildings we are somewhere in North America. This is not Russia nor Mongolia or some other godforsaken frozen tundra. I believe we are in Canada." Little said "Good show, Howard. I was so angry I haven't even looked out of the window."

Lovering continued, "A number of months ago a Russian trading company and a Chinese company asked the Mann Company to bid on a laser system. The solicitations were given to me to look at and see if we might be interested in manufacturing them. I did some cursory research and determined that the approach might be able to work but the interest for the Mann Company to manufacture it was low to say the least. It was a good exercise but, at that time, I didn't think it was for Mann.

Voss and Little had not seen the proposals Lovering was talking about. That would not be unusual since their companies were huge in comparison to the Mann Company. The proposals probably got into the hands of the marketing departments and never advanced from there.

The hour quickly flew by and there was a knock at the door. The magnetic fields for bracelets were energized as Little shouted, "Shit! God-dam it! I hate these things." Four women entered and started to escort Voss and Little back to their rooms when one of the escorts, in broken English said, "9 o'clock meet again." The door was closed and Lovering's bracelets went limp.

Lovering walked to stare out of the window with a positive thought that help was on the way. He was wondering how Helen was. Just then, in one of the unfinished buildings two spotting scopes on tripods were taken down and two men dressed as workmen started down to the construction offices. The men were specialists in reading lips. They had read the lips of the three scientists as they were standing by the window and figured out the entire conversation. They were on their way to prepare a report that was to be ready for the 9 o'clock meeting.

CHAPTER 11
MEI CAO LIU AND CHANG INDUSTIRES

My wakeup call rang at 7 and a voice told me that the weather was expected to be clear today. I decided to do my Canadian Air force Exercise routine, which I'd learned almost ten years ago in our training facility in Virginia. The routine has served me well: whenever I returned for refresher programs I found I was able to keep up with everyone, and that made me feel terrific.

Breakfast in the Felix room on top of the hotel with its spectacular view of the harbor was a sight to behold. I ordered an American breakfast that was served from elaborately decorated covered sterling silver tureens. I made my choices of scrambled eggs, bacon, home fries and muffins. Traveling to another country and to a different style of cooking, I found it was always a good idea to start the day off with something familiar and comfortable. The rest of the day I could handle anything.

After reading the newspaper and taking a very easy morning I decided to walk to the Star Ferry. From there I made my way to the Chang Industries building for my meeting with the Mei Cao Lin people. Along the way I noticed the same person, who was in the same place that I was in yesterday, was there again today. I thought I might have been followed or shadowed yesterday but I wasn't sure. Well, it now appeared I was.

He was a slight young man in a light brown sport shirt and blue sport jacket with the preverbal newspaper that seems to always accompany a tail. As I was walking I put my left hand to my right armpit to reassure myself that I was carrying my .45 caliber pistol. I guess it was just habit but it felt good to know that I had something to protect myself with.

I tried to project nonchalance but kept a close watch. I got to the Chang Industries building and my tail did not go inside. I went to the eighth floor, where Mei Cao Lin had its offices. As I mentioned, eight is considered lucky: Chinese chauffeurs stand on line at the Hong Kong Motor Vehicles Bureau to get license plates with as many eights as possible.

I opened the door to the Mei Cao Lin Company at 9:45 and was surprised to see the simple, rather messy open, bullpen office layout. All the desks were grey metal and the chairs looked well worn. The office was busy with phones ringing and people talking. I quickly counted twenty-two or twenty-three people. A young worker came up and asked in unaccented English, "How may I help you?" "I have an appointment with Mr. Cao and my name is Robert Schein." I was shown to a small sitting area where Chinese newspapers and magazines littered the coffee table and chairs.

I cooled my heels for about twenty minutes before anyone came to report "Mr. Cao was on the phone and will be ready to meet with you in about ten minutes." I said, "thank you" and picked up one of the magazines and pretended to read.

All along I was watching the operation of Mei Cao Lin Company. I noticed two directors at the head of a row of desks; the younger members would walk over to them to report on their phone calls. The calls were in Chinese, English and German. A German speaker was only about twenty feet from me and seemed to be very comfortable with the language.

Finally, the young woman indicated that Mr. Cao was available to see me. We walked past the rows of desks and entered a small, clean and simply appointed conference room. Mr. Cao walked in as I was about to be seated. He said, "good morning" and made no indication to shake my hand. "Would you like some tea," he asked. I nodded and said, "That would be fine." The young woman left the room and Cao asked, "How may I help you?"

I thought that he was being direct and that was unusual for a Chinese. I expected some small talk and was slow in reacting. Cao surprised me by having a strong resemblance to another member of his family. That Mr. Cao was assassinated before my eyes in Japan about ten years before.

"My company, TAG Photographic, Inc. is interested in expanding its product lines into LASER products. We are interested in cutting and measuring instruments. We are a key supplier to the David W. Mann Company. They forwarded your unsolicited proposal to us. TAG is the distributor of Nikon products in the States and we have an excellent relationship with the Nikon factory in Japan. We believe that there is some synergy between LASERS and photography. It is our desire to stay ahead of the competition and that is why we are strongly interested in what you have proposed."

Cao thought a moment without saying a word. I made my presentation and remained silent. It would be a break in protocol if I said anything. If necessary I was prepared to remain silent until lunch. Cao finally said, "We didn't authorize the Mann Company to forward our proposal to you.

This is a breach in confidence and we are not very happy about this." I shot back, "Did they sign any agreement with you stating any point of confidentiality?" Cao said, "No." "Then I don't think you can blame the Mann Company for trying to help you by finding another manufacturer or supplier."

Cao looked directly at me and said, "If we wanted to go to Nikon we wouldn't have needed you or your Company. We would have done so directly." "Yes" I said, "But you didn't. Now, let's not make an issue of this and see if we can bring this to any conclusion so that both of our companies can get something out of the project's possibilities."

Cao said, "We have already contracted with another source and are already underway with the project. The proposal you are reading is out of date and no longer of interest to us. New requirements have been suggested and added. So Mr. Schein, we ask that you back away from this and when and if any product or products are derived from the project we will make sure you are contacted."

That was an interesting response, I thought. OK, he obviously will not give me any more; I decided to see what his reaction will be when I mention other parties. "Mr. Cao, is Mashpriborintorg involved with the project?" There was no expression change or response. I pressed further, "Can you tell me how Madame Chang of Chang Industries is involved?" That brought a slight bit of surprise to his face. Cao was now sitting up straight on the edge of his chair when he responded – "Madame Chang is not involved with this project. How dare you involve her name as if she was a common person off the street? She has been very helpful and generous with her time as a member of our board of directors. Mr. Schein, thank you for your visit our meeting is now at an end." Cao stood up and walked out of the room before I could say anything else.

I thought this was surprising and amusing. I obviously hit a nerve with the mention of Madame Chang. It was curious he would lose his composure so quickly with the mere mention of her name. His assistant came to escort me to the door. As I was looking around the office on the way out I saw Cao's corner office; he was on the telephone, angrily gesticulating and standing as he was talking. That immediately put me on guard. My relationship with the other Cao was, if you didn't agree with him he had you taken out. That made me a little nervous. It was certainly food for thought.

I exited the Mei Cao Lin Company and pressed the elevator button up. It was now about 11:30 and I was on my way up to Chang Industries. I stepped out of the elevator and the area around the elevator doors was a hubbub of activity. People in conference on one end, others sitting and waiting while others were walking in and out of the area.

At the reception desk I asked to see Hyacinth Chang. "Who shall I say is calling?" "Robert Schein." "Just one moment please." The operator started a conversation in Chinese and I heard my name mentioned." She then looked up and seemed startled. She said, "If you will please wait a moment, Madame Chang has requested to meet with you." "By all means," I said. I found myself an unoccupied couch and plopped myself down to wait.

About five minutes later a pretty young woman came and asked me to follow her. I was led through a couple of corridors with open office doors and into a glass, enclosed conference room. It was a very plush setup with comfortable chairs, fresh flowers, beautiful appointments and a view of Hong Kong Harbor. I sat down and waited for Madame Chang to show herself.

Twenty minutes later the door opened and in walked Madame

Chang. Much to my surprise she was unaccompanied - Hyacinth or an assistant was not shadowing her. I thought this unusual. She was gracious when she said hello, she offered her hand and I kissed it. She was dressed in a tailored suit that seemed to be a little large on her. She wore large rose-colored pearls around her neck and wrist. She looked quite a bit older than the last time I saw her and very tired.

I asked how she was and she replied that she was fine. We talked about the camera industry in the States for a few minutes and then about her U.S. distributor, Al Bernard. She said, "Everyone is getting older but you look the same Robert – maybe a little more mature and filled out but just about the same." I thanked her for the compliment, and returned it by saying, I was happy to see that she had recovered from her illness. She was being very pleasant so I was girding for the outburst that I was certain to come.

She continued, "You are aware that I know of the real mission of your company. Why have you come to Hong Kong now – at this time? What is your interest in Mei Cao Lin? Finally, I rarely involve myself in my daughter's affairs outside of business but I am not happy that you two are seeing each other." That hit me in the face as if she'd thrown a right-handed punch and hit its mark.

I had to say to myself – OK Robert, pull yourself together. This is a wise and difficult lady. Be very careful what you say. "First, I am here because of TAG business. Sigma has opened a Hong Kong factory and I promised Mr. Yamaki that I would visit it. Second, David W. Mann Company, one of our top customers for specialized lenses, passed on two laser proposals and we became interested in them. We believe that lasers and photography have a future together.

"Finally, there is nothing – I repeat nothing – going on between your daughter and me. Is she attractive – you bet she is! Do I like being around her? – I certainly do, she is good company. Have I gone to bed with her? – NO! Do I intend to go to bed with her? NO! Do I think of it? – YES! However, I also think of my wife and I think of my children. Going to bed with your daughter is not one of my plans."

Madame Chang was stoic and stared at me as if she could see through me. After a few moments she said, "I do not believe you are telling me the truth." She held up her hand before I could interrupt. You came to see Mei Cao Lin because of a missing scientist. I am an investor in Mei Cao Lin. It is my penance for having the elder Cao son assassinated in Japan. Nippon Kogaku [Nikon] will not build the type of laser my associates are interested in. You are lying.

"If I don't believe you for the first part of my question why should I believe that you will not bed my daughter? I don't believe you." She raised her voice a decibel or two and continued, "I do not interfere with Hyacinth so I will not stop your trip to Repulse Bay. Please take this as a warning, Mr. Schein. Whether it will be you or my daughter to blame is not my concern. You both will have to wear the guilt and I will not enjoy that result."

Well, if the cards were really on the table I had nothing to lose. "Then tell me, do you have Howard Lovering?" "No," she snapped. I was surprised she didn't say Howard who? "Are people in your organization holding Lovering?" Equally as firm she said, "No." "Where is Lovering being held?" "Mr. Schein, this is getting boring, so I will help you. I am an investor in a project with Mei Cao Lin and other people. That is all I know or will say about the project – period, end of report." She got up and left the room.

CHAPTER 12
BACK IN THE SCREENED BANQUET ROOM

The three scientists were seated as they were in the morning; their hands locked in magnetized bracelets. There were footsteps and chairs shuffling on the other side of the screen. Suddenly the magnetic field was turned off and their hands were free.

The voice started: "Gentlemen, have you come to a decision?" It was agreed that Lovering would be the spokesman. "We have decided," he said. "We will participate as long as our families are not brought into this and they are safe. If they become involved we will stop immediately. We ask to talk to our families periodically so that they have no need to worry. They must also know we will be coming home after 30 days." Lovering stopped speaking.

The voice started and was interrupted by Alasdair Little. "At the end of this meeting we expect to have the confirmation that one million US dollars has been forwarded to our accounts. We have written down the routing and names of the banks. Mine is in the Isle of Man, Lovering's is in the Cayman Islands and Voss is in Switzerland."

The voice said, "That will happen as soon as you have assured your families and your business establishments that all is well and you are taking a short leave of absence." Lovering objected, "That was not the original agreement." The voice said, "It appears that you are negotiating about the time you are spending with us. You have already broken the terms of the agreement."

Lovering looked at his companions and they both nodded. "All right, we agree." The voice continued, "We are reasonable people and we will adjust your time with us to 45 days instead of 60. Thirty days is believed to be too brief to accomplish what we are looking to do. Are we in agreement?" Lovering asked, "What are we supposed to be working on? What is the project?" The voice said, "You have had an indication that it involves a laser. That is all we will say until you have talked to your families and business organizations."

"You will be in our laboratory tomorrow at 8 AM to meet the staff you will be working with. They will introduce you to the project. Then each of you will be presented with a contract that you will sign and then, and only then, will we be able to continue our relationship." Lovering asked, "Will a copy of the agreement be sent to our families?" "If that is your wish, the financial part of the agreement will be sent to your families for their safekeeping. It is our intention gentlemen, to live up to our agreement. The only way to break it is to sabotage the project, which would bring down the wrath of the principals. Are we agreed?"

Voss spoke up, "I would like to have these bracelets taken off. They impede my work because they remind me of the time I spent in a concentration camp during the war. They disturb my thinking, and if we have signed an agreement why would you have to worry about three old men causing a problem?" There was a hush and people started talking fast on the other side of the screen. But their words were muffled and could not be understood by the three scientists. Lovering, listening determined that he heard one woman's voice and three or four men's voices. He also thought one of the men spoke with a thick Slovak accent and the other man had to be Asian.

The discussion went on for five or six minutes. Everyone stopped talking, it became quiet and the voice said, "We agree to remove the bracelets while you are working in the laboratory. However, they will be put back on when you return to your rooms or go to dinner. Gentlemen, we do not have a very large security force and we do not want to weaken their effectiveness by having to observe you all the time. Are we now agreed?" Lovering looked at his two colleagues and both reluctantly nodded. "We agree."

CHAPTER 13
REPULSE BAY

I waited in the conference room for Hyacinth to arrive and after about thirty minutes the receptionist came and said that Madame Chang and Miss Chang were meeting and were not to be interrupted. Miss Chang suggested that I return to my hotel and she would pick me up at 4 o'clock. I thought, I would love to be a fly on the wall at that meeting, but said, "Please tell Miss Chang that I will be waiting for her arrival."

At 4 on the dot Hyacinth drove up in her Jaguar. It was a beautiful day, the top was down and a very solemn Hyacinth Chang met me. I jumped into the passenger seat and without a word we took off. I chose to look straight ahead and refrain from small talk. I figured that when she was ready she would start talking.

Repulse Bay was about an hour's drive and at thirty minutes into the ride Hyacinth started to relax. I could almost see her tension disappear. She took a deep breath and let the air out and asked, "What did you and my mother talk about?" That hit me by surprise, "She didn't say?" "If she did, would I be asking you what you discussed? Now, what did you talk about?"

"She mentioned the possibility about there being an 'us' and I told her that was impossible." "That wouldn't make her this angry. What business did you discuss?" Interesting, I thought and said, "I have a friend missing and I wanted to know if she knew anything about it." Hyacinth asked, "Did she?" "She said she did not," "Do you believe her?" I had to be careful here, "I am not sure." "Then you don't believe her." "Hey, don't put words in my mouth or put me in the middle of a family squabble." Hyacinth took her eyes off the road for a second and said, "This is very serious Robert, this is no joking matter. If you mess with my mother the Tong; [Chinese Mafia] will move in and you do not want that to happen." No, I thought, I do not want that to happen.

"What is going on, Hyacinth; why are you so upset?" "When my Mother doesn't tell me what is going on it usually means that she is trying to protect me. It can mean it is a dirty and dangerous business. Robert, I will spend the afternoon and evening with you and tomorrow morning I will drive you to the airport to make sure you get on your plane to Japan. I can't bear the thought that you could be injured or killed over this. I am taking no chances."

Huh, a Chang is protecting me from a Chang. This is a different turn of events. But why kill me; I don't see the gain in it. Unless the mere thought of someone snooping around is enough. I have to think about that for a few minutes. We both sat quietly after Hyacinth's pronouncement and did not speak the rest of the way.

The Repulse Bay Hotel is a beautiful old colonial hotel. Down the middle of a vast lawn was a concrete walkway to the beach with flower planters along the way. It looked like a river of red geraniums.. Looking to the left of the hotel was a small mountain peak that was defended by the British during World War II. This place sheltered British civilians and fought off the Japanese until the magnitude of the invading force overwhelmed it.

It was a beautiful sight to be sitting on the veranda in wicker lounge chairs looking out to sea. We agreed that we would not go swimming. I told Hyacinth I didn't want to tempt fate. Her Mother could be proven right and I just wanted to sit and not give in to whatever animal feelings I might have for her. Hyacinth laughed and we decided to sit, relax, drink and later have dinner in this historic building.

I was drinking Chivas on the rocks, looking at the bay and glancing at Hyacinth when I thought that my scotch didn't quite taste right. I ignored it, thinking it might have been because of the ice, and took another sip. Suddenly, I felt woozy. I closed my eyes trying to shake it off and the veranda started to spin and I felt nauseated. I again closed my eyes and tried to stand up when I heard Hyacinth ask, "What is the matter, Robert." I got one word out - "sick" - and passed out.

There was a dreadful pounding in my head; I felt the room was spinning. I could hear a couple of voices speaking in Chinese. I peeked through my closed eyelids and realized I was on a bed. Two Chinese girls were talking while undressing. I shouted as loud as I could, "What the hell is going on - get out of here."

The girls ignored the outburst and came onto the bed. "Look, our big boy is coming awake. How are you big boy? We are going to take care of you – have a good time. Just wait a minute." One girl got off of the bed and finished undressing and stood there so that I could see her naked. The other girl quickly did the same. They both stood there, arm in arm, and said "We are all yours."

"Get out" I shouted, "Out." Instead, they started to fondle me and undress me. As they were doing this, I almost started to give up the fight and give in when I heard a click. It was a sound that I was very familiar with. I heard the click again. It was a distinctive sound. I ignored the girls and looked around the room. There was a large mirror across from the bed. I started to flail my arms around and clipped one of the girls in the mouth and she fell off of the bed. The other girl backed away for fear of also getting hit.

I struggled to the dressing table, picked up the chair and banged it against the mirror. The chair just bounced back. I looked around the room and saw a glass coffee table on a metal stand. I was now in a rage. I lifted off the heavy glass and picked up the metal stand and rammed it against the mirror. The mirror cracked. I rammed it again. It cracked some more. The girls were screaming and one started to punch me on my back. I turned to her and hit her with the steel base and she collapsed. The other girl grabbed her clothing and went screaming out the door.

I turned back to the mirror and with one final thrust I rammed the steel base through the mirror. It broke and crumbled into a hundred pieces. There were two people behind the mirror in a small closet-sized space. There also were two cameras on tripod, one was a Sankyo 8 mm movie camera and the other a Nikon 'F' 35mm still camera. It was the sound of the Nikon camera shutter that got me out of my daze. The expression of fear and surprise on the faces of the two women when their shooting position was given away almost made me laugh. They quickly turned around, leaving their camera equipment, opened a door and fled the room.

I reached in and grabbed the equipment, tripods and all, opened both camera backs and exposed the film to the light to destroy it. Even though I had a massive headache I was angry and still working on adrenaline. I was so pissed I picked up the cameras, by their tripods and flung them against the wall across the room. I didn't know what I was doing. I ran across the room, picked them up and slammed them against the wall again. I can't ever remember being this angry and this crazy. I felt as though I had the strength of a bull and if anybody got in my way I would kill him.

I pulled myself together, ran out of the room and saw that I was in an apartment building. I found the stairs and ran down to an exit and freedom. I emerged on the street in a poor neighborhood of either - Hong Kong or Kowloon. I had no idea where I was. I put my hands into my pockets and found that I still had my Hong Kong dollars. I walked a block and hailed a taxicab. I asked to be taken to the Peninsula Hotel. The driver looked at me curiously but did not ask questions. He took off and we soon arrived at the hotel. We'd been just a few blocks away. I over-tipped him and entered the hotel. I guess I didn't look terrible because I didn't feel that anyone was staring at me. I got my key at the desk and made it to my room.

I stripped off my clothing and ran the shower. I made it as hot as I could stand and let it beat on my back and head for what seemed a half hour. Dried and refreshed, I walked to the bed and sank down, trying to put together what happened.

I called the front desk and asked them the time and day. It was Wednesday, 11 AM. I had lost a full night. What the hell happened to me? I decided to call the office and talk to Doreen on the other side of the world. I didn't know if she was in the office or in her apartment. I needed to talk to someone and I chose her. The phone rang and she picked up. She seemed to understand my predicament. I guess she lived through something similar to my experience a number of years ago with Luke Albert. Unfortunately Albert wasn't able to destroy the film results and it haunted him all the way to Washington. When Albert had his incident he was in Hong Kong with a prostitute and under the influence of opium. The person who set up the charade was none other than Madame Chang, the

Dragon Lady. That is her trademark. Embarrassment and blackmail are how she controls people. It didn't work with Albert even though she had the incriminating film. It sure as hell didn't work with me. It made me feel vulnerable but it also made me very angry.

I talked the evening out to Doreen, reviewed everything I could remember and I started to understand what happened. I thanked her for listening and helping me. She seemed tired and said, "As soon as you can get out of Hong Kong and get to Japan." She then said, "I will book you at about 4 PM today, Hong Kong time, which will bring you to Haneda Airport at about 6:30 PM Japan time. We will keep your arrival under wraps so you won't have factories lining up to meet you in the airport. I will arrange for Bob Claypool to pick you up." "Thank you" was all I could say. We hung up and I felt a lot better.

I thought I had to get some normalcy back in my head so I decided to call home. I woke Debbie; it was very early in the morning. She tried to make some sense out of our conversation while her head was still asleep. She wanted to know how I was doing and I told her "Everything was fine." I said, "I just wanted to hear your voice." That brought her fully awake. "What's wrong, Robert?" "Nothing," I replied. "I will be on my way to Japan this afternoon. I will call you then."

"Robert, stop it. I know you too well. You are very conscious of the time you call me and you don't usually sound so upset. I can hear it in your voice. What is going on?" "Debbie, I am just tired. I am sorry to have alarmed you. I forgot the time, it is very early for you and that is that. There is nothing to worry about." "Are you sure," she asked. I firmly replied, "Yes, I am positive. Send my love to the kids, give them a kiss for me and go back to sleep. I will call you tomorrow from Japan." We hung up.

That puts my life back into perspective, I said to myself. I am always surprised how perceptive Debbie is. She reads me like a book. I have to remind myself of that the next time I call.

CHAPTER 14
PLACATE FAMILY AND BUSINESS

T he three men returned to their rooms and were told that at 10:30 their phones would be open for them to call their families and firms.

The script was to say that they have been asked by their respective governments to take a leave of absence and work on a highly secret project that is vital to national security. The government apologizes for any difficulty, inconvenience or anxiety it might have caused because of the men's sudden disappearance. Unfortunately, the project was moving rapidly and there was no time to properly alert local authorities. It is expected they will be out of touch for a little more than one month.

It was a weak script but Lovering thought it might work. On the other hand, he said to himself, I have to think of some way to send a signal that my captors would not understand. They surely will be censoring each call and will probably cut the call or have it on a delayed response. They most likely can add static and probably imitate a small telephone voice. That way the people on the other end would be totally unsuspecting. I have to be very careful.

At 10:25 PM there was a knock on Lovering's door. As one of the female escorts entered the room, the magnetic field was activated and his wrist bracelets came together. The escort plugged a headset into the stationary telephone and dialed Lovering's home number. Helen said, "Hello?" Lovering responded with "Hello, honey." Helen screamed. "Thank God it's you. Are you all right? Are you hurt?" Lovering stopped her questions and dutifully repeated the script.

Then he added: "I am doing fine and the work is challenging. I am sorry I will not be home for our anniversary, and send a happy birthday greeting to Robert." Helen was puzzled by this request and said, "Robert was just here. I am sure he will be happy to hear that I spoke to you." "Good," Lovering said. Lovering was being given a signal to end the conversation. "Goodbye, dear, I hope to call you soon. Before Helen could respond the telephone went dead.

Helen stared at the phone and said, "I didn't say goodbye." The FBI agent said, "We recorded everything. Did you think anything was out of order, Mrs. Lovering?" Helen thought a minute then said, "Yes, it is not our anniversary and I do not believe that Robert has a birthday this time of year. If I remember correctly it is in September. Our anniversary is in June. I can't imagine why he brought that up." The agent said, "He might be trying to send a signal. We will study the tape and see if we come up with anything else."

Lovering then repeated the same litany to Burt Wheeler at Mann. Wheeler was ecstatic to be able to talk to Howard. Wheeler, of course granted the leave of absence. He asked if he had spoken to Helen and Lovering said, "Yes."

Wheeler then asked, "Howard, we are having trouble with uneven illumination on the Texas Instruments Photo Repeater. Can you give me a hint where to start to correct the problem?" Lovering looked at his escort and she nodded. Lovering thought a second then said, "Adjust element #7 up and down a couple of millimeters at a time and retest." Burt said, "Thank you, I will call and look after Helen while you are away." The line went dead.

Burt Wheeler didn't know that the FBI had obtained permission to tap his telephone, for national security reasons and for Wheelers safety. Burt Wheeler was about to call Helen when he realized that there was no element #7 in Howard's illumination system. Wheeler immediately called the FBI local office from the business card that had been left with him.

Lovering's escort was on her way out when his bracelets' magnetic field was turned off. These bracelets are very bothersome, he thought. I hope I got my messages across.

I have always had a feeling that Robert was involved in some way with clandestine activities for the government. That is why I decided to mention his name at the last moment. I hope I am correct. I think Burt will understand and get to the right authorities. Lovering figured he covered all of the bases he possibly could have in the censored short telephone call with his wife and Burt. God, he thought, Helen sounded terrible. I pray to God we get through this.

CHAPTER 15
A VISIT TO JAPAN

I boarded my Cathay Pacific flight at about a quarter to four. I found my seat and plopped down like the weight of the world was on my shoulders. One thing that everyone remembers about Cathy Pacific was the tall leggy stewardesses they employed. Each one of them could be a fashion model. They were all beautiful. Watching them lightened the load.

One stewardess in particular reminded me of Hyacinth Chang. She asked me if I wanted a drink before takeoff, "A Chivas over ice will do fine." Before I got myself settled and started to close my eyes the drink was on my tray-table and served with a large warm smile. I smiled back and took a cautious sip. My last sip of scotch knocked me out and I lost a whole night. This glass of scotch was exactly what Chivas was supposed to taste like. I took a large pull and slowly closed my eyes.

Before I nodded off I was thinking about Hyacinth Chang. She didn't call when I returned to my hotel. She truly seemed surprised when I could say nothing else except the word "sick." I find it hard to believe but, maybe - just maybe - she really knew nothing about my conversation with her mother. Maybe she did not know anything about knocking me out and trying to set me up in that cheesy apartment. There are too many maybes. That is way too much of a coincidence to believe but, I guess it is possible. There is another maybe; maybe she was trying to send a message when she mentioned the Vancouver project. I don't know I'm too tired to think straight and nodded off as the plane took off.

The wheels locked into place, jolting the plane, and I immediately awoke. We were on our final approach into Haneda International Airport. We turned in over Tokyo Bay and quickly we were on the ground. The new jet-way, connecting us to the terminal, was jockeyed into place and the planes door was opened.

My red diplomatic passport got me quickly through passport control and into the baggage area. I was waiting by the carousel when I felt a tap on my back and turned. It was Lt. Robert Claypool (Ret). I was happy to see a friendly face. We shook hands and Bob said, "You look like shit. What the hell is going on with you? I see you only a week ago and you look great, then you go to China and you would think you walked the entire way. What gives?" "It's a long story that I will tell you about over a drink in the hotel. Where did you put me up?" Bob said, "In the Okura Hotel just as you requested." "Great."

For years we went to the Frank Lloyd Wright designed Imperial Palace Hotel. After a long run of more then seventy years the classic old hotel was torn down to make way for a more up-to-date modern facility. Most of the people of the photo industry switched over to the Okura. The Okura was opened in 1960. They even named a couple of their restaurants after the old Imperial's restaurants in hope to attract the Imperial's guests.

It seems there is always room for luxurious, five-star, first class hotels no matter where you go in the world. The Okura has got to be at the top of the list. When you visit the Okura, for the second time, it is like returning home. That is probably the best thing you can say about the quality of service for any hotel.

The Okura Hotel is situated near the center of Tokyo right across the street from the American Embassy. It is a brisk walk to the Ginza or the Imperial Palace. We arrived and the cab driver opened the back door with his lever. The doorman, collecting my B-4 bag, recognized me and said, "Welcome back Mr. Schein. It is good to see you." "Thank you," I said and went inside. As soon as the manager saw me walk in he grabbed my room key, came from behind the desk and bowed. We shook hands and he started to take me to my room with a bellhop toting my bag.

The hotel is built on the side of a hill and the lobby is on the fifth floor. My room was on the sixth floor, number 637. Bob said he would meet me in the Starlight Lounge as soon as I was organized.

The manager showed me into a very comfortable sectioned off bedroom. The drapes were drawn because it was about 8:00 PM and the bed was turned down with some chocolates on the night table. There was an ikebana fresh floral display and bowl of fruit (apples, oranges and grapes) on the small conference table. The manager said, "I hope everything is in order." "Yes, thank you."

I handed him a yellow receipt for the contents of my locker to be brought to my room (a service for their regular customers). "There is no rush, anytime this evening will be fine." "Very well Mr. Schein, enjoy your stay." I unpacked, freshened up, and then went up to the top floor of the hotel - Starlight Lounge - to visit with Claypool.

The lounge was crowded but Claypool found a couch and chair

combination near the window that was relatively quiet and private. I brought him up to date with everything I could remember that happened in Hong Kong. Bob asked, "What do you think? Do you believe the daughter is ignorant of the activities of the mother? Do you think she is putting on a façade and is right there with her?" "Good questions, I'm not sure what the answer is. I am as confused about this as you are. My heart says, I hope Hyacinth is not a part of it but my head tells me she must be."

"I agree" said Bob. "She has got to be a part of it. Even if she might not be we have to assume she knows what is going on." "OK, where the hell does that leave us?"

Bob continued, "They obviously wanted to shut you up for some time. They figured if they could embarrass you, your creditability would have been shot. That would have caused some delay in trying to evaluate your information. If you got too close to what they really are doing they probably would not have tried to embarrass you, but, most likely you would have been killed or injured. I guess we are not quite there yet but we are on the edges of what Madame Chang is involved in." Sarcastically, I said, "Thank you very much. That makes me feel a whole lot better."

Bob laughed, and started his report. "Mei Cao Lin has been very active in Japan flogging their laser proposal around the optical and electronics industry. Cao himself has been here to try to interest factories in what he is looking to build. Once Cao met the people at potential manufacturers and they turned him down he went after some of the employees. I understand that he has hired ten or twelve people at high U.S. dollar contracts and has taken them out of the country.

"I also learned that only Chang Industries sub-contractors in Japan were contacted by Mei Cao Lin with their proposal. I called a couple of companies that weren't doing business with Chang Industries and they had no idea of who Mei Cao Lin was."

"Bob, what the hell are they trying to build? This is an expensive operation. Contract salaries, abduction, I am finding this to be very disconcerting. What do you think?" "I agree, this has got to be something very big. There is a lot of money involved and they haven't yet declared what they really want to build."

"The only people I know who would pay for something involving lasers at this level are governments or extraordinarily wealthy people who feel that something can be developed to sell to governments, the military or mass markets. You know Bob; I think I know what it is. They want to build a weapon. I think a frightening weapon. It has to be that. Why else would they abduct three of the world's foremost scientists and hire a staff of scientists? It is the only thing that makes sense to me."

"Let's call the office tomorrow, get their update and try to decide where and what we should be doing. In the meantime I will visit Nikon and set up meetings with Mamiya, Sigma and Fuji in the hotel. That will save a lot of time and I will be able to hit the road in a couple of days." Bob then made a point of caution – "Robby, if Madam Chang thought you might be getting close to what is going on, she tried to discredit you and failed - I don't think she will stop because you went to Japan. She just might employ her good friends the Yakuza to take care of you."

"You are right. I will contact Chief Ichiro Hiro of the Japanese Domestic Crime Agency and bring him in on this. He has been a friend in the past and I am sure we can count on him to assist. He most likely will put a tail on me to let everyone know that I am being protected. I don't think that will stop anyone but it wont hurt either."

Claypool decided that I should get a good night's sleep. "You still look like shit," he said. I'm afraid I felt that way as well. I conceded I would go to bed. We planned to stay in touch after my meeting with Nikon. We then took an unattended elevator down and I stepped off at roku ki (6th floor) and Bob waved as the doors closed. I felt it had been a long day. I had an eerie feeling that it was not yet over.

I put my key in the door and out of nowhere a man tapped me on the shoulder. In one motion I spun around got on one knee and pulled out my .45 cal. pistol with my left hand and cocked it with my right hand. I must have surprised my intruder by his reaction. He stepped back and put his hands up to show he was unarmed. "Choto mata kudisai" and again, "Choto mata kudisai," (please wait a minute, please wait a minute) he shouted. In broken English he said, "Hiro Sacho-san meet you tonight." I stood up and started to breath again. "OK, lead on McDuff." In the meantime, I felt as though I'd had the crap scared out of me. Whew!

We went down six flights of stairs and out the Okura's back entrance. I was walked up to a large black Mitsubishi four door sedan and as I was recognized, the back door opened and I was asked to jump in. All of a sudden I became a little wary and slowed my gait and put my left hand on my pistol. A familiar voice called out "Come on, Schein-san it is only me – Ichiro Hiro." I relaxed and moved faster.

We warmly shook hands and I teased "Making house calls now. Business must be slow." Hiro laughed and said he'd received a call from Luke Albert. "Luke brought me up to date and said that you would arrive tonight. After what happened to you in Hong Kong I think I will attach a couple of men to you daily while you are in Japan." "Hiro-san, you must have been listening to my conversation with Bob Claypool. That is exactly what we decided we were going to ask of you."

"Good, then it is settled. Do you have any more clues regarding the whereabouts of the three scientists?" "Not solid ones yet" I replied "But I will be sure to run them by you before I leave in a few days." "Wonderful. It is good to see you so fit, Schein-san. Have a good stay and remember that I am only a phone call away." "Thank you, Hiro-san, thank you very much." "Robert, it is my pleasure - besides being my duty - Oyasumi-nasai (goodnight)." I echoed his parting phrase, stepped out of the car and watched him drive away.

I went back to my room and called my wife to check in as promised. Everything seemed to have cooled down and I guess I sounded better. I told her I had a big day ahead of me and I was going to get some shut-eye as soon as I hung up. We said our goodbyes ending with "I love you."

I then called the office number and got Doreen's surprising report that "Our three missing scientists called their homes and offices saying that they are on a 'leave of absence' and that all were well. The only one who tried to indicate that all was not well was Howard Lovering. He signaled by mentioning he would miss your birthday party and his wedding anniversary, which are not until later in the year. And, when he was talking to Burt Wheeler he gave instructions for a non-existing element in the illumination system of a photo-repeater."

"Good old Howard, always thinking," I said. "What does Luke say about this?" "Nothing changes, we keep on looking." "I agree. After the nonsense in Hong Kong we think that the Yakuza might be brought into the picture. Madame Chang is no one to fool with. Luke must feel the same way Bob and I feel. He contacted Chief Hiro before we did. Doreen, please tell Luke that Hiro is providing some sort of watch team while in Japan. We agreed to this only a few minutes ago." "Good, Luke will be happy to hear that."

"I am hoping that Nikon will be able to decipher the information from Howard's notes," I said. "Maybe we will get an idea of what is so important that they are trying to build it in such secrecy." Doreen said, "Luke arranged a meeting with you, Shirahama and Miyahara tomorrow morning at the Nippon Kogaku head office. They will send a car for you. I believe they then would like you to visit the factory in Ohi-Machi and possibly have dinner with them."

"Great, he saved me a few telephone calls. Goodbye for now from Tokyo" I grandly said. Doreen jumped all over me: "Cut it out Robert. Please take care of yourself. I don't want to have to train a new person because you were careless." "OK Doreen, goodnight" and we both hung up. It was now two hours later than when I had my premonition that the evening was not quite over. In another ten minutes I had my lights out.

CHAPTER 16
PREPARING TO VISIT NIKON

y wakeup call buzzed and the voice said "It is 6 AM
Mr. Schein and the weather is mild today at 13°
Celsius, about 55° Fahrenheit." I got out of bed and
did my exercise routine until I worked up a good sweat. Then
hopped into the shower, got dressed and went down the
elevator to the Camellia breakfast room.

I was looking around when an old friend, Abe Fiegelson waved
and beckoned to his table. I got a big greeting and a hug from
Abe who said, "Please join me. I just got here myself."

Abe Fiegelson is the president of Anglo-Photo of Canada and
is the Nikon distributor in Canada. He is a gregarious, funny
man who loves to play practical jokes on anyone at any time.
Sometimes I think he goes overboard but his response is, "that
it's all in good fun." "I'm surprised to see you here this time
of year, Abe, how come?" "You guys in the States have been
so successful with Nikon that it's spilling over the boarder into
Canada. I've had to increase my letter–of-credit with the
factory. I am going to pitch them for some open-account credit
relief. Always having to open a letter of credit is killing me.
It's time consuming and costly."

"I wish you luck. That's a tougher job then you'd think. You
know the Japanese government may have to get involved with

that issue. They like to see merchandise shipped from Japan with some secured documentation - cash in advance or L/C. They really do not approve of open account credit unless there are no other choices and the buyer has a type 'A' credit background." Abe indignantly said, "Are you implying that my credit stinks?" Laughingly I said, "Yes." "Humph," Abe said turning up his nose up looking away from me. As I said, Abe is fun to be around.

Abe then asked, "Did you notice Jerry Littman on the other side of the room?" Littman is Fritz Scheonheimer's right-hand manager of sales. Intercontinental Marketing Corporation is Scheonheimer's company. He usually makes the trip to Japan so it is unusual that Littman is here alone. I looked across the room, Littman and I made eye contact and we both waved. "You know, after all these years Scheonheimer is still embarrassed because of what happened with Minolta. When he had to give Minolta up because Yashica complained, that was a very bad moment for him. He just might not enjoy visiting Japan that frequently and sends others in his place."

While we were being served breakfast I asked about the winter Olympics preparation in Calgary for 1976. Abe was jubilant about the games coming to Canada. He said, "We have more building and more foreign investment than we expected throughout the country. It is also going to be great for the photo industry. Photography will make out like a bandit." He tweaked my interest when he said foreign investment. "Abe, Calgary is not that far from Vancouver. Will Vancouver be used for any of the events?" Abe replied, "No, everything will be in the Calgary area. However, I repeat, all of Canada will gain from the Olympics."

That hit me like an arrow and I thought that maybe Hyacinth was actually trying to tell me something. We finished our breakfast and I said, "Abe, I have to call the office. I am sure we will bump into each other here or in the factory." "I know we will because we are having dinner together. Shirahama has invited us both this evening. He told me that yesterday." "That's super; I look forward to this evening." I got up slowly and returned to my room. I dialed my office number and reached Doreen. "Has anything been discovered about the Chang development in British Columbia?" "Not a whole lot," Doreen answered. "They are developing a community in the mountains not far from Vancouver and I gather it will be for the fairly wealthy."

"Doreen, I think this might be a little far-fetched. It doesn't really add up in my mind yet but, let me try something on you." "I'm all ears." "The plane holding Howard Lovering files a flight plan to Toronto. It never arrives in Toronto and no one gets suspicious because the flight controller might have gotten a call that the plan was cancelled. In the meantime, the plane somehow flies between Quebec and Ontario all the way to Hudson Bay. It then hangs a left and heads west over Manitoba, Saskatchewan and Alberta, then flies down into British Columbia into the Vancouver area. The Chang's development, just outside Vancouver, includes a private airstrip. That airstrip has yet to be approved for normal traffic by the government. The plane lands and is somehow covered and stored. It might even have taken off again and returned to Hong Kong. Who would ever have thought that the plane would end up on the other side of Canada? I know this is very sketchy but from what Hyacinth said to me I can't let it go. What do you think?"

"It's a bit thin all right, and it might be a crazy enough of a stretch to look into," she replied. "I don't think we should call out the Mounties or go parachuting in with guns blazing – but we should check it out. I will talk to Mr. Albert and see if he agrees. Maybe we can get Harry Collins to take a look-see. He was going back to Canada this week to try to find out what might have happened to the Chang plane anyhow."

"I feel a lot better now. I just don't want to let any stone go unturned. Thank you again Doreen." We both said goodbye and hung up. As I was walking to the bathroom the phone rang, I picked it up and a voice said, "Hello, Robert." "Hyacinth?" "You sound so surprised," she said. "You bet I am. When you didn't call or try to find me and were not present when I woke up I figured you were finished with me." "How can you say that, Robert? When you passed out I ran into the hotel to get help. When I returned you were nowhere to be found. We searched the grounds, I had the manager call the police and you disappeared. I only thought to call the Peninsula Hotel yesterday to see if you still had a room there and you were avoiding me. I was told you checked out. I had my secretary call the major hotels in Tokyo and she found you at the Okura. I figured you acted like you were sick because of what my mother said and fled the Repulse Bay area. I thought it was my fault. I am calling to say I am sorry for whatever I did or what my mother said."

I was bowled over. This was either a crock of shit or she is very naive and her mother really pulls the puppet strings. "Look Hyacinth, I want to believe you but when I ended up were I did all trust went out the window." "Where did you end up?" "I think it is best you ask your mother that question. For now, let's stay friends until we straighten out everything. I want to be sure you are not a part of a scheme of some sort." "What is my mother going to tell me Robert? Answer me, please?" She sounded about to cry. Wow, this is not the Chang family style, I thought. Could she be telling me the truth?

"Let me sleep on it for a day or two. I will call you in your office." She said, "I am going to Vancouver for a few days and will return next Monday. Leave a message with my secretary and I will reach you. Is that OK?" She sounded like a college kid.   Either she is a great actress or I am just a gullible pawn. "OK, it's a deal.   As soon as I know where I will be I will leave you a number.   Hyacinth, I have a car waiting downstairs so I have to get going, goodbye for now" and hung up.   I stared at the phone.   This can't be real I thought.   You can't make up things like this.   What was her game? I have to think about this. In the meantime it was time to go to work.

CHAPTER 17
THE CONTRACT AND THE LAB

The three scientists were rounded up at about a quarter to eight in the morning. With their bracelets magnetized they were marched to the elevator, then through the basement of the building, out a back door, through an outside wind screen and finally into a mobile laboratory. In actuality, there were three labs connected end to end. Their wrists were released and they were asked to put their hands, one at a time, into a black box. They did and their bracelets broke in two and fell into a receptacle. Howard thought to himself, "Talk about high tech items. These bracelets are a pain in the ass but you have to admire the technology."

There were four men dressed in white lab coats waiting for the scientists. One of the men approached Lovering, put out his hand and said, "It is good to see you again Mr. Rovering." Lovering startled blurted, "Do I know you?" "Yes" he replied, "I have recently worked for Zenji Wakimoto at Nippon Kogaku. My name is Kawakami." Lovering stared for a moment. "Yes I do remember you. What are you doing here?" "I joined the project a couple of weeks ago," Kawakami replied.

He walked over to his colleagues and introduced them. "Dr. Ping from China - a chemical specialist; Dr. Rabinovich, from Russia - a weapons designer; Dr. Klieber, from East Germany -

an electronics specialist; and I am a lens designer from Japan. The men were directed to a small conference room where seven chairs were waiting and they just barely fit in the room.

The door was slid closed and Kawakami started the conversation. "The four of us have been briefed on your backgrounds and some of you we know. We have chosen, to participate in this program. There are six laboratory assistants whom we brought along; they also freely decided to join. We understand that may not be the case with you three. That does not affect us in any way. All we are interested in is the development of the product and of course the money we have received and will be presented with once a product decision is made.

"I also would like to add that the people in this room represent some of the finest scientific minds in today's industrial world and it is an honor to be with you and work with you. I hope we can come to a quick conclusion so that we may all return to our homes as soon as possible. In the past two weeks this operation was moved from another remote location. Everything is very portable and can be moved on a moment's notice. I mention this only because of the secrecy of the project."

Alasdair Little interrupted, "Excuse me, but whom are we working for?" Kawakami continued, "The name of the company is REC, Ltd. but, in a one word answer, Communism. Three Communist nations have a large stake in this project. The information on the weapon to be developed will be equally shared between China, East Germany and Russia. Lovering asked, "What is the weapon? Other then our shaking hands and saying hello, no one else has said a word."

Kawakami, obviously the leader of the four scientists, continued, "In analyzing recent wars, conflicts we saw the advantage of a battlefield weapon that would incapacitate – but not kill – an enemy soldier. We learned in Korea that a wounded soldier usually requires at least two men to help him to an aid station. The result is, three men have been taken off of the line thus reducing the firepower of the team the enemy is fighting.

"A dead person obviously doesn't need any help. A wounded person needs help and brings a bunch of other fears, anxiety and guilt to a soldiers mind. It polarizes them.

"That is one of the reasons why MASH units were moved as close as possible to the front lines in Korea. It saved time, it cheated death and the helping hands of the soldiers not wounded were not kept away for long periods of time from the front lines and it didn't reduce the firepower needlessly.

"From a humane point of view I don't want to kill anyone. However, the weapon we are trying to design will permanently blind an enemy soldier. The laser beam will hit his face and his cornea will be burned irreparably." Lovering blurted, "That is inhumane! A weapon like that must never be developed."

Kawakami continued, "Is the atomic bomb humane? My country can tell you it is inhumane. Nevertheless, East and West are stockpiling atomic weapons. Does that mean they shouldn't be produced? Maybe someday that can happen but not today – not in 1962.

"Gentlemen this weapon will be built. It will be called - Personal Tactical High Energy Laser - PTHEL. It will be a weapon that can be carried by one soldier and can be used in battle. If we do not build this weapon, I promise you, someone else will build it. If we build it, then we can learn about it and understand it and maybe even figure out how to combat it as well. Indeed, it might be considered unpatriotic if an individual has the opportunity to learn about a dangerous weapon and also learn what makes it tick to help stop it. The people we are working for would not hesitate to let this type of information out to the public. It would ruin our careers if we personally said no."

The room got very quiet and Lovering said, "Well, we got the soft sell and the hard sell and they both stink." He looked at his two colleagues and they both nodded. "I guess we have no choice – we are in." Klieber opened a file folder and handed out three contract, letters of agreement. Upon signing each would receive one million dollars, then nine million more if they came up, within 45days, with a way to build the weapon. The last financial point was off the chart. It was a percentage of sales from the manufacturer of 1% for the life of the patent. That could mean untold millions of dollars for each of them. Finally, the seven men were listed as patent holders. It was a very generous agreement.

Reading further, the agreement labeled sabotage and untruthfulness as being the major deal breakers, and a hint of further repercussion. A letter was to be signed by each scientist. The holder of the agreement was a world-wide consortium called REC, Ltd. (Russia, East Germany and China).

Once the paperwork was done the scientists were shown around the laboratory. The machinery and tools were state of the art and under normal conditions this would be a great place to work. Some interesting pieces were shown but no mock-up or any test results were seen. Lovering thought this to be unusual but figured they might be waiting to see if the three of us were really onboard. Than can wait until tomorrow.

After the tour they were escorted back to the first trailer and

the infamous black box. Each man stuck one hand in at a time
and squeezed two parts of a bracelet together. then stepped on
a floor button. The color of the light in the box changed and
the bracelet was bonded onto the wrist. Each of the three
scientists repeated this action. When they were ready to exit
the trailer they were told to hold their wrists together and the
magnetic field was reestablished. There was the anticipated
pinch and their wrists were locked together.

CHAPTER 18
VISITING NIKON'S HEAD OFFICE AND FACTORY

As I was gathering my papers the phone rang and I was told that a car was waiting for me. I thought it was kind of early at 9:15 in the morning because the office is maybe ten minutes away. I went downstairs and saw a familiar 1959 blue Buick. This brought a smile on my face. As soon as Alex Triguboff saw me he got out of the car and gave me one of his Russian bear hugs. He squeezed the breath out of me. "Alex, you look great." In his thick Russian accent he said, "Miyako [Alex's wife] sends her regards. Why do you look so terrible, Robert?" "I don't feel terrible but between you and Claypool telling me how bad I look I am beginning to wonder."

We got into the car and Alex drove it out of the way of the hotel traffic and parked. "Luke and Doreen filled me in where we are with Lovering and your Hong Kong trip. Robert, how are you really doing?" "I'm fine, a little angry with myself for falling into Madame Chang's trap but other than that I'm OK." "Well, the result wasn't too bad and there doesn't appear to be any evidence to worry about. However, Madame Chang is a vindictive woman and I am concerned that she will call upon some of her Yakuza friends to reach you." "That might be true; that is why I have already talked to Ichiro Hiro. He is having some of his people shadow me while I am in Japan."

Alex said, "I noticed them on the street waiting for you to come out. OK, it is what it is."

"Miyahara called me and told me about this morning's meeting with Shirahama and then going to the factory. He asked if I wanted to be present. I naturally said yes and that I would pick you up. If you have any objection I can bow out of the meeting." "Of course not, I am happy that you will be with me. It feels good to have some friends around." Alex started up his car and we headed for the office. As we made the turn out of the hotel driveway I saw that a black Mitsubishi sedan was following us. "I guess our friends have joined us."

I asked, "When are you going to replace this heap." "It still has some life in it. Besides, if I purchased a new American car it bears a 100% duty price entering Japan. I can knock it down a little by purchasing the car in the States, drive it around for a month or two and then bring it to Japan as a used vehicle. The duty is only about 45% in that case." "Whew! They really protect their products." "Right and I won't buy any of the Japanese crap. I'm an American citizen [General MacArthur's staff issued citizenship to Alex and Miyako for duties performed for the U. S. Army during the occupation] and I will drive only American cars."

We drove to the new Nikon headquarters, across the moat from the Imperial Palace. We were now in a prestigious neighborhood with new office buildings that had underground parking and connections to buildings with an arcade for a wide selection of restaurants. We parked in the Nikon lot and took the elevator to the top floor. The head office area was done in teak and stylish furniture.

President Shirahama came out to the lobby, which is a high honor, to shake our hands and bring us to his spacious office. He was shadowed by a young woman in a uniformed jacket, brown penny loafers, white socks and plaid skirt. In my mind, I laughed at the thought they didn't want Shirahama to get lost. It very rarely happens that the top executive of a Japanese company would go to the lobby to receive a guest. This was a compliment reflecting the success we are having with the Nikon 'F' camera. As we walked to his office everyone stood up and silently bowed as we passed. For a westerner it was a strange feeling, like a soldier saluting an officer as they passed each other.

Miyahara, director of export, joined us. Alex and I sat in the comfortable side chairs in front of Shirahama's desk while Miyahara brought over a straight-backed chair to join us. Miyahara started by saying how concerned he was about Howard Lovering. "Mr. Rovering has been a good friend to Nippon Kogaku and we are all wondering if he is well and will he be all right." I took a moment before I answered. Because of my previous action in Japan, everyone in the room knew of my CIA involvement. It is a secret that no one talks about but everyone knows.

I chose to take the assuring and comforting company line. "Mr. Lovering recently called his home and office stating that he was taking a leave of absence for forty-five days. He appeared to be sound of mind, committed, strong and in control of his faculties. He and the two other scientists involved were granted leave by their companies. To our knowledge everyone is in good health and not under any duress." As far as I was concerned that was a complete fabrication of the facts.

Miyahara translated for Shirahama. Shirahama speaks English fairly well but Miyahara wanted to make sure his president had the latest word accurately on the Lovering situation. Shirahama smiled and said, "Good." The old man looked away a moment and I realized he didn't believe a word of what I'd said.

When Dr. Nagaoka died, Shirahama became president. Nagaoka was a physicist and studied optics in Germany during the war. Shirahama was a marketing man and has been with NK for almost forty years. Getting the product to market and listening closely to his engineers' problems is how Nippon Kogaku has gained great respect with their parent company, Mitsubishi. The bottom line is obviously better and the company is now able to look at many more projects.

Shirahama said our projections and orders have been excellent and thanked us for our business. His theme was that we are 'happy partners.' We all smiled and said, "May this go on for a very long time." Shirahama mentioned that we were going to have dinner in an old restaurant that he frequents and he was looking forward to the evening. He also indicated that he had invited Abe Fiegelson from Canada to make sure we have fun. "Fiegelson-san always makes the night lively."

Miyahara asked if we were ready to go to the factory and I nodded. We said our goodbyes and made our departure. Triguboff was asked to leave his car and join us in a company car. The ride to the Ohi Machi factory was about thirty minutes. We paid a toll and got on a highway and soon we were at the factory, passing the guardhouse pulling into the courtyard. I got out of the car, cautiously looked around - I remembered being shot at in this very spot. My friends and working partners came out of the building as our escort of Hiro's men pulled into the courtyard. I'd been wondering if they were with us.

Zenji Wakimoto came bounding down the steps as if he were a kid of fourteen rather then a man of forty-five. He stuck out his hand and loudly said "Schein San, welcome to Japan." I smiled, "thank you." Right behind Wakimoto was Segawa, manager of the mechanical shop and Nakano, director of the factory. It was nice to see everyone again. We all walked into the building, climbed the stairs and entered a small conference room where the obligatory mugs of tea and cookies were waiting for us.

Alex and I greeted everyone. I asked Segawa how he made it back from Canaveral and he said, "Mr. Summits of Life magazine helped me to get to the airport. From there on it was no trouble - Orlando to New York to Tokyo - it was a long day to get home. I thank you and TAG Photographic for your hospitality and the opportunity to see the Mercury Seven flight." "You are quite welcome; it is not every day we get to see history in the making." During our conversation everyone else was listening intently. I thought it better we just move on.

I started the meeting by giving a summary of what was going on with Nikon sales in the States. We were slowly conquering the newspaper industry by giving cameras to newspaper staffers around the country. In theory this was our cheapest advertising angle: When an amateur saw a professional photographer using a Nikon on the job he decided he wanted the very same camera. It was a straight prestige angle, a keeping-up-with-the Joneses, and it was working beautifully.

Another key to our success was the service staff we had in place. In New York we had ten factory people and they were just wonderful to work with. We went out of our way for the professional photographers and the word got around. Our timing and our marketing approach couldn't have been better. Everyone, including our parent organization, was very happy with our financial results. The money was flowing in and the product was being shipped. We were breaking our own sales records, especially when we started doing one million dollars at wholesale prices per month. This was the success we dreamt of when we first saw the Nikon 'F' camera almost ten years ago.

I handed over TAG's projections and everyone at the table started looking at the numbers. This was unusual because normally they would have given the projections to their office staff to evaluate. However, production was having problems filling the orders and the key players who decided what and how much was going to be produced were sitting in this room. They were like kids who couldn't wait to open up their Christmas presents.

There was a lot of shaking of heads and the word "difficult" muttered over and over. Difficult to the Japanese means – NO! I interrupted their conversation and perusal of the paperwork. "I don't need an answer today but I will be leaving within two days. An affirmative answer would be very helpful at that time. We will meet in my hotel at about 10 in the morning and hopefully I will be able to convince all of you that the schedule can and must be met.

"Remember, Canon, Olympus, Pentax, Miranda and so on, would love to hear that we will not be able to supply our dealers' requests. The competition will run strong promotions to sell their equipment – stock up the stores – and that forces the dealers to sell the product because of the cost of inventory sitting on his shelf. They will take a major portion of our product market share if we are stymied and stuck in the mud."

Everyone was quiet. They knew I was right and they would have to put their heads together and figure out how to meet the schedule. Wakimoto broke the ice and said he wanted to show me some new lenses he was working on. He had them on another table covered with a red cloth. Out came the jeweler's pads and he placed a couple of unusual lenses on them. One was a 35 mm f3.5 distortion correction lens and the other was an 8mm f5.6 fisheye lens. When I looked closely at it I thought of it as an actual eye of a fish. That would have been some size fish.

Both lenses were mounted on 'F' camera bodies. They looked like jewelry, and holding them and looking through the fisheye special optical finder was exciting. The fisheye had such a short back focus that when used on the 'F' camera you had to have its mirror locked up. The image result was a full 180° circle.

The distortion correction lens allowed the photographer to correct angles of view similar to how you use a view camera. The lens straightened out converging lines in the viewfinder. I thought it is development of lenses like these that will keep the Nikon 'F' System way ahead of the competition. I was very happy with what I saw and we all relaxed.

While everyone was feeling good I figured I would spring my surprise. I reached into my bag and brought out the Cousteau Calypso camera. I didn't say anything, just demonstrated it. The camera was a bit smaller than the 'F'. It had three major sections. One was an enclosed lens that had to be twisted counter-clockwise and pulled out of the body when taken off. It did so with an airtight pop. Then the mechanics of the camera were lifted out of the body, and that was where the camera was loaded with a standard roll of film. The third part was the base of the camera that held it all together.

The camera could go down to 300 meters in water with no additional protection and no problems. Wakimoto reached for the camera first. He played with it for a few shots then passed it around the room. Everyone was fascinated by it. They wanted to know whom to talk to in Monaco, and I handed all my information to Miyahara. Everyone thought this could be a perfect product for Nikon's specialty list. A self contained undersea camera was just the ticket. If you put a Nikon 'F' into a plastic housing and tried to work the controls with extensions it was just too awkward and bulky

– and you could never attain the depth of 300 meters.

Everyone was handling the Calypso and talking about it when three young women walked in with trays of food. Because of my short stay in Japan we were having a working lunch. The first course was a bowl of suimono (clear soup), then unagi (eel) over a bed of rice in a wooden bento box. Pickles and ginger were on the side. Each person was given a bottle of Kirin beer with a tall cold glass. I commented, "Isn't beer unusual in the factory?" Wakimoto said, "You should come more often Schein-san, the beer is served in your honor and I like beer." We all laughed.

The conversation quickly got around to Howard Lovering. Their concern seemed genuine. These men had worked directly with Lovering when he visited. I stayed with the company line, "All was well and Lovering has contacted his family and the David Mann Company to ask for a forty-five day leave of absence which was granted."

The statement seemed to satisfy everyone and the conversation shifted. We talked some shop and about how their colleagues, who were servicing the cameras in the States, were doing. The servicemen, who were in the States for one year, were without their families and living together in rented apartments.

After lunch Alex and I were shown around the factory and we saw the high rate of production and lack of space to comfortably expand. They were sure they would have to build additional facilities but were not completely committed to the idea yet. Their answer for the present was to run two and three shifts around the clock.

Alex was an easygoing person to shadow me during the meetings. He chose not to speak during our negotiations. If he had a thought he would write me a note. He was constantly observing and trying to be as inscrutable as our hosts were. After the tour Miyahara, Nakano and Wakimoto said they would see us for dinner. Alex and I got into a car and I was returned to the Okura and Alex was taken to his car.

CHAPTER 19
THEY ARE PLAYING FOR KEEPS

Harry Collins, our affable Irishman, had a conversation with Doreen Parks and decided that the Vancouver lead was worth looking into. His BOAC ticket took him from London to Toronto, and then it was Air Canada to Vancouver. Vancouver is a stunningly beautiful city, with a bustling center and surrounded by spectacular natural beauty including the Coast Mountains. Because it is framed on three sides by water, residents here enjoy one of the most temperate climates in Canada.

Collins made a couple of stops to pick up equipment then pointed his Avis red Ford Mustang toward the mountains. He mapped out where the new development of Chang industries should be. When he was only twenty miles from the city he noticed that there wasn't anything but the road and the mountain range. People, cars and roadside stops seemed to disappear. There was very little snow and the road was clear.

As he got deeper into the mountains, about fifty miles out of Vancouver, Collins started looking for some sign that a development was under way. He was hoping for a sales office so he could pick up a map of the development, pretending to be a serious buyer. However, all he saw was a twisting road with not even a dirt path exit. Collins was starting to wonder if this was a wild goose chase when he saw a small hand-written cardboard sign with the word

101

"trucks" and an arrow. He slowed and made the turn.

Collins bumped his way to another rise in the mountains and saw nothing but more of a trodden down lightly snow-covered road. It was very quiet: no people, no traffic. "This is some hell of a fun community," he said out loud. He came to another rise and saw a chain link fence and a small guardhouse. Collins stopped the car and backed down the road until he was sure he was out of sight of the guardhouse. He pulled the car off to the right where he saw a group of boulders and some trees.

It was a little hairy trying to maneuver off of the road but he spotted a bald spot where the wind had blown away the snow. He slipped and skidded until he felt he could, more or less, hide the car from immediate view of the dirt road. The Mustang might have some trouble getting back on the road but he was counting on its sturdy snow tires. He felt he was being ultra careful but, to see a guardhouse and a fence covering a large area in the middle of nowhere and not see any kind of development made him decide to take the path of caution.

Looking around, Collins noticed a reasonably high hill about thirty yards to his right. He was happy he'd stopped at a sports shop - Gart Brothers - in Vancouver for some climbing gear and warm clothing. He started his climb slowly and carefully, breathing easily. Fortunately it was not icy and his footing felt secure. He climbed about a hundred yards up the hill, breathing heavier, decided to turn and look around to see if any of his view had changed. It had -- dramatically.

Down the other side of the hill a large complex came into sight. It had one completed tower and two others under construction. He took out his 7 X 50 binoculars and started a slow scan over the site as if he were on a sailboat looking for a distant buoy. He noticed people walking in straight lines.

They would go to one end then turn around and cover the same ground. The men were sentries. Collins peered into his binoculars looking for a weapon of some kind but could not make any out. They were unarmed. Why the hell would someone stand guard without a weapon?

He started to rationalize what he was looking at. They were walking the same path because they didn't want to have to establish a new path in fresh snow. It would be wetter and colder that way. I bet they have weapons in a warm location if they ever needed them. After all, who would be crazy enough to come out here looking for trouble? No one at all. Collins decided to make himself more comfortable and sit on a fallen tree, take off his backpack and study what was before him.

Lovering was looking out of the window of his suite. He was starring at nothing in particular when he saw a glint of light on the left side of his window in front of the mountain range. No, he said to himself, I must be imagining that I saw something. Then he saw another glint. There is somebody out there. I can't make out anything but maybe I can signal back. He went into the bathroom and tore the shaving mirror from its mount. He went back to the window and tried to catch something of the dying light. "There!" He shouted, "He saw my reflection."

Collins sat up straight as a quick reflection of light passed just before him. He realized his binoculars must have reflected light. I better get moving. He jiggled his binoculars back and forth hoping to show whoever sent the signal that he saw it. Whose signal it was he didn't know but he did know he had to get moving. If he saw the signal, then others might have seen it as well. Collins made a mad run down the hill and did it in a few minutes rather then the thirty minutes it took to climb it.

He threw his gear in the red Mustang, got his pistol out and got behind the wheel. He struggled getting the car in position to get back on the road. He was giving it too much gas and had to ease off and take it slower. The snow tires finally gripped but he wasted precious time. He got back onto the dirt road and started a controlled dash back to the highway.

One of the guards at the top of the tower saw the same glint of light that Lovering saw. The guard had high-powered – 8 X 300mm - binoculars on a tripod. He confirmed that a man was watching the complex and picked up his radio to alert his superiors. In back of the completed tower was the heliport and airstrip. A Bell two seated, bubble type helicopter started to warm up as one of the security crew was running to the passenger side holding an AK-47 machine pistol. The chopper took off and started in the direction of the road and the intruder. The chopper quickly picked up the red Mustang and flew to its side with a warning – "Pull over. You are trespassing on private property."

Collins ignored the chopper and kept on going. He was going fast and knew if he braked he would skid. It was tough keeping the Mustang on the road. His only route was straight ahead. He would certainly spin out if he tried to zig-zag off of the dirt road to get away from the chopper. He was in a bad spot when the chopper opened fire. The bullets stitched across the hood of the car. He kept going. The chopper came in low and fired a volley through the glass and one of the bullets hit Collins in his left shoulder.

Now it was very hard to hang onto the wheel and keep the car straight. Somehow he continued. The chopper came directly at him and the AK-47 firing. He was shooting back when a bullet from the chopper hit Harry Collins between the eyes. He slumped over the wheel and the car went into a spin and turned over then exploded in flames.

Collins, an expert marksman, also hit his target. One of

Collins's bullets found the chest of the pilot. The chopper teetered back and forth and finally went down on its side plowing a huge track in the ground as the prop dug into the dirt and fell apart in pieces. The chopper came to rest about fifty yards from Collins. Both men inside were dead.

CHAPTER 20
A CALL TO THE OFFICE

As I entered the lobby of the Okura I saw Bob Claypool sitting in one of the comfortable leather chairs waiting for me. He waved and we decided to go to the Camellia room for a cup of coffee. Bob asked how my meeting with Nikon went and I said, "It would have been great if they could have said that they were able to reach the production levels we are asking for. They parried a little here and a little there. I will know by tomorrow whether they will be able to manufacture what we are looking for. I seem to be having the same problem with the Ultra Micro Nikkor lens manufacturing. Mass production is tough when very high quality and precision are involved."

Bob said, "I have some information regarding the Mei Cao Lin Company. I think you might be a little surprised. The other partner in the company is Mama Cherry. Mei is one of her forenames from her mother's side – she was Chinese." "Are you sure of this?" "Absolutely, we have checked it back and forth with both the registry in Hong Kong and Japan. Alex and I had long discussion about this and he confirmed it. There is no question that these two ladies, Madame Chang and Mama Cherry, are still close partners."

Mama Cherry was a famous restaurateur in Japan. Among her many assets was that she owned the Copa restaurant and had close ties with the Yakuza. The Copa is *the* night spot to visit while in Japan. Upstairs on the mezzanine you can have one of the best steaks served in Tokyo, listen to a dance band and have a paid escort sit at your table or dance with you on the crowded dance floor. It was all topped off by a gaudy high kicking show twice a night.

Cherry's connections with the Yakuza were infamous. If you wanted to find someone, do something that wasn't quite legal or arrange something with various government parties then the dreaded Yakuza were the people you wanted to speak to. Mama Cherry had a direct pipeline into the organization.

I remember her saying, "If you were a successful business *woman* in Japan that meant you were a prostitute, a restaurant owner, a madam or held some important man by his gonads. I have had the pleasure of mastering all four areas." Women in the 1960's were not in the top management of any major businesses in Japan. I had previously run into the Chang-Cherry combination about ten years ago. They were tenacious and ultimately violent. They proved to be a very difficult combination of negotiators to do business with.

"Bob, there is no doubt in my mind who is involved with the Lovering abduction. There may be other partners such as a Russian party but, the people calling the shots are most likely Chinese," I said. Bob thought a moment. "Chang and Cherry have fronted the Red Chinese before. They obviously are still doing it but now through the Mei Cao Lin Company. I guess Chang's involvement with the Cao assassination ten years ago angered their benefactors and that is why they now have the company with a Cao family member as a partner." "Has this been reported to Luke Albert yet?" "Not yet," Bob said, "I wanted to tell you first before I went any further." "Let's use one of the Okura offices." We went to the hotel's business center and made our request and were told that a room would be available in five minutes. I ordered up some coffee.

We were soon ushered into a small, elegant conference room set up for us with coffee, water, fruit and cookies. Pads, pencils and pens were on the conference table. We made our call and sure enough Doreen's voice said, "TAG Photographic." All of the outside 'employees' use a special number and that is why we were always able to make contact. "Hi, Claypool and Schein reporting in" I said. "Hello gentlemen. I believe Mr. Albert was hoping to make contact with you today. Hold on while I transfer your call and attach the recorder."

Through the speakerphone we heard, "Albert here." "Bob and Robert here, Luke." "Hello guys, do you have anything new to report?" Bob filled him in on Mei Cao Lin and I filled him in on my Nikon visit. Albert continued, "Harry Collins is overdue by about ten hours. He went to see the Chang development in Vancouver and has not reported in. Collins is very reliable and when he says he will make contact he does. I am getting concerned and have already called the Royal Canadian Mounted Police. I spoke to our contact, Inspector Hahn. He said he would check out the development tomorrow. In the meantime I requested two of the Company's personnel, Speziale and Held, to backtrack everything we knew Collins was doing - rental car, hotel, equipment purchases and airline. Maybe we can re-establish his itinerary and figure our where he was and when. We know where he was supposed to be going."

"Luke, I just remembered something: Hyacinth Chang said she was going to visit the Chang development in Vancouver for a couple of days. I wonder if she has arrived yet. It could be an innocent coincidence but you pretty much proved to me over the years that innocent coincidences are not so innocent."

"Good," Luke said, "I'll have Hong Kong follow her trail and then turn it over to our team to follow up. It may be nothing but I doubt it. Do you have anything else guys?" "That's about it for now," I said. "I'm having dinner with Shirahama and Abe Fiegelson this evening." "Knowing Abe I am sure you will be having a good time. So long guys, report in tomorrow." We all hung up.

"I wonder what Harry is up to, Bob, what do you think?" "I don't think we have enough information. However, I have worked with Harry before and he is a stickler for keeping his schedule. I don't think he would miss a call in unless he was in some kind of difficulty." "Well, let's keep our fingers crossed and hope he is just delayed." "Sure, but I am not very convinced." "I will see you tomorrow about 8 for breakfast. I'm going to take a shower and change for tonight. We have meetings with Mamiya and Sigma in the hotel conference room. Bob, if you hear anything reach me – OK?" "Right, see you tomorrow."

When Lt. Robert Claypool retired from the Navy about five years ago he decided he wanted to stay in the Orient. Luke Albert hired him for the TAG Photographic Far East Office and made him a full fledged CIA participant. Bob is a good guy with a lot of contacts. He works well with Alex Triguboff which is very important. What you need in a good broker and agent is someone who is amiable, has a ton of contacts and is not afraid to try different things. Bob with his military background fits the bill on the money.

CHAPTER 21
DINNER WITH NIKON

After a long hot shower and a fifteen-minute power nap, I felt refreshed and was looking forward to the evening with Abe, Alex and the Nikon people.

As I was dressing the Hyacinth Chang issue was still bothering me. Does Madame Chang run separate lives with each of her companies – I doubt that. How can you be so close to one another and not know what is going on or, at least have a hint of what is going on in the other company. Hyacinth must know something or she is completely insensitive. I don't think so, she has got to be a part of this, you can bet on it.

OK, now that is clear in my head, what am I going to do with it? Good question, I thought. Why did she decide to go to Vancouver now? Why did she inform me of the development when she didn't really have to? She was trying to tell me something. She might not agree with what her mother is doing and this was her way of retaliating. This is kind of far-fetched but it has possibilities. I decided to call the office.

"Doreen, Robert here. I think I have to get to Vancouver and should leave first thing tomorrow. I will cancel my meetings and maybe come back later in the month. With Harry missing, the indication I might have gotten from Hyacinth Chang, and the possibility that the Chang plane ended up in Vancouver makes everything pointing to that city. Let's have our team and the RCMP hold off one day until I can get there. I think I would like to be present when we confront Hyacinth Chang."

Doreen said, "OK, if you like I might be able to get you on a military flight in the wee hours of the morning. What do you think?" "OK, I always wanted to fly copilot on an Intruder of some sort." "Yokosuka Naval Base is the closest to you and probably our best bet. Let me see if I can make arrangements. I will leave a message at the desk if I am successful. In the meantime, enjoy your dinner with Nikon. If this works out I will either cancel your meetings with Mamiya and Sigma or tell Bob Claypool to handle them. Remember you gain a day crossing the International Date Line. I don't have to hold up our people because you should arrive in time if all goes well." "Super, let's make it happen."

I could feel the adrenaline starting to run through my veins. I have to calm down and slow down a bit, I chided myself. Easy big guy, you have a whole evening ahead of you. As if on cue the telephone rang. "Mr. Schein, your car is waiting." I put on my tie and sports jacket and walked out of the room. On the way down the elevator I noticed a man standing in the corner. I thought I knew him. Yes, he is one of Hiro's men. God, I never noticed any of his people earlier; they must have been with me all day. Neither Bob nor I noticed them. That is a little scary. Our antennas aren't working, I have to change that, I thought. "Come on Robert, wake up or you could be pushing up the daisies instead of smelling them."

Alex's blue Buick was waiting and Abe Fiegelson was already in the front seat chatting away when I got in. "Hello guys, how long a ride do we have." Alex replied, "About forty minutes. We are going to the Sansuyso Ryokan in the Kanto District. This area is where Shirahama Sacho-san lives and the inn is not far from his house. It is an old inn and I think you will like it." We all settled down for the ride with Abe chirping away to

Alex. I tuned out, settled back in the comfortable car and thought of what I had learned today. I still wasn't one hundred percent sure about Hyacinth but for Howard's sake I had to try.

We drove off of a busy street and into a curved driveway. As soon as we stopped two kimono clad girls came to the car to lead us inside. We got to an alcove, took off our shoes and were helped on with slippers. Bending over carefully so that we didn't hit our heads on the low overhanging beams we came to a small, five tatami room (tatami mats are woven together from tall grass and are specific sizes – approx. 40"x 60" each. A five tatami room would be five tatami mats). We took off our slippers and walked into the room where Shirahama, Wakimoto, Nakano and Miyahara were waiting.

Next, off came our jackets and were put to one side against the wall. I carefully put my shoulder holster and pistol in the fold of my jacket. In the middle of the room was a foot well. In the center of the well was a burning potbelly stove with an open fire at the top. The stove was in the center of a table and the top of the stove was even with the tabletop. You slipped your legs into the well and it was like sitting at a warm dinner table.

It was now wintertime. The older Japanese inns with their paper-thin shoji screens didn't have central heating systems. In each of the rooms there would be some method to safely burn wood or coal. Our room, with the stove in the center, was set up to keep feet and hands warm, the idea being the rest of your body would feel warm. It works pretty well for the front but I could certainly feel the cold on my back.

Suntory Japanese scotch whiskey was being poured very liberally by Miyahara. There was no ice in the glass; it was being served neat. As soon as we had our drinks, Shirahama would say, "kampai" (bottoms up) and we would down a full jigger of scotch. Everyone warmed up very quickly.

I was sitting next to Wakimoto, who was grinning. He tapped me on the knee, leaned closer and whispered, "We have a special surprise for Fiegelson-san. I can't wait." I didn't ask what the surprise was but I know that both Miyahara and Wakimoto had been the butt of a number of Abe's practical jokes over the years. This should prove to be interesting, I thought.

A waitress knocked on the shoji screen and carried in our first course which was steaming hot miso (bean) soup. She also brought a tray of seven hot sake decanters and small cups. The tradition is that you try to keep your partner's sake cup filled and he tries to keep yours filled at all times. It was rude to fill your own. Our waitress filled our first cups and again Shirahama said, "kampai" and we all repeated "kampai" and drank the cup of sake.

Our waitress left and we were making small talk about our families. Abe tried to tell some jokes and he was getting frustrated because no one was laughing or responding. I found them funny but our Japanese hosts either didn't understand them or were just not in a humorous mood. The sake kept on flowing and we all seemed to be getting a little louder after each toast of "kampai."

Again we heard a knock and two waitresses brought fresh courses. This time we were served small bowls with tiny cuttle fish, grilled sardines and grilled shrimp heads. When you looked into the bowl the eyes of the shrimp heads appeared to be starring back at you. It was a little disconcerting. I ate them very fast and didn't look down at them once I had captured them with my chopsticks.

Another waitress came in and put some beautifully prepared red snapper before each of us. However, nothing was put in front of Abe. Everyone kept busy eating and not looking in

Abe's direction when one of the waitresses came in with a tray
and one item on it. A huge, complete (sack and all), fish eye,
most likely from a large tuna. To Abe, Miyahara said, "This is
a manly specialty we have had prepared for you. It is very
special and cannot be purchased in many places. Please enjoy
it; I am sure it will do you some good for your overall health."

Everyone continued busily eating, not looking up. Abe was
perplexed. This gelatinous eye and sack was sitting before him
and he took one of the chopsticks to stick it into the side and all
the sack did was move and jiggle a little. I understood Abe's
problem; during our visits to various parts of the world we
have been faced with unusual food. We have eaten monkey's
brains and snakes and tiny beetles. I wasn't sure if this was a
joke or our hosts expected him to really eat the eye. I wasn't
certain what I would have done if it was served to me.

Abe slapped it again with his chopstick and it jiggled again. I
could see what was formulating in his mind. His plan was
going to unfold for all of us to see. He pretended to grab the
eye with the chopsticks and it rolled closer to the center of the
table. Then with one strong grab with his chopsticks he forced
it into the fire in the center of the table. Everyone was very
quiet as we heard a loud hiss from the boiling fluid of the eye.

I started to smile and Abe said, "I truly apologize, Shirahama-
san but I just couldn't grab the eye properly and it just slipped
away from me. I realize how special this was and I feel terrible
about it." Miyahara looked up and made eye contact with
Shirahama and with no expression said, "Fiegelson-san, it is
quite all right, we have no problem, we can take care of this -
because we have the *other* eye!"

There was silence in the room, then everyone started to laugh
and Wakimoto hit me and said, "That is a good one isn't it?"
"Yes," I agreed. Abe caught on and began pantomiming what

he had done. He started by playing his part then imitated the eye with great exaggeration by shaking his stomach like a belly dancer. We all had a good laugh.

From that point on the evening continued uproariously. Abe didn't have to tell any jokes, all he had to do was shake his stomach and everyone would start to laugh again. The sake continued to flow and the meal continued with a large pot of sukiyaki being prepared by our waitress in the center of the table. The sukiyaki was a little salty from the soy sauce and that made us thirsty. The result was we drank more sake. It was a loud and boisterous night. I can't remember when I laughed so hard at one meal.

CHAPTER 22
AN UNUSUAL NIGHT OF TRAVEL

We got back to the Okura Hotel a little before midnight. Abe and I extricated ourselves from Alex's car with the help of one of the doormen. Abe was completely blitzed. He couldn't walk a straight line. I felt good but I didn't want to have to walk that straight line either. Alex, who drove us here, didn't seem fazed at all from all of the drink we had. I remember drinking vodka at a breakfast he invited me to at the Jewish Community Center of Tokyo. Alex and Miyako, are major benefactors of that establishment. I think he drank five decanters of vodka about the size of a sake decanter that morning. He drove me back to the hotel then also. I guess he has a high tolerance for alcohol.

As I walked into the hotel the front desk manager flagged me down. He said, "Mr. Schein, there was a telex marked urgent for you." I ripped it open and it was from Doreen. "Robert, Mr. Albert has pulled out all stops. A military vehicle will pick you up at 2:30 AM and take to Yokosuka Naval Air Base. We were in luck and got a ferry pilot who was bringing a Phantom F-4 to Seattle for refitting. There will be one stop somewhere in the Pacific aboard an aircraft carrier for refueling and part of a qualification program for F-4 carrier landings. The Phantom will then divert and take you directly to Vancouver where you will meet with agents Speziale and Held. Your ETA in Vancouver is about 10 AM on the same day you left Japan. Leave your bags at the Okura Hotel and we will organize them once we know your schedule. The military base has your size information and will fit you out with flight gear and winter parker. That clothing and your pistol is all you will need. Have a safe trip." It was signed, "Doreen Parks, TAG Photographic, Inc."

My mind was racing; I have a couple of hours to get packed and ready. I'd better take a shower and freshen up. I'm not sure what all this alcohol will do for me, other then keep me pickled during the trip. I've got to try to sober up fast. I asked the manager to send a pot of coffee and a ham-and-cheese sandwich to my room. I also said, "I will be checking out and will return within a week or two." The manager nodded.

In the meantime I had to deal with Abe, who looked like a lost soul sitting on a couch near the elevators. I had to get him into his room and somehow get him into bed. I went over and picked Abe up and slung one of his arms over my shoulders and practically carried him into the elevator. As I got in a bellhop stopped the operator and handed me Abe's key. He then asked if I needed help and I shook my head no. Abe is a little guy so he wasn't hard to handle.

His room was a few doors from mine and I managed to get him in okay. But as I laid him on the bed him and started taking off his shoes he somehow scampered into the bathroom to vomit and make the classic statement, one I am sure he has made many times over the years: "I will never do this to myself again. No more drink for me." I laughed, went into the bathroom to help him back to bed and he said, "Thank you, Robert, but I can take it from here. See you tomorrow." Though I knew I would not be seeing him I said, "Sure, see you tomorrow."

As I was walking out I thought, Abe always leaves you with a smile on your face. The next couple of hours passed so quickly I hardly realized it. I called Bob and brought him up to date then called the floor attendant to organize my luggage and items for my locker. I went down to the desk to sign my bill and as I was doing so an army sergeant walked into the hotel. I asked, "Are you looking for Robert Schein?" He saluted and said, "Yes sir." "You got him; I will meet you outside in a minute." He spun around on his heels and I finished signing my bill.

The sergeant was driving a jeep with a canvas top. As I walked over he got out and handed me a parka. "You will need this, sir. It is going to be a cold ride." "Thank you." During the day I guess Yokosuka would be a ride of an hour to an hour and a half. But at this time in the morning I guess we made it in twenty-five minutes. The sergeant didn't say a word and that was fine with me. We checked in at the gate and he then drove me to the Bachelors Officers Quarters. The Sergeant helped me out, saluted and drove off.

Inside, I was directed to a room on the first floor that had all my gear laid out. An Air Force flight sergeant introduced himself, "I am Sergeant Richard Murphy, sir, and I am here to get you all together." I put on the pressurized flight suit, fatigue coveralls - he suggested I keep my sweater - then a pair of lined boots. Murphy said, "Your parachute is already in your seat and I prepared it for you about an hour ago." He handed me a football-style helmet with an oxygen mask and said, "Let's take a walk."

That was easier said than done. The pressurized flight suit was tight-fitting and heavy. The rest of the gear seemed to pile up on top of that. Wow, this is a load, I thought. We got outside and climbed into an open jeep. I was holding my new parka and helmet as we bounced our way to the flight deck where a number of Phantoms were lined up.

We went down a whole row to the very last one and stopped. A tall man in flight gear was walking around the plane and walked over to us. "Good morning, I am Lt. Cmdr. Charles Broome. I am your pilot for today." "It is a pleasure to meet you, my name is Robert Schein," I said. "Thank you for letting me tag along with you." "Huh," he said, "Some tag-along. You have long arms sir, they reached all the way into that funny building they call the Pentagon. I don't know what kind of deal this is but I am surprised to be diverted to Vancouver." "Is that a problem?" I asked. He looked at me as if I had two heads. "No sir, I follow my orders." He turned his attention back to his flight checkout. Murphy whispered, "He will come around, sir, don't worry, whenever things change everyone makes a big deal out of it. He will warm up." "Thank you, sergeant."

Murphy then helped me into the right navigator's seat. The navigator runs positioning and fire control. This flight was only a ferrying flight so any navigation could be handled by the pilot. The seat was a little tight and getting my feet around the secondary set of controls was an effort. I strapped into my parachute and seat belts as Murphy stood over me like a careful parent. The pilot then climbed in. In the Phantom F-4 the navigator and pilot sit side by side. Lt. Cmdr. Broome continued his check out. Murphy tapped him on his helmet and a few moments later Broome gave him a thumbs-up. The sergeant then climbed down and positioned himself in front of the plane a little to the left so that he could make eye contact with the pilot.

Broome asked the control tower for permission to start his engine. Permission was granted. Then he asked for permission to taxi and take off. We were now starting to roll when Murphy stood at attention and saluted, Broome saluted back. We were on our way taxiing to get into position to take off.

Broome was busy flipping switches and talking to the tower. I watched him in awe and said nothing. I certainly didn't want to distract him. Finally, he was ready and got permission from the tower to take off. We roared down the runway and as if we were kicked from behind while being pressed in our seats we took off in a steep angle. We got to our planned altitude of 30,000 feet and our cruising speed of 585 mph. After about ten minutes at that speed Broome seem to relax as he put the plane on auto-pilot.

He called over the sound system, "You all right, Schien?" "Yes sir" was all I could muster. Broome continued, "In about 1,200 miles we will find the Forrestal, make a landing, stretch our legs and take off within an hour. Until then you can grab some Z's if you wish." "Thank you, but I think I will just take it all in." There was a heavy cloud cover below us so there really wasn't much to see. I was concentrating on all of the instruments on the control panel. It was lit up like a Disneyland ride and I was trying to make out what I was looking at.

A couple of hours into the flight I could hear Broome talking to aircraft carrier control. The Forrestal was sending out a couple of planes for normal patrol and to check us out. In short order another pilot said he had a visual on us and all of a sudden a whoosh flashed by that took my breath away. The pilots were talking and the one from the carrier was telling Broome that the wind and wave conditions below were negligible.

We went into a turn and out the front of the plane at about 11:00 o'clock I could see a speck, in the distance in the water. In amazement and maybe with a little fear in my voice, I tentatively asked, "Are we landing on that spot?" Broome said, "Yes and do not I repeat, do not touch anything. Leave the controls alone" The Phantoms started to land on aircraft carriers the previous year, in the latter part of 1961. It took about a year for the plane to qualify for carrier operations. This landing and subsequent takeoff would be recorded as one of the qualifying landings.

I think I opened and closed my eyes continuously hoping I was not seeing a mirage. You can't imagine what this looks like, particularly in the dark, unless you experience it. You are landing on a dime, on a black spot with some lighting, somewhere in the middle of the Pacific Ocean. It was a weird feeling. As we made our final approach, flaps down, engine cut back, we kept watching the "Christmas tree" of lights telling us to raise or lower our wings or altitude. And then – BAM! – we hit the deck as if we were in a bumper-car ride in Coney Island. After the wheels touched down we hit what felt like a wall that strained the seat straps as the Phantom's hook caught the cable stretched across the flight deck and the jet came to a very sudden stop. I felt as though I'd been slapped in the face – hard! We taxied over to the side onto one of the Forrestal's three huge elevators. It took us below decks. Engine off, we were towed inside the carrier to a fueling area to gas up. The top bubble opened and a number of people saluted us as we scampered out of the plane. God, it felt good to stretch.

We were directed by an ensign to the flight ready room for coffee and sandwiches. An aircraft carrier is pretty much self-contained. In the ready room Broome was saying hello to some of the other pilots. I was happy to find one of the comfortable wide leather chairs and have a cup of coffee. Before I knew it, over the speaker system they called Broome's name and we were on our way back to the Phantom.

A petty officer helped me get settled and strapped in. We were put onto an elevator nearer the bow of the ship. Our bubble came down as we rose to the flight deck. A deck-crew horsed the plane into position for a hydraulic-assisted catapult takeoff.

Broome was talking to the crewmen and carrier control when he was given permission to start engines.

The Phantom's tail was attached to the catapult. Broome pushed the throttles forward and the pitch of the engines rose as the plane shook. Broome saluted the deck officer then he let go of the brakes and WHAM! I was pressed against the seat and couldn't move as the F-4 was thrown out into space. The Phantom's engines took control and climbed to our cruising altitude. We settled in at our 585 mph cruising speed, which uses fuel as economically as possible. We had another 1,300 or 1,400 miles to go, which happens to be at the limit of the Phantom's range.

The landing and takeoff from an airplane carrier is an experience I don't think I will ever forget. What a hoot. "Chukko," which is Charles Broome's nickname, was being hailed over the sound system. "Tell the guys in Seattle we are not far away. Another month and we are there." "OK Spider, Chukko out."

Broome said, "Well, we are on the home stretch. About three hours and I'll have you in Vancouver." "Thank you, it's been a fun ride so far." "As long as there are no problems it is a great ride. I have wanted to ask you – who the hell are your godfathers? Your orders come from way up high. There is no way I would have been diverted otherwise." "Well, then you have your answer. I don't think I can go beyond that." I was sorry I had to put it that way but I was being as honest as possible. That pretty much curtailed any further conversation with Cmdr. Broome for the rest of the flight.

I must have dozed off because I opened my eyes when I heard a lot of chatter between the Vancouver control tower and Broome. Broome said we were low on fuel because of head winds and he was considering landing in Fairbanks.

Vancouver and Broome confirmed that his fuel was enough for a straight in shot into runway two. Since there was no other major air traffic he decided to go in. We quickly went on final; banked in and landed at about 11 AM Mountain Standard Time, an hour later than Doreen anticipated.

We taxied over to the Canadian military part of Vancouver International Airport, where a team of soldiers were ready to assist in refueling and to get me out of the plane. Broome decided he would continue his flight to Seattle as soon as he was refueled. We both got out of the plane and I walked over to him and shook his hand. He saluted me and I said "Thank you." He didn't say a word and walked away. He wasn't sure whom he was talking to and decided it was better for him to be military and as formal as possible.

CHAPTER 23
THERE IS A CHANGE OF VENUE

overing, Voss and Little each received a 4 AM wakeup call. They were told that they would be moving within the hour and going for a plane ride. Lovering wondered why so early, and then figured they wanted to hide what they were doing under the cover of darkness. He decided to prepare himself by showering, shaving, and making a cup of coffee. Thank God they have coffee in this room, he thought.

A little after 5 AM two young women dressed in yellow coveralls entered his room and his bracelets magnetic field was activated. He joined the procession of Voss and Little to the elevator then to the basement floor. They were stopped for a moment and the magnetic field was released.

Each man put his hands into the black box and the bracelets were taken off. They were going to board a plane out of the back door. While Little and Voss were having their bracelets removed Lovering tuned his back to everyone and took a ballpoint pen from his vest pocket and leaned against the doorframe. With the point of the pen he scratched his initials – HL – in the doorframe. He put the pen back in his pocket before he turned around.

They were now ready, the door and the steps of the plane were in position. The men were hustled out the door where a blast of cold air hit them and took their breath away. The plane was about 20 yards away and then it was up eleven steps into the protection of the cabin. They ran the entire distance because of the wind and biting cold. That was an exertion for these not-so-young men. They were all breathing hard; the cold air was burning their lungs when they got inside.

They finally got control of themselves and started warming up. A couple of the girls who guided them to the plane started to organize their seating. This was a luxurious aircraft with wide leather seats. There were four in the front cabin, a conference table with comfortable seating for eight amidships and four seats in the rear of the plane. The plane was a long-range Lear jet that was fitted out to the specifications of its lessee, Chang Industries.

No sooner had the three men settled in at the conference table seats than they were joined by their new colleagues, Kawakami, Ping, Kleiber and Rabinovich. A few minutes later a young Chinese man arrived and stood at the front of the cabin and announced: "I will be accompanying you to our next destination. I will act as your facilitator. I will help you to get the discussions started regarding what we are looking for you to develop. For now I am sure you would all like to rest before we talk. We have plenty of time today and will be flying west. Oh, my name is Tsung, - Inouye Tsung. The ladies will provide you with some refreshment should you wish any. In the meantime, please rest and relax."

Lovering immediately recognized the man as "the voice" they had been dealing with from behind the screen. There was no attempt to disguise the voice. I guess he was always meant to escort us. His English was excellent. Lovering thought that was interesting for such a young man. Well, maybe I am being fooled trying to determine the age of an Asian. He just looks very young.

The plane's stairs were retracted and the front hatch closed. The party of seven scientists, four young women and the 'facilitator' settled in for takeoff. The Lear started up its engines, taxied a couple of minutes then set its brakes, turned up the throttles, released the brakes and rumbled down the icy runway. About 25 seconds later the wheels seemed to jump off the ground. The plane then faced a very bumpy ride until we reached the planes 15,000-foot cruising altitude. The plane leveled off as the powerful Roll Royce engines clawed at the frigid air. There were no further announcements and the mood in the plane eased considerably.

Three Mack tractor-trailer trucks were hooking up to the three trailer laboratories while the Lear jet took off. In a few minutes, after the trailers left the complex, a clean-up crew came into the area just as the sun was starting to rise to make sure there were no signs that the trailers had ever been there. At the same time a cleaning crew was fastidiously going through the rooms of all seven scientists. The scientist's assistants along with some of the security guards were on the way to Vancouver International and were assigned to fly on a commercial airline to Beijing.

By 9 AM the Chang development was clear of any association with anything other than sell expensive condominiums to wealthy customers in what will be a state of the art community. A trailer was placed on the main road where the paper truck sign had been. The trailer was an office set-up with information on the future community. Tours of the new community were organized through the personnel in the trailer.

CHAPTER 24
WAS THE VISIT A WILD GOOSE CHASE?

With all my heavy gear on I trudged to the pilot's room where flight plans were filed. I was met by agents Victoria Speziale and Hunter Held. Speziale was a tall good-looking athletic young woman about 25 with a shock of short cut black hair; she had recently joined our team after earning her doctorate in oceanic studies. Held, a former Navy lieutenant, came onboard about five years ago. He was muscular and tall, about 26 and very self-assured. He had one of the highest ratings for a recruit graduating from the Company's training complex in Virginia. His major in college was Science.

Both agents came to greet me as I walked through the doors. They helped me off with my uncomfortable gear and we moved to a corner of the room. "Mr. Schein," Speziale said, "Welcome to Vancouver. We have a helicopter organized. The RCMP is standing by waiting for instructions." Held continued, "I was surprised they let us take control of this operation since it's in their jurisdiction."

"Don't be surprised, we have some very strong backing in Washington and we have a hostage situation. The Mounties don't want to be responsible for a mishap that might get the hostages killed and/or cause an international situation. I think they are very willing to take the back seat. That way, if anything goes wrong the blame is not on their shoulders." I excused myself and went to the men's room to get out of the pressurized flight suit and put back on the coveralls and sweater.

When I returned the two agents had organized a table, chairs and coffee in a quiet area of the large room. They appeared eager and ready to get the operation underway. I thought I had to slow them down before someone gets hurt. "Is there any update on Harry Collins?" Held replied, "Everything he did from arrival to picking up gear at Gart Bros. checks out with no holes. He told Doreen what he intended to do and as far as we have been able to follow his trail he did exactly what he said he would do. We covered his steps to his rented Avis car where the attendant helped him with instructions heading to the north or the mountain range. No one has seen him since."

"OK," I started, "Whatever we do today we do not want anything to look like a show of force. Victoria and I will go by helicopter and try to create the impression that we are looking at the condos for acquisition by TAG Photographic. Our story will be we are looking towards the Olympics in '76 and would like to have a couple of apartments for our factory executives to stay in. I will tell them that my invitation comes from Hyacinth Chang. That happens to be true and that should add some credibility.

"Held, you will travel with the RCMP as a member of their team. Play on their concern that there appears to be air traffic, landings and takeoffs, on their yet-to-be-approved landing strip. Your goal would be to examine their log books and check with the control tower personnel. Your group should arrive by car about the same time the chopper arrives. That puts a little pressure on them, in that they have to respond to two areas, and gives us the backup protection of a couple of more people on our side at the site. Questions?"

Victoria said, "We will have to wait about 40 minutes to bring the helicopter in at the same time of the arrival of the RCMP vehicle at the complex." I said, "Fine; that works for me and gives me a chance to pick up some clothing in the airport that doesn't look so military." "Doreen had me pick up some clothing yesterday." He handed me a bag containing slacks, socks, shoes, belt, shirt, sports jacket and tie.

After sitting down and working out the details with the RCMP we were ready to start our operation. It was now 2 in the afternoon and we had to get the lead out if we wanted to do this in daylight as efficiently as possible. The RCMP car left with Held and three Mounties. I changed my clothing, put on the warm military parka and got into the helicopter with Speziale about thirty-five minutes after they left. Our pilot started his engine and got permission to take off.

Speziale's calculation of time was on the money. As we started to circle the complex we could see the RCMP vehicle leave the office trailer and make its way to the facility. From overhead there was no sign of Collins' Mustang, nor did anything look out of place. There was little security that I could see other than cameras on high poles. The helicopter landing site was next to the complex between the completed building and the airstrip.

We made our final approach, hovered and set down on the helicopter tarmac. As soon as we turned off the engine and were secure two men, dressed as bellhops, came out the door to assist us. I took off my parka, handed it to the pilot who said he would wait in the chopper. Victoria and I went into the building. I asked one of the bellhops where the manager was and he started to guide us to him.

A man in a grey-and-black morning suit met us in the lobby. He was Japanese and bowed when I walked over to shake his hand. He said his name was Hairu and he wanted to know how he could help us. I went through my spiel ending with the Hyacinth story. The man looked up and smiled. "You are in luck, Mr. Schein. Miss Chang is present with us today."

As if on cue, Hyacinth Chang appeared and walked over and planted a kiss on my cheek. I introduced her to Victoria Speziale and said that she was in charge of media communications for TAG Photographic. Both women stood there sizing each other up and I felt I had better get between them or there might be words.

Hyacinth said, "I am so happy you chose to accept my invitation to visit our complex of the future, Robert. I will be most happy to show you around. Have you changed your mind about being able to afford one of our condominiums?" "To some degree I have," I answered. "I have convinced the management of TAG that it might be a good investment and a place for us to have meetings as well as a vacation site for the companies we do business with. It just might turn out to be a nice perk for some of our people."

I thought it was such a good lie I might even start to believe it. Hyacinth invited us to have tea in the lobby before she took us on the tour. She asked, "Have you given any thought to our last conversation, Robert? I was very disturbed by it." I thought it highly unusual to have this conversation in front of a stranger but I participated by playing hard to get. "Not really, I have been very busy and have not had the time to sit and ponder what has happened." Victoria smartly sat and listened and remained quiet.

As we were sitting there was a commotion at the front of the building. The bellhops ran outside and eventually escorted in two red-jacketed Mounties, an inspector in a navy blue uniform and a civilian in street clothes. The manager rushed to the door from the front desk. Hyacinth stood up and said, "Pardon me for a minute, please. I would like to see what all of the fuss is about." She walked over and immediately got into the conversation. She was smiling so I don't think she felt threatened in any way.

She came back and said, "They are concerned that we are using our airstrip and it has not been fully approved by the Canadian Air Authority – CAA. They wish to check our logs and control tower activity. I told them to please satisfy themselves if we are in compliance or not. I believe we are in compliance." She smiled and drank some tea. I think she was onto why everyone was here. However, she was playing along with the game.

"Now," Hyacinth said, "Let me show you around." She took us on the tour of rooms and completed facilities. She was being very much the tour guide and enjoying it to the limit. She kept as close to me as she could while we were walking from one room to the next room or banquet rooms or in the hallways.

The accommodations started at $300,000 and went to $800,000. The penthouse was drop-dead gorgeous, and a flat $2,000,000. All in all at the end of the tour I felt that Hyacinth had spent a lot of time in the planning stages of this establishment and was very proud of it. It was an elaborate facility that I was sure had possibilities, but that was not why I was there.

I asked her, "Were there any accommodations that might include a laboratory or some other working facility." She said, "We had an extensive carpenter's shop that supports the construction crew." She took us down to the bowels of the building and there was an excellent carpenter's and machine shop.

131

"Hyacinth, thank you for your time. Miss Speziale and I will make our recommendations to our board. I have to be getting back to Vancouver because I was en route and stopped off to follow up on your suggestion to take a look. It was also an opportunity to see you again and try to make up my mind regarding what we had discussed." Did you come to any conclusion," she asked. "Not yet, that will take a little more time." She then asked, "Do you really have to leave this moment?" "Yes, plane schedules are pretty precise." "Please let me know where you end up so we can talk. Leave your telephone number with my secretary as we had planned."

Hyacinth then asked, "Shall I lead you directly to your helicopter or do you have a need to go back to the lobby?" "The quickest route will be fine." We came to a back door where some snow removal equipment was stored. Victoria went ahead to let me have a few moments with Hyacinth to say goodbye. As she walked out the door my eye caught Howard Lovering's initials scratched on the doorjamb. It was a series of straight lines – three straight up and down and two across, one crossing the center of two lines and one at the bottom.

I was talking to Hyacinth but the scratched lines distracted me. She asked, "Is something wrong?" She looked around to see what I was looking at. "No, but I wonder if the facility had received any visitors recently." Hyacinth said, "Yes, there was a medical meeting here for about a week but other then that no one. We really aren't ready to receive large numbers of people." I thanked her for her hospitality, kissed her on the cheek and said, "You have a beautiful complex under construction, I wish you a lot of luck with it." I turned to go out the door and braced for the cold.

I started to jog to the plane and said out loud, "Son of a bitch! Sorry I was late, Howard." Victoria could see I was upset as I got aboard the helicopter. "What's wrong?" "Howard

Lovering was here and we must have just missed him."
"Hyacinth Chang told you that?" "No, I saw his initials
scratched on the doorjamb. I noticed them as you were walking
out of the building."

The engine was reaching its liftoff revolutions and the copter
was hovering over the tarmac. We held that position for a few
seconds and then made a sharp right turn and started our trip
back to Vancouver International. My thoughts were about
Howard and the facility. The RCMP crew was shadowed by
the facilities manager while they were there and they had left
about fifteen minutes before we did. I wonder if they
discovered anything. I needed to talk this out. When the hell
are we landing?

Thirty-minutes later we circled Vancouver International and
got permission to land. I was on edge. I have to call the office
and tell them what I had discovered. No, I better wait and see
if Held and his group come up with anything. I decided to
have coffee and wait for the Mounties to arrive. There was no
question that I was agitated. Victoria kept her distance as I
paced back and forth.

Held and the RCMP team finally arrived. As soon as they
were seated, before they could control the meeting, I asked,
"Were you able to find out anything significant?" The
inspector said, "I don't think so" and left us all hanging. I
thought that was odd. Either he was inept or he was holding
back his information until he spoke to his superiors. I couldn't
let this continue. I began telling them what we learned. "I am
certain that Howard Lovering was at the site. I can't speak for
the others. On one of the doorjambs I saw Lovering's initials
scratched in the paint. He was obviously trying to leave a sign
before he left the building. Do you have any information that
might corroborate my assumption?"

The inspector thought for a moment. I guess Held had had all he could take of the man's procrastination all afternoon and blurted out, "I believe the log shows that a plane took off from the airstrip about 5:30 this morning. The same plane identification numbers had landed early yesterday morning. I imagine that is when Miss Chang arrived." I interrupted, "Was a flight plan recorded?" "To some degree," Held said. "All it had was the longitude and latitude and that it was flying west north west – about 290° - out of Canadian territory. It did not have an ultimate destination." "If they stay on that course they will end up in Russia. However, I personally feel their final destination is in China. This development is all Chinese, it has very expensive Chinese furnishings and most of the personnel are Chinese. It has got to be China."

I guess the inspector had enough. He politely said, "I have to report in" and apologized for having to leave. That was fine with me. My next action was to call the office. I dialed our special number and Doreen immediately came on the line. Speziale and Held were sitting at the table opposite me and they were intently listening to my side of the conversation.

Doreen asked, "How did your 'raid' go today?" "It wasn't much of a raid," I replied. I reviewed everything we had to date. I ended with, "We saw no sign of Harry Collins or his vehicle. We are certain that Howard Lovering was at the complex but we could not find out anything more. I think that their escape route will take them somewhere in China. I imagine their range is no more than 3,000 miles. That should put them down somewhere in Russia to refuel. Russia is a big country. My guess is that they will then continue to China. This is not much to go on but it is all we have."

Doreen suggested, "I will give it to our logistics people in Virginia to see what they come up with. At the end of the call give me the details of the call letters of the plane – that will help our people figure it out. We are very concerned that you found nothing regarding Harry Collins. We are starting to think the worst. Tell Speziale and Held that they should stay there and continue to search for him. What do you think is next, Robert?"

"I have this feeling that I will end up in China. In the meantime, I want to follow up with Mashpriborintorg. Just as I did with Mei Cao Lin I want to visit their Moscow office to talk to one of their principles." "Robert," Doreen said, "The Russians aren't like the Chinese. They are very difficult to organize meetings with. If they feel threatened it could turn dangerous."

"Have Luke talk to the American Embassy; they can be present. I just want to see if I can get a rise out of them. If we go after both of the organizations who made proposals in the open market they will talk together and possibly show their hand by trying to stop me. I am going to use myself as bait." Doreen insisted, "We need permission for that type of decision." "I know all about that. However, this is what I recommend: Fly into Moscow, meet with them and then fly out the same day to Beijing. We won't give anybody time to organize anything special. It would be nice to have Bob Claypool meet me when I get to China so that I have able backup. I feel very comfortable with Bob."

"Robert, cool your heels for an hour and I will get Luke into the loop and let him decide if that is a viable plan. In the meantime I will start setting everything up. I am not very happy about this but it isn't my decision to make." "Thank you and don't fret about this," I said. "It will work out fine."

While waiting for Luke Albert's call the three of us came up with a plan to find Collins. It included visits to garages, hotels, and automobile recycling and junkyard facilities. Fearing the worst I believed we would find our answer there. We looked up automobile recycling and junkyards and there were only a handful in the book. I suggested they start there. "Ask the manager of the yard if they have crushed any red Ford Mustangs recently - within the past week."

While we were talking the phone rang Luke Albert; was calling. "Robert, I think your plan is farfetched but it appears to be the only plausible lead we have. I will approve the plan under the condition that you are in and out of Russia within the day. Mashpriborintorg is near Lenin's Tomb, about three blocks away in the government's Industry & Trade building. I will set up the meeting for you through an old friend. You go into the airport in Moscow; the embassy will meet you at the airport, take you to the meeting, and then get you back to the airport. No additional stopovers, no photography, no sightseeing and no unescorted activity. Understood?" "Yes sir," was all I said.

Albert continued, "The call letters of the Chang plane you gave us is a specially outfitted long-range Learjet. It could reach Beijing if it had to but our people feel as you do that it will make a refueling stop in Russia. That indicates that Russia, which is very protective of its air space, is in on the deal." "It is interesting that Russia and China, two countries that have had major border confrontations almost daily, are working together," I said.

"This project has to be out of the ordinary realm of business." Albert said, "It can be a number of highly secret committees that have direct approval from their prime ministers. That has happened before. Doreen will give you your itinerary. Be very careful in Russia and remember we do not have many friends to call upon in China. I have also approved for Claypool to be with you in

Beijing." The call ended and we all went about our missions.

I was going to spend the night in Vancouver then take an early flight to Moscow, arriving at 10:45 AM. I was scheduled to fly out of Moscow at 5 PM to Beijing.

CHAPTER 25
A MEETING AT FIFTEEN THOUSAND FEET

About two hours into the flight Tsung called the first design meeting to order. Each scientist was given a Mont Blanc fountain pen and laboratory log book. They were asked to write their names and the date in the book. "At the end of each meeting or laboratory work period the log books will be collected and transcribed. That way all of the information can be shared before the next meeting," Tsung said. It also meant that their benefactors would be kept up to date.

Kawakami started the meeting. He brought everyone up to date with what was accomplished before Lovering, Voss and Little arrived. Quite frankly, other than outlining what the project was, Lovering thought very little work had been accomplished. Just about every scientist at the table was a member of a large company. Lovering was the only one with any real hands-on business experience because the David W. Mann Company is a small business when compared to the giants – Rank Industries, Philips, Nippon Kogaku, etc.

Lovering said, "If we are going to get any results immediately let's stop all the side chatter and recognize what is before us. We do not have our usual backup staff or management group to answer to. So our decision is all that counts. Our objective is to design a method to transport a light wave at least 5,000 meters and with enough power that when it flashes the eye of a person that person will be damaged. The weapon according to our benefactors is to be called - Personnel Tactical High Energy Laser, or PTHEL.

"Fortunately, I had done some work on the proposal that was brought to my company. I had to decide whether or not we wanted to bid on it. Now that I know the ultimate goal, a lot of what I had learned can be useful to us.

"The ruby laser, the product that started this whole thing is our beginning. The ruby stone was excited to the point that a concentrated laser beam exploded out of the stone in the visual spectrum and made history. The visual spectrum is 400 to 700 milli-microns (mμ). If we go to the ultra-violet, which is a short wavelength, below 300 milli-microns, I think the exciter will end up being too large to be hand carried. My guess is to go to the infrared, above 1,100mμ. That is a much longer wavelength and we might be able to use it in conjunction with a chemical exciter that will bring the weight down and allow us to hand carry the unit.

"We want to give PTHEL enough power to cause a blind spot in the retina. That can be accomplished in the infrared part of the spectrum. If we can get high enough into the infrared spectrum we can then cause damage to the cornea and/or the lens of the eye.

From my research I learned that with a carbon dioxide laser beam that can reach 10,600 nano-meters would most definitely affect a burning pain at the site of exposure on the cornea and sclera. To go higher in the spectrum, only a few nano-meters more, the ray becomes particularly dangerous. The beam is invisible to the human eye and the retina lacks pain sensory nerves. Photo-acoustic retinal damage may be associated with an audible 'pop' at the time of exposure."

Lovering decided to stop here and let what he said sink in.   He thought he might have missed or confused something by how quiet everyone was.   He was about to say something when Little spoke up: "This is a dastardly, dangerous and inhumane weapon. I am frightened at the very thought of it." Lovering sat back.

Kawakami agreed, "The weapon might be evil, it hasn't yet been developed. I am sure a weapon like this will ultimately be invented. This is a lot cheaper to manufacture than to go through the development of an atomic weapon. I'd rather fight this weapon than an atomic one."

Voss said, "If we had the right type of glass we certainly could design a plasma tube to hold a highly volatile chemical, which would become part of the exciter.   Ping, the chemical specialist, said, "I believe there are a couple of combinations that just might work in something like this."   Rabinovich added, "The weapon could be constructed in two parts, power pack and weapon part. It might very well be constructed lightweight enough for an individual to carry it."

Kawakami confirmed, "It was harder to find glass that will allow very short wavelengths of the UV to pass through it. We would be better off looking at higher wavelengths in the IR just from the materials that are available." Kleiber and Little, the electronics wizards, felt they could build the required power pack. "It would be an enhanced unit to make it powerful enough to stimulate the plasma tube. The design of the power pack would have to accomplish multiple flashes, or firings, before having to be recharged."

Summing up, Lovering said, "We are looking to develop a plasma tube that can be excited from an external laser power supply, design a high output reflector within the laser-head, and tie it to a transmitter, photocell and beam splitter to throw out a stabilized evenly illuminated beam or ray. We ultimately want to put that equipment into some sort of package so a man will be able to carry it and be able to shoot or flash it a number of times before it needs recharging.

The scientific challenge was now before them. There was no more discussion. Several of the men started writing in their laboratory books while the others pondered their parts of the project. The challenge hooked everyone at the table. Their scientific curiosity took over. There were no more comments about the danger or destruction or how inhumane the weapon was.

Lovering sat back, had an elbow on the arm of the chair and his chin in his fingers. He looked closely at his colleagues. He smiled to himself as he thought how he might be able to stop the ray with a simple pair of goggles. At least that is what I think. The only way we will prove that will be to build it and then develop a counter measure. If the goggles protect you from being blinded, then all we have to see is what, if any, side effects there might be.

I guess I am convincing myself that this weapon can be defeated and that's the only way I would be able to work on it, Lovering thought. One thing that has come out of this session is that I can take command of the meetings without much difficulty. That will serve us in the future should we have to operate in concert. These are wonderful people but they seem to have all been brought up with a silver spoon in their mouths. It is tough for them to make a straightforward decision without a lot of discussion.

Tsung, who hadn't said a word since he started the meeting, was pleased with the first session. He said to himself, these scientific men are no fools but they can be sold a bill of goods. We can get our way very easily with them. The one I have to watch out for is Lovering. He seems to demand and is given

141

the respect of the group. I have to keep my eye on him.

The hum of its engines was steady and as the plane approached land the scientists broke off into small groups or decided to close their eyes. Suddenly one of the men said, "There is a Russian fighter plane alongside us." That got everyone up and looking out the starboard windows. "What's this all about; there is another one." Tsung said, "They are friendly and are escorting us to a military airfield where we will be refueling. There is nothing to worry about. Please return to your seats. Thank you."

But they kept starring at the sleek Mig-15s. There were two, one on each side, a little ahead of the Lear jet. They had camouflage markings and looked like a very able piece of machinery. They dipped their wings as the Lear passed them and they climbed to a higher altitude to circle the field while the scientists' plane made its final approach.

In the middle of nowhere was a snow-covered, fenced-in military base with a long landing strip. The flaps came down, the wheels locked in place and suddenly the Lear touched down, rolled the length of the runway and was taxiing over to a tanker truck. The scientists were told to stay strapped in. The cabin door opened and the stairs motored out to touch the ground.

The pilot and navigator came out of their cabin, a female pilot and a male navigator. They went down the stairs and started talking to a couple of the men working on the plane. They obviously were Russian. Since World War II women have been a major factor in the Russian military. An officer approached them, saluted, and they engaged in an animated conversation. The pilot took off her head gear and exposed a long brown ponytail and a beautiful face. As the plane was being topped off the navigator started his ground check while the pilot went up the stairs and walked into the cabin. "Good afternoon, gentlemen," she said in perfect English. "I am Captain Samantha Nicolaskaya of the Russian Military Air Defense Force. I know a number of you through your papers that I have studied in university. I was on leave going to school in California when I was activated to bring you here and to our ultimate destination."

Lovering spoke up, "Where might that be?" "I will let your benefactors answer that when we arrive. For now, we are on Russian soil in Siberia on a Russian military air base." "Where in California do you go to school and what do you study?" Lovering asked. Captain Nicolaskaya didn't say anything for a moment and everyone had their eyes on her. She was obviously thinking over her response before she answered.

She continued, "Well I don't see how this can hurt if you know this, so, I go to UCLA and I am working on my doctorate in physics." Aha, Lovering thought, that would explain why she had read some of our papers. "It is kind of unusual for a Russian military person to be studying physics in the United States, wouldn't you say?" "Not really, when your father is an American citizen from New York and your Mother is a Russian citizen from Odessa. I am blessed with both passports." "How did the military accept that one?" Little asked.

Samantha Nicolaskaya was very open, obviously a very proud person with a sizable ego. "When you are the best in your class with the highest marks ever recorded in Russia's testing procedures there is no problem of acceptance. Gentlemen, it is time for us to get underway." She then turned, entered the cockpit and closed the door. Shortly after that the navigator bounded up the stairs and before you know it, the Lear was aloft again.

CHAPTER 26

A SHORT VISIT BEHIND THE IRON CURTAIN

I made my Aeroflot flight with time to spare in Vancouver. I had never been on one of the slick-looking Tupolev planes so I was curious to see what kind of amenities it had. In a simple word the answer was 'few.' The seats were not very comfortable or heavily padded, even in first class. The plane was a turnaround flight so it wasn't very clean but the point that got me concerned was that at least one of the five lavatories was out of order. They'd had time to fix it in Vancouver but decided to let it go. I hoped that same attitude didn't apply to aircraft maintenance.

The TU 114 rumbled down the runway and at liftoff took a very steep angle. The noise of the wheels retracting sounded like the BMT train in New York City. I wondered if the plane was coming apart. When we finally leveled off at our appointed altitude, the ride was fine. The service crew, a mixture of men and women, was efficient but not brusque.

The lunch was more or less tasty. First a stiff glass of Chivas on the rocks, then a bowl of potato soup, a course of herring, a hard-to-cut piece of some sort of grey boiled beef with potatoes and peas served with a glass of Russian red wine. The coffee was strong and black and the best part of the meal for my part was the Courvoisier brandy. That took away all the taste of the meal so that I was able to close my eyes and sleep the flight away.

I awoke to the clanking sound of the landing gear locking into place. The flaps were down and we were on our final approach into Vnukovo International Airport, which is about 28 km from Moscow. Walking into the great hall of the terminal gave me a weird feeling. The room felt cold and unfriendly. It was all marble walls and floors with people milling about. The great hall is also the transit area and the cross section of people waiting for their flights was like looking at a cross section of all humanity. Every type of dress, race, creed and color was pacing or sitting, talking or sleeping. It was a busy area.

There were pairs of Russian soldiers walking around and when they approached a group that group would stop talking and watch them closely. I got the feeling they stopped talking out of bone-deep fear rather than having something subversive to hide. As I went into the hall my red passport got me quickly through the first point of control. At the second point, military or customs, the situation was different.

A soldier asked, how long did I intend to stay? I replied, "Only a few hours, I will fly out this evening." "What is your final destination?" "Beijing." "Why are you staying so short a time in my country? There is a lot to see and do." "I am here on business and already have my schedule in Beijing." "What is your business in Russia?" I thought a moment said, "I believe my passport is a diplomatic passport and these questions do not have to be answered by me. Is that correct?" "That is correct Mr. Schein, I was only being friendly." Sure, like a cat to a mouse, I said to myself.

"We will hold your passport until you leave the country," he said. "As you exit, it will be handed back to you." I replied, "I understand that is what you do with in-transit people but my passport is diplomatic." He ignored me and said "Next." "I guess I have to get advice from my embassy to see what course of action we should take." I wrote down his name and marched off to the baggage area where I was to meet representatives of the embassy.

While standing in the baggage area a young man tapped me on the shoulder. I turned and he asked, "Are you Robert Schein?" "Yes." "I am Justin Connor special assistant to the ambassador. This is Madison Maxine, our translator. We are here to take you to your meeting with Mashpriborintorg and then back to the airport to make an evening flight. Do you have any bags?" "No, I was just waiting for you here. We can leave whenever you are ready."

We walked out of the terminal and I followed my escorts to a black Lincoln Continental with two flags, one American and the other the ambassador's flag. We were obviously using the ambassador's car. Conner was about forty with thinning blond hair; he looked a little out of shape and was friendly in conversation. Maxine was young, with long brown hair, good figure, pretty and very quiet. In fact, since we met she hadn't said a word; all conversation was carried by Justin Conner. I guess her position as translator was to do just that and listen when it came to other conversation.

It was a short ride into Moscow. The city had been largely rebuilt since the Germans practically leveled it in World War II. The streets were wide and austere. It was interesting driving through Lenin Square; from pictures I had seen I expected it to be much larger. We made a few turns and ended up in front of the Ministry of Industry and Trade. We got out, went into the building, checked in with a guard and were directed to the stairs to the second floor to the Mashpriborintorg Trading Company.

When we got to the second floor another guard directed us to the trading company's door. We entered an alcove with a glass window and a woman asked, in Russian, "May I help you?" Madison Maxine started a long response and we were told to wait for a Mr. Malenkov. After about an hour of sitting and not speaking for fear of listening devices, a door opened and we were led into a small conference room. We couldn't see any of the office area because it was blocked by a wall. The room had a picture of Stalin on one wall; the other walls were bare. There was a samovar and cups next to it on a small table. The furniture was all grey metal.

Gregori Malenkov, a stocky bald man, walked in, handed me his business card and started speaking in Russian. Madison Maxine started to translate. As quickly as he spoke, she was right there with him. It was like listening to a conversation with an echo. I leaned over to Conner and said, "She is good." I saw a flicker of recognition of what I had said which meant to me that Malenkov understood English.

Malenkov was welcoming us to Mashpriborintorg and according to the embassy information he received he was prepared to discuss the proposal that was presented to the David W. Mann Company. I started to talk and Maxine started to translate English to Russian as fast as she had translated Russian to English. "Sir, your business card states you're the Director of Trade for the United States market. Can that also mean that you speak English?" Malenkov smiled, like a kid caught with his hand in the cookie jar, and after thinking about it for a moment said, "Yes, I do."

"Good. That way we can have a more direct conversation. Are you still interested in the proposal the way you had presented it in your solicitation?" Malenkov thought for a moment and was about to answer when he sat back in his chair and asked, "What difference does it make to you? You either respond or don't respond. Anyhow, the time limit for response has passed so it is a moot point, isn't it?"

"My company, TAG Photographic, is interested in laser-oriented products that are currently manufactured and what might be manufactured in the future. We believe we can be a positive factor representing you in the United States." Malenkov said, "Before you came to us I had our people research your company and yes, you might be the people who can help us establish a product in the States. You have done a particularly good job with Nikon. We are aware of your company and if we had desires to bring a product to the world market we would probably visit you for your advice and or participation in the U.S. market. We do not have such a product or interest at this time."

"Mr. Malenkov, is Mashpriborintorg in partnership with Mei Cao Lin of Hong Kong?" Malenkov simply said, "Not to my knowledge, nor would I state that we were in partnership if I had such knowledge. We might consider that to be proprietary information." I pushed further, "Does the name Howard Lovering mean anything to you?" "No. I have no idea who he is." "How about Walter Voss or Alasdair Little; are those names familiar to you?" "Mr. Schein, this is getting tedious and I think it is out of order. I have no knowledge of these people."

"One more question, please." Not waiting for his reply, "Was the ultimate goal of your solicitation to build a weapon?" Malenkov continued, unflustered that I could observe, "The solicitation response date has long past. I see no need to answer that question. Mr. Schein, please take the following advice as one business colleague to another business colleague. Don't pursue this subject any further; it can only bring difficulty and possible harm to you. The solicitation is off the market, there is no need to look any further."

"That is an ominous statement Mr. Malenkov. Is that a threat? Please elaborate." "Mr. Schein, I have warned you, now I think I will take my leave. It was interesting to meet you, thank you for your visit. My secretary will show you out."

When we got back into our limousine the mood was somber. No one said anything other than to tell the driver to take us back to the airport. We worked our way out of the city to an open road to Vnukovo.

I was thinking about the meeting when out of nowhere – kaboom! – The front of the Lincoln jumped up in the air and came down hard on all four wheels. Our driver calmly turned to us and said, "Do not open the windows or doors. This car is like a tank and has bulletproof glass. He picked up a military walkie-talkie from his seat. "This is Ambassador 1 to base – Mayday 4 – Mayday 4" (indicating there were four good guys). "Base here – alarm sent - help on the way. What's your location?" "We are on the Lenin highway four miles from the airport – Lenin highway four miles from airport. We are being peppered by small-arms fire. All four passengers are in good condition." "Roger." The base repeated the information to reconfirm and our driver said, "That's a roger; better hurry, the firing is getting more intense."

The only thing we could see out of the windows was smoke. I had drawn my pistol and was holding it in case we had to get out or the doors were opened. The small arms firing stopped and the smoke started to clear from the wash of a helicopter that was landing very close to us. Four marines jumped out and made their way to us. One marine knocked on the window of the door and shouted, "Let's go!" We shoved the door open and as we got out Madison quietly said, "I think my leg is broken."

I got out first, Madison stretched out her arms for me to pull her out of the car as Justin helped lift her so that I could carry

149

her. The three of us headed for the helicopter as another chopper landed on the other side of the road. The shooting had stopped when the marine knocked on the window and there was no additional firing. Whoever it was had scattered when the helicopters arrived. We loaded onto the chopper and it took off towards the airport. We covered the four miles in no time and landed in a secure part of Vnukovo that is reserved for incoming foreign military.

An ambulance was waiting as we came down to the helicopter landing area. Our chopper landed and shut its motor. A medical team was at the door as it opened. Madison Maxine was put onto a stretcher and carried to the ambulance. Justin was to ride with her but first he shook my hand and said "Your visit was not an ordinary visit. I'm glad you weren't hurt and I hope to meet you someday in a more peaceful way and have a drink with you." I replied, "You did well; thank you and the drinks will be on me. Goodbye."

A jeep pulled up and a couple of Russian officers walked over to a marine captain to get a report. I was quickly walked over to an airport vehicle and brought to the main terminal. My driver, a Lieutenant Fox said, "We don't need for you to get mixed up in all the paperwork. There'll be hell to pay because we did a military action on Russian soil. There are going to be a lot of apologies from both sides. Have a good flight." I said "Thank you and please thank the limo driver - he did a magnificent job." "All he was doing was following his orders and a standard exit plan. But I will tell him you said he did a good job." The marine saluted as I walked away.

I had an hour before my flight loaded, and I was starved. I found a coffee stand and had a hot cup of thick Russian coffee that held me until my flight was called. I walked to the gate, handed the attendant my ticket and she handed me back my passport. I was whole again.

150

CHAPTER 27
TIANJIN

aptain Nicolaskaya announced over the PA system that "We will be landing in the next 30 minutes on a private airfield near Tianjin.   REC Ltd. operates a large industrial facility and that is our destination. That is all I have been told to say, gentlemen. It has been an honor transporting such a notable group and I thank you. Samantha Nicolaskaya clicked off and started the process of landing her plane.

Tianjin is an industrial city, with the second largest port in China.   Approximately eleven million people live in the municipal area. Beijing is about an hour and a half auto ride to the north, which makes Tianjin the entrance city to the Capital.

The Lear made a sharp left and lowered its flaps and landing gear.   The airstrip looked short and surrounded by factory buildings. The plane touched down and Captain Nicolaskaya immediately hit the brakes hard and reversed the engines. The plane was almost at the end of the runway before its forward motion completely stopped.   It then taxied toward a control tower and airplane hangars.

Three or four service vehicles drove up while two vans parked below the plane's door. Before it was opened Tsung said, "We have an excellent laboratory and dormitory set up for you. Unfortunately the sleeping facility will not be as plush as it was in Vancouver but it is clean and should be quite adequate.

We have seriously considered Dr. Voss' suggestion and discarded the use of the magnetic bracelets. We are in China; we are in control of the area so there is no need for additional security. On the other hand, if there should be some kind of infraction, we will revisit our security issues."

The door of the plane motored upward and the stairs motored outward and down until they touched the ground. The scientists exited the plane and climbed into the vans, which drove across the landing strip to a large hangar. The doors were opened and the vans drove inside. On both sides were walls about fifteen feet high that ran the length of the hundred-yard-long hangar.

Stepping from the vans, they were guided through a door in the wall on the left side. The scientists saw a well-lighted modern laboratory facility. At the far end, all the way to the back, was a complete model and tool shop. The laboratory was divided into sections, each with the expected equipment for a particular specialty -- chemical, illumination, electrical, etc. In the center of the lab was a conference table that could accommodate thirty people. Lovering said, "It looks like our benefactors have thought of everything."

The tour continued out the door of the lab to the corridor where the vans were parked. They went across the driveway through a door just opposite of the laboratory door and seemed to step into another world: plush carpeting with comfortable looking leather chairs, mood lighting and gaily painted walls. Soft classical music played – Vivaldi, Lovering thought. Several young women wearing white Susie Wong-style dresses escorted the scientists to their bedrooms. The rooms were brightly lit with a king-size bed, desk, and toilet facilities including a shower. There were four jumpsuits hanging on a pole and a small chest of drawers with underwear and polo or golf shirts. Lovering thought, someone has gone to a lot of trouble to make us as comfortable as possible. This is impressive.

Soon they were led to the common area and asked to make themselves comfortable. "This is where you will spend the next month or so," Tsung said. "We have made it as comfortable as possible within the time we had to set it up. Your benefactors, REC Ltd., hope it meets with your approval. We had to move the laboratory twice in Canada because the authorities were becoming curious. That will not be happen in China.

"We will consider this a travel day so please take some rest or continue your work. Whatever you would like to do is fine as long as you always remain within the walls of this structure. If you need any equipment or funds for a product or project please let me know immediately so that we can acquire it for you. By the way, that is one of the reasons why we chose Tianjin. Much of the material you might request can be found within this large industrial municipality."

Pointing, Tsung said, "We have a small commissary at the far end of the building for all of your meals and/or any snack, in the late evening. It will be open to you 24 hours a day, 7 days per week. That is all I have for now. Enjoy your free time; I will leave you and will return at 7:30 tomorrow morning."

"Oh," Tsung continued, "Your assistants will be joining you tomorrow. They also are staying here in slightly smaller sleeping units down the line closer to the commissary. Enjoy your time off." Tsung walked out of the common room followed by half of the women escorts. The scientists all seemed to start talking at once and Lovering said, "Stop; please remember that we most likely are being monitored. Please be careful with your remarks and criticism." That seemed to take the wind out of everyone's sails. The men had never been so closely monitored and were unaccustomed to this type of restraint.

Lovering continued, "If we want to share information now then let's call an official meeting. If you want to break off and do your own thing then let's do that. What do you want to do?" Kawakami spoke up, "I am not ready to share my information. I need some more answers before I can do that." "So do I," said Ping. The others agreed they needed some time to put their thoughts and notes straight before they could intelligently share their information.

"Good – I guess we break off into small meetings or work individually. See you at dinner." Howard got up and left the common area for his room. Rabinovich sought out Little and Ping and they all went into the lab. Voss and Kawakami teamed up and Kleiber went to his room.

CHAPTER 28
BEIJING

All through the flight to Beijing I was trying to figure out why I'd been attacked. Orders for the hit had to have come from high up in the government. The effort was weak and poorly constructed; they probably didn't have enough time to work it out. I was lucky that it was a short run from the Mashpriborintorg offices to the airport. That didn't give the attackers much time to set up. Malenkov had to give someone the results of the meeting before they attacked. That all takes time - unless the attack was planned before I ever got to the meeting.

They probably weren't expecting me to use the ambassador's car and that was why the bomb didn't blow us open. God, that car was certainly built like a tank. Had I been in a standard vehicle we wouldn't have had a chance before the marines arrived. I guess they, whoever 'they' is, thought if they put me out of commission or kill me, they would slow up the search for the scientists.

That might be true but how would they know that? I haven't done any more than what any investigator would be doing. I am following up leads and hunches. From all appearances – on the outside – I am just following orders. How would they know if I have a larger role in this? I wonder if they are getting information directly from my office. Nah, can't be. That thinking is way too devious. That can get you into trouble.

On the other hand, Harry Collins is still missing and there has been no word where he might be. He probably has been taken out. These people just do not want anyone sniffing around. Unless Harry made an error or was expected, they would never have known that he was there or he was just visiting. Something isn't right. A lot isn't right.

After about five more hours we were on final approach to Beijing airport. It's amazing how much clout the red passport has. I just waved it and walked through inspection. I got into the baggage area and continued my walk out of the controlled area. I entered the terminal when someone to the left of me asked, "Are you in a hurry?" It was Bob Claypool. My face lit up, it was good to see a friend after this morning's incident.

"Boy, I rarely get an ear-to-ear smile like that." "When I fill you in you will understand why it feels great to be with a friend." We shook hands and Bob said, "I have a limo waiting to take us to the Beijing Hotel. The Beijing is about the best business hotel in town and the one used by foreigners. We will be able to use it as our base." My response was a relieved, simple, "Good." I was happy someone else was helping to make some decisions. My mind just seemed a jumble of unanswered questions.

On the ride to the hotel I filled Bob in about my hectic trip to Russia and the attempt on my life. His reaction echoed mine. "Why the hell take you out? Just to slow us up in our search for the scientists gives a lot of credence to how close we might be. They must be very nervous. I wonder what the fuck they are building."

We got to the hotel and settled in by unpacking and meeting in the lobby to go to the bar for a drink. I started to make notes on a yellow pad and after a few minutes of review we went to the guest business office and rented a conference room to call

New York. As always, old reliable, Doreen Parks answered and passed us on to Luke Albert.

Luke was not a happy camper. He was angry, upset and surly. When I inquired what was going on he said, "In one of the auto junk yards they found a crushed red Ford Mustang and the VIN number matches the car rental ticket number for Harry Collins. Agents Speziale and Held were in the process of searching all junkyards in Vancouver and this is one of four red Mustangs they came across. It was crushed into a five-foot by four-foot by two-foot mass of metal. The car had been badly burned but the serial number tag was readable. The number was recorded by the junkyard as required by Canadian law. The RCMP is having it transferred to their forensics lab in Toronto.

Bob and I sat and starred at each other silently while Luke rambled on that Collins had no backup and had not followed orders to the hilt. I interrupted, "Harry was a stickler for following procedures. He probably didn't have much faith in this visit because he didn't plan any backup. I don't think he can be blamed for being sloppy. We just might not know what he was up against." Luke could see that this was going nowhere and changed the subject. "Are you set up in Beijing yet? Do you have everything you need?" "Not quite," I replied, "We will have to make some purchases on the street."

Luke was now all business, "Mei Cao Lin has a major customer and is doing quite a bit of business with REC, Ltd. They have an active landing strip in Tianjin just south of Beijing. The strip is protected by a number of industrial buildings and hangars. That is where I think you should start looking." "We're on it," I replied, "We will get back to you as soon as we check it out."

"Nothing more then just a checkout, understood?" Bob and I chorused, "Yes." "You are in unfriendly territory and we do not have many rights in Communist China. Let's make sure we play it as straight as possible." The call ended with Bob and me scratching our heads. "Luke is very upset. Harry was an old good friend of Luke's. They go back a long way, to when Luke was active in Europe."

Bob and I made for the streets of Beijing. As soon as we walked out of the hotel we could feel the pulse of the city. There were very few autos, but thousands of bicycles, and every imaginable item was somehow transported on a bike. You could see hot meals, large pieces of window glass, and businessmen in suits – all on bikes. Beijing was a city on wheels, bicycle wheels.

We were just a block from the Forbidden City, a beautiful piece of history that even the communist government respected and protected. On the way to the Forbidden City we were looking for shopping arcades or street vendors so we could purchase binoculars, a compass, wire cutters, flashlights, dark clothing, rope, knives and other items. I guess we would call it the ultimate camping equipment excursion.

After about an hour of walking and bargaining, plus spending about U.S. $500, we found just about everything we were looking for. Beijing is teeming with people, we didn't have to go very far for what we needed. There seems to be a cart, a shop, an alley for almost anything. You can find it on the streets of Beijing if you are persistent enough.

As far as weapons, Bob had his 9mm Beretta, a 10-shot pistol, and I had my 45 caliber, 7-shot pistol. With the firepower we were carrying we might be able to start a war, but we certainly were in no position to finish it.

We went back to the hotel and ordered a black Ford Mustang from the concierge. We left instructions to have it parked and ready to go at 4 AM in front of the hotel. We decided to have a bite to eat in our suite. Over an American dinner of cheeseburgers and French fries we checked the map we had purchased and made our plans before turning in. I was thrilled that I had Bob to work with me. Lately I have been doing this by myself and it is a lot easier with a dependable backup. It was a good call bringing Bob to Beijing.

We had a tenth floor suite that included a modern living room with fireplace and two bedrooms. We were up at 3 AM, had room service deliver breakfast were set to go about 4:15. Pretty much on schedule, I thought. We wanted to do our scouting around in darkness, so timing was important.

CHAPTER 29
TIANJIN BY CAR

The black Mustang was parked in front of the entrance to the Beijing Hotel. Bob decided he would drive and that was fine with me. He must have had a great image of the trip in his memory because he did not check the map or ask me any directions. I just followed the map as the navigator and was amazed how Bob seemed to have memorized our route. When we hit the main road to Tianjin, a relatively modern highway, Bob starting hitting speeds of 100 mph and would increase it wherever possible. There was only light traffic with a few trucks at this time in the morning,

An hour later we were on the outskirts of Tianjin with about ten miles to go. The land opened up and everything was much flatter as we approached the southern part of the Bohai Gulf. The REC, Ltd. airstrip and complex came up quickly. In fact we almost passed it. We decided to continue to drive a little further, park and then hike back. Bob found a perfect spot that was normally used for fishing from an overpass. We turned off the road and with the help of the structure and a little housekeeping hid the car.

If anyone was following us we were not able to detect it. We were sure someone had to know we were out of the hotel but where we went had to be the question. Unless there is a transmitter in the car we felt we were alone. After all, this was communist China and the government liked to know where visitors were at any given moment. So we decided to operate as though we had company. We hid near the car to see if anyone was following. After ten minutes no one had arrived.

We started the half-mile hike to the complex. We were unable to get any kind of night-vision gear so the binoculars were our distance eyes. We walked a good quick pace – it was 5:45 AM and the sun was supposed to rise at 6:37. We had to get the lead out. I got Bob's attention, pointed to my watch and pumped my arm and he started a steady jog. Soon enough, the building came into view.

The airstrip was on the other side, set among a number of buildings. Bob held his hand up and pointed at the razor wire spread around the grounds. It was particularly heavy around one of the hangars in front of us. The air control tower was across the field and we were not in a position to see it. Bob hit me on the shoulder and we went down to the ground. I looked up as two guards passed on the other side of the razor wire fence, gabbing in Chinese.

Bob whispered into my ear for me to look at the peak of the hangar. I could make out all sorts of communication gear and smokestacks but nothing else. He motioned me to look through my binoculars again. I saw it. At the very peak of the hangar, just below the eaves, a man was lighting a cigarette. Around his neck he had a large pair of binoculars. He was an observer and probably had some kind of weapon. He was talking into a walkie-talkie, which possibly meant that there were other observers in strategic positions. Finally, the security men wore uniforms but were not government soldiers. This was a private army. My conclusion was simple: Why the muscle in a country where the government is on your side? You must be protecting something very valuable. I was sure we had found our scientists. Now, we had to figure out how to get at them. I signaled to Bob that I'd had enough and he returned thumbs up and we were on our way back to Beijing as the sun started to come up.

We were driving and talking about the extreme security measures we'd seen when all of a sudden we heard a sharp CRACK! The rear window had shattered. Without another word Bob floored the car and we started to fly. Traffic was still light and Bob was weaving in and out of the cars and trucks. When we had one of the trucks for cover I climbed into the back seat and punched out what remained of the window. I reached for my pistol and on my knees, propped myself in a ready position to see if I could find who was shooting at us.

I shouted, "Bob did you pick up anything? I don't see anyone." "Not yet!" Bob yelled back. I have no idea how fast Bob was pushing the Mustang but it had to be over a hundred. He was aiming the car more then driving it. Thank God it was a straight road. "There! Did you see that flash?" A couple of thuds hit the trunk of the car. A black car without lights was making its way towards us. I steadied myself on my knees, holding my 45 as firmly as possible and squeezed the trigger twice. The chasing car slowed and ducked behind a truck.

I turned to Bob and said, "These guys will try to stay with us to knock us off the road before we reach Beijing. Slow down and maybe I can get a better shot and get them before they get us." Bob dropped our speed down into the low fifties. This brought us about twenty yards from the truck that was concealing the car.

It came from behind the truck and started up fast, looking for us, not expecting us to be almost in front of them. I squeezed off three shots. One of my bullets hit the right front wheel. The driver did all he could to steady his car but he was going too fast. He hit the soft shoulder of the road and the car rolled over a few times and came to a stop then burst into flames.

Bob yelled over his shoulder, "Good shot," and picked up speed. I could see trucks and cars stopping at the wreck as we took off. We were back in our hotel within the hour and quietly having breakfast in our room. It was quite a morning, I thought. A good shower and a conference call with New York will wrap it up perfectly.

My reverie was shattered by a knock on the door. I looked through the peephole and there were two police officers with their hands on their holsters. I opened the door and said, "Good morning." The officers stepped inside uninvited and one of them in excellent English asked, "Do you own the black Ford Mustang that is parked in front of the hotel?"

I said, "No, but we did rent a black Mustang and it was parked in front of the hotel." The officers pulled out their pistols. One went over to Bob and one stayed beside me. "Do you have any weapons," he demanded. Bob and I both replied, "Yes." "Hands up, where are they and let me see your identification." With my hands at shoulder height I walked into my bedroom while Bob did the same and we got our diplomatic passports. As soon as they saw red passports, the tension eased.

"Where are your weapons? May we see them?" "What's all this about?" I asked. "A black Ford Mustang was seen leaving the scene of an accident. The hotel reported that a damaged car was parked in front and we were asked to investigate. We discovered that the automobile had bullet holes in it and its rear window was missing. We checked with the front desk and were directed to your room. Now, may we please see your weapons?"

Bob and I got our pistols, cocked the chamber and released the clip. We then handed the empty pistols to the officers. The officer covering me said, "This weapon (my 45) has been recently fired. The other one appears to be clean. May we have an explanation why the weapon was fired?" "I'm afraid not," I said. "I believe my diplomatic passport allows me not only to carry the weapon but to fire it. I'm not at liberty to explain why it has been fired."

The cop was barely controlling his emotions. In measured terms he said, "If there is any evidence of any wrongdoing using this weapon you will be expelled from China. I will confiscate the weapon now and have a ballistics check on it before we return it to you." "I'm afraid not," I said. "I stand by my diplomatic immunity and formally state, in front of witnesses, that you make your request to the American Embassy. For now, I believe the weapons will stay here."

The police officer stared at me, seething but silent. You could almost see the wheels turning in his head. He was not sure of his ground nor was he sure whether I was right or wrong. He did not want to lose face. He particularly did not want to look bad in front of his partner, who obviously spoke little English. He nodded, put his pistol back in its holster and his partner did the same. "We will check in with our superiors and get back to you and the Embassy if need be." I nodded slightly and said, "Thank you." The crisis was over; Bob and I had our room back.

Bob said, "How did you know all this diplomatic mumbo-jumbo." "I didn't," I replied. "I was bluffing all the way. It all just sounded logical to me." "Whew, I'm not playing poker with you." "Well, what we can say for sure is, thank you Luke Albert for making sure we had red diplomatic passports." "Amen to that," agreed Bob.

CHAPTER 30
THE WEAPON BECOMES A REALITY

Howard Lovering rose about 6 AM, showered, rang for some breakfast and walked across the driveway in the hangar to the laboratory. The lab was humming, it was brightly lighted and the operation went on 24 hours a day. Lovering thought it was like being in Las Vegas, you never knew what time of day it was.

In the few days they'd been in Tianjin a great deal of progress had been made. In fact, Lovering thought too much progress was being made. Well, maybe if we get done ahead of schedule our captors will let us go earlier. That is, if they ever let us go. It was an unsettling thought but it was reality. I just hope my signal got across and our people don't forget us.

He walked over to the lens development section of the lab where Kawakami was waiting for him. Kawakami had been working on some lens and illumination pieces that Lovering had ordered to be manufactured. He said, "I think these are what you were looking for. It was very hard to make this kind of convex curvature with the elements so thin. We were able to do it by being very resourceful, using a condom to hold the glass in place. We must have cracked a dozen pieces before we got the knack how to do it."

"I think they will work out just fine," Lovering said. "We have to start some sort of breadboard assembly to see what is out of place and what has to be adjusted and adapted." Kawakami said, "Good, I will have my assistants get right on it." "Remember, it will be hard to focus the illumination system, keep trying to adjust the nodal separation of the elements. That is how we will come to a focus point." "Ah so, Lovering-san, the secret of the David Mann Photorepeater illumination system is now coming to my understanding."

Lovering turned beet red. All he could say was "Go about your business." He turned away and found his desk. When he sat down he looked around to make sure no one was watching him and pounded his desk. I don't know if that makes me feel any better but it releases some frustration.

Ping had developed a critical mass of volatile chemicals for the exciter. He wasn't sure that it could be safely handheld. He turned to Rabinovich and posed the problem. Rabinovich looked at it and in his thick Russian accent said, "I will develop a carrier tube out of high grade stainless steel that should hold the chemical safely. Then I will design it into the gun position with a series of buffers that will serve as shock absorbers. The only thing to worry about will be when the weapon is unattended. It will act as a bomb if it is mishandled or mistreated. We have to have a shut down or safety holder where the weapons can be stored when not in use."

Voss was working with Little and Kleiber. Voss was designing the trigger mechanism, Little and Kleiber were dealing with the portable side of the electronics package. They were having trouble trying to pack enough power into a handheld device. They finally gave up and started to design a powerful battery could fit into a backpack. That way they would have a two-man team; one would carry the weapon, aim it and shoot or flash it, the other would carry the battery package. He would also keep track of the battery levels and would be able to take certain measures, such as shutting the system down, to preserve the power for the PTHEL. A two-man team fire team is not unusual: a mortar or bazooka team consists of two men.

During all this activity Tsung was periodically collecting all lab books and notes. He then had them meticulously copied by hand and returned in a matter of hours to the scientists. Tsung made an announcement over the PA system that within the hour there would be a briefing so that he could bring the latest information to the administrators of REC, Ltd. There was a lot of grumbling, most of the scientists wanted to move ahead so that they could get done and get home. They all felt the meetings that Tsung ran were a waste of time.

The key scientists were sitting at the conference table when Tsung was about to open the meeting. Howard Lovering stood up before Tsung could speak and said, "Gentlemen, according to what I have seen and the reports I have read I believe we are ready to put together a working breadboard to prove out our theories. After all, we have been working independently and I think it is time to see if all this can mesh and come together."

Tsung was doing a slow burn at having the floor and attention taken away from him. The scientists looked at each other, some checked their papers, and then Ping and Rabinovich said, "We think you are correct! We should marry as much as we can together and make a trial run." Little interrupted, "I am not sure we are ready with the power pack but, for the mockup we can use an external power source."

Lovering said, "Then we are agreed. Let's try to get something operational within the next two days for a demonstration." The meeting broke off into small groups with animated conversations. Everyone got up and went back to the work areas and Tsung was left at the table, totally ignored. Lovering stayed seated and looked at Tsung and said, "It looks like we are on the way, do you agree?" Tsung was livid but, after all it was the project that mattered. He said, "Yes," got up and left the laboratory. Lovering sat there with a smile on his face and said out loud, "Got you, you bastard."

CHAPTER 31
A PLAN IN THE MAKING

Bob and I finished our repast and decided it was safer to use the hotel's business center for our conversation with New York. We were certain that our room was bugged. We never bothered to look for the bugs, we just took precautions. We made sure there was either a radio or television on, fairly loud, if we had to talk business.

We were cautious, too, with the information operator in the business center, when she designated a conference room for us to use. I decided that we should occupy another one. This seemed to fluster the young woman. I said, "Room 2 is empty and it has a view of the lobby. We would like to take that one." She stared at me for a moment and finally said, "That room was reserved, but I will change the reservation to another room." I said, "Thank you, my business associate and I will take the room now." I guess you can never be too cautious. I don't know what that was all about but I bet she had instructions for foreigners to use specific rooms because of listening devices.

Bob started for the conference room and as I was giving the telephone operator the number I wanted called in New York, I heard a commotion at the hotel's entrance. I looked up and said, "I don't believe it." Hyacinth Chang was walking into the hotel with a couple of bellhops and managers in tow. She wore a skintight white business suit with a short skirt, black stiletto heels and a white magnolia in her hair. She had on a black blouse that was cut low to show off her ample bosom. The only thing that was out of place was a pair of large, black-rimmed and very dark sunglasses. She was talking to one of the managers and was being led to the front desk. The lobby of the Beijing Hotel is brightly lighted with uncomfortable chairs and pretty floral displays.

Bob came up to me and said, "What the hell do you make of this?" "I have no idea. Bob, take the room; I will only be a minute." I walked toward the front desk and she looked up and saw me. Hyacinth wasn't rude but she pushed aside the manager she was talking to and walked over to me and said, "I was hoping I would find you here." "What's this all about, what is wrong?" She seemed upset but I couldn't see her eyes because of the sunglasses so I wasn't sure. "Is there a place where we can talk?" "Yes, Bob and I have just reserved one of the conference rooms in the business center." "Fine," she said, "I will join you in a few minutes."

I walked back to the conference room and told the operator to hold up on our call to New York. I told Bob what happened and said, "This might prove to be interesting, let's sit tight and see how this pans out." About ten minutes later Hyacinth Chang walked into the conference room. She didn't have her usual air of confidence and forcefulness. She even asked, "May I sit down?" I said, "Of course." There was an uncomfortable silence for a few minutes while she gathered herself and finally said, "I am here to help you recover the scientists."

Bob and I looked at each other in complete surprise. Hyacinth continued, "I have been against this business project since the first day I heard of it. My mother is involved with the project through the Mei Cao Lin Company. I think what they are building is a mistake and against society that we know. I have

170

wanted to keep Chang Industries as a clean, apolitical business operation. I have wanted us to be recognized as a legitimate competitor. We are doing a creditable job of product development and have an excellent bottom line. We do not need to be associated with a product, actually a weapon that is so abhorrent and dangerous to mankind."

I interrupted and asked, "What kind of weapon?" I think this took Hyacinth by surprise. She must have assumed that we were aware of what weapon was being developed. She paused a moment, then, as if she was preprogrammed, she rambled on with an explanation in a monotone voice.

"As I said, I have been against this project when I first heard of it. My mother and I fought about our involvement many times before you arrived in Hong Kong. When you arrived to talk to Mei Cao Lin I recognized that there was some urgency because of the missing scientists and you were against the project as well. That is why I made the arrangements for you to meet Mei Cao Lin to see if you could dissuade them in any way.

"My mother allowed the meeting to take place because she wanted to know whatever information you might have about the project. After the meeting she tried to discredit you even though she knew you really didn't have enough information to hurt the project. You were quick enough to catch on with the two prostitutes and spoiled her attempt.

"I told you about the Chang Industry's residential development in Vancouver because I knew the kidnapped scientists were working there. You arrived on the scene a few hours after they had left. I was happy that you understood that I was tipping my hand and trying to give you an indication where the scientists were. When we said goodbye in the basement of Tower #1 in Vancouver your eyes wandered and distracted for a moment. After you left I tried to figure out what caught your attention and I saw the initials HL scratched on the doorjamb – Howard Lovering. I knew then that I had to tell you the full story.

"I returned to Hong Kong to plead with my mother to pull out of the project. She became angry and I met with the full power of her wrath. She told me not to become involved or I would face horrible repercussions. I made the mistake of again saying that this was wrong and decided to challenge her. She slapped me in the face and said, 'You have no idea what you are talking about. How dare you challenge me? If you are not careful you could be blinded for the rest of your life.' 'To your own daughter you would say that?' I shouted, 'How could you?'

"My mother called in one of her trusted bodyguards and whispered instructions to him. He walked over to me and before I realized it he swiftly punched me in my left eye. I was stunned and stood up straight and covered my eye and was about to say something when he hit me again, this time in my right eye. I now had my hands over my eyes and he pulled down my right hand and hit me again in the eye very hard. I fell to the floor weeping and my mother shouted 'STOP!'

"I could hardy see, everything was a blur. I was sobbing. My mother walked over to me and said in a voice spoken through clenched teeth, that I should enjoy my sight now because it could be a very fleeting thing should I decide to go against her and the family. She promised that there would be no pain the next time. All you will see is a light and you will be blinded for the rest of your life. She then turned on her heel and walked out of the room leaving me on the floor hurting and crying. She didn't even send any help into my office. She just left me there on the floor like I was a toy that she was finished playing with. She didn't care."

Hyacinth then took off her sunglasses. Her face was a mess. Her right eye was swollen and partially closed and her left eye was black and blue. I walked over to her and put my hand on her shoulder and said, "I'm sorry. Thank you for telling Bob and me what happened. I am sorry you had to go through this. Why don't we take a break for a moment, have some tea and see how we can help each other." Hyacinth put on her sunglasses and said, "We can't waste any time. Let's push on." I could see she was determined and very angry. Her mother, the matriarch of the family, had terribly let her down and she wanted revenge. In Hyacinth's mind it was pay-back time.

"I gather from what you're saying, the weapon we are talking about is built around the use of a laser. That is similar to the original unsolicited proposals that Mashpriborintorg and Mei Cao Lin were looking for. From what you are saying the weapon is a specially designed laser that if the ray hits you in the eyes you go blind, correct?" Hyacinth nodded. I continued, "Well, if we know about it in advance we then can protect our people with special goggles."

Hyacinth interrupted, "Not necessarily, in World War One they had mustard gas and gas masks. The gas masks stopped the majority of soldiers from getting gassed but those who were gassed caused major problems in the trenches, drawing able-bodied men to deal with the gassing victims and heightening fear among their comrades. This resulted in a weakening of the trench defenses. The purpose of this weapon is similar. Imagine a number of blind soldiers thrashing about on the front lines. It would cause chaos. Also, if you didn't have the right wavelength to stop the light ray, your goggles might be useless."

"OK, I understand," I said. "I think it is time we call our office." Bob went out of the room to tell the operator to put the call through and I said to Hyacinth, "Thank you for coming forward. I am sure this was a difficult and dangerous decision for you. This is very important to me as well because I have a good friend in Howard Lovering and I would hate to lose him." Hyacinth said, "We still might lose him if we do not do this correctly." That reality sent a shiver down my spine.

As usual, Doreen Parks came on the phone and said that Luke Albert would be with us momentarily. I asked Doreen to speak up because the speakerphone attachment was not particularly clear. I also mentioned that in addition to Bob, Hyacinth Chang was in the room. Luke got on the phone and said "Hello everyone." I then recounted everything to the moment Hyacinth Chang finished her report. Almost an hour had passed, including Bob's input. Hyacinth sat quietly and listened. Our visit to the Tianjin facility and the shooting that followed was completely new to her. She took everything in, did not show any emotion and didn't say a word.

Luke said, "Please wait a minute, I want to check with Doreen to make sure your report was recorded OK." A few moments passed and he was back on the line. "Robert, please pick up the phone for a minute." I did and Luke said, "I realize you can only answer with a yes or no because Hyacinth is sitting in the room. Bear with me. Do you believe she is telling you the truth?" "Yes." Luke continued, "In my thinking a Chang working against a Chang is just not possible." "It may be possible in this instance," I said. "Does Claypool feel the same way?" "Absolutely." "OK, you can put me back on the speakerphone."

"I am going to put a call into the Command Office of Navy Seals - Pacific. I am going to try to contact Captain Andrew Hardwick who, you will remember, worked successfully with us some ten years ago. He was a lieutenant commander at that time off the aircraft carrier Intrepid. He now is in charge of all Seal teams for the

174

Pacific theater. Doreen is trying to tie him in as we talk."

In a short while, a booming voice said, "Captain Hardwick here." Before anybody could say anything Claypool shouted, "How's it hanging, Andrew?" "Oh my, that's a blast from the past, is that Bob Claypool?" "None other. I also have Robby Schein with me." "If you guys are together then I know we are in trouble. How is everyone?" Luke Albert interrupted, "Sorry to break up this reunion but we have business to discuss." Everyone stopped talking and Luke outlined a plan after a quick briefing for Hardwick's sake.

"We need a team of eight to ten Seals to get into Beijing as unnoticed as possible. Check in at the Beijing Hotel as regular guests, then formulate an attack plan after we get a little more intelligence. That is where Hyacinth Chang can help us. Can you visit the Tianjin facility, Miss Chang?" Hyacinth said, "I will do whatever I can to help rescue the scientists and destroy the weapon." Luke said, "Good. What do you say, Captain Hardwick, are you in or do I need to get some more information and authority to convince you?" "No, this is good enough for me, I just need an authorization in writing and we are on our way." "You will have that within thirty minutes." "Fine, see you all in Beijing," and Hardwick hung up.

Luke asked for me to pick up the telephone again. "Robert, I still do not trust Miss Chang. I want you to be very careful and watch her very closely. Madame Chang is machiavellian enough to have staged this whole beating to get your trust and sympathy. I don't want to send in my people and the Seal team just to get them killed. This has to be a clean take with as little shooting as possible and with good intelligence. We have to get in and get out quickly. Unfortunately we will be creating quite an international incident. Walk on eggs with this one. I will let the politicians work that out. Be very careful. Have Bob watch your back." I replied, "Yes sir" and hung up.

CHAPTER 32
THE BREADBOARD

The laboratory was working at a feverish pace. It was like the birth of an unknown being. Lovering's thoughts were that they were creating a Frankenstein's monster. Everyone was into what he was doing. Tempers were short and there was a lot of screaming and hurt feelings.

Lovering called his colleagues together and once again reviewed the project's parameters. "The ability of the laser we are building has the following critical factors to be concerned with: the laser wavelength, pulse duration, pulse energy, and size of the laser beam when it hits the eye. Each of us has worked on a special section of the project. Now we have to see if we can make the parts fit together. Gentlemen, let's try to do this as calmly and professionally as possible." The message got across.

The breadboard was in the hands of Rabinovich, the weapons design expert. The others were feeding their parts to him and his two assistants. When another section was to be added the assistant who had worked on it was added to Rabinovich's team.

In the meantime the tooling shop was machining parts to Rabinovich's specifications and drawings. As the rough breadboard started to take shape it looked like something from outer space. Lovering never imagined that the complicated seating of the volatile exciter to the complicated lens and illumination design would end up looking this futuristic.

The weapon was about four feet long with a shoulder rifle stock. Imagine a hunting rifle with a scope on top of it. This looked like three scopes on top of one another. Under them, where you would expect the rifle to be was a tube with a diameter the size of a mortar of about 8". This was a big weapon but the shiny stainless steel made it look like something other worldly.

In general, when the PHTEL weapon is powered up the topmost barrel was the aiming device or laser measuring locator to find the enemy. The next two barrels dealt with the optical parts of the system. The illumination and lens combination squeezed the light through a catadioptric front surface mirror system that determined the diameter and distance the light ray would travel. The bottom tube, the largest of the four, housed the volatile chemical exciter, the electronics package and the firing mechanism. Attached to its side was an electronic eyepiece that would tell the shooter when the target was in focus and when the PTHEL could be fired.

Plans called for a link to a portable battery pack that would be carried by the second crew member. This wasn't ready for the initial testing and a standard 220v (50 cycles) electrical power source was to be used.

Rabinovich worked feverishly on the equipment giving sharp orders. Except for the electronics people everyone was staring and commenting on what they were watching. Lovering said, "I think this would be a good time to break for dinner and give our comrades a little space." Reluctantly everyone agreed and walked to the commissary.

As the meal was ending Lovering tapped his glass with a spoon and got everyone's attention. "Gentlemen," he started, "I think it only proper that we take a moment and reflect on what we are building. I remember a photograph my father showed me from World War One of a line of blinded soldiers being led from their trenches by comrades after being exposed to phosgene gas. The outcry from the public was decisive. The cruelty and inhumanity of chemical warfare led to the adoption of the 1925 Geneva Protocol banning the use of chemical and biological warfare. I researched this information when the original unsolicited laser proposal was shown to me. David W. Mann Company chose not to be involved with the project.

"We are building a weapon that we assume will have the results of damaging the retina of the eye or at the very least cause hemorrhaging near the retina. The result will be irreversible blindness. Once this weapon is demonstrated, I am sure the public will object and I imagine manufacturing bans will ultimately affect the production of weapons like the PHTEL. However, today we are embarking on a trip for scientific history. Many problems have been solved to be able to build this prototype. I salute you and toast you: Success to our demonstration!"

Everyone was silent. No one raised his glass – or knew how to deal with what Howard Lovering had just stated. They stared at their champagne or into space. The room was quiet when Tsung decided he had to save the day. "Everyone, stand up," he ordered. "A toast, a toast to a successful demonstration." The doctors and assistants looked at each other and the mood was broken. One of the men shouted, "Yes, a toast to our hard work!" The glasses were raised and emptied. Everyone drank the champagne except for Howard Lovering. He sat and stared at his glass.

CHAPTER 33
THE GATHERING IS FILLED WITH SURPRISES

I sat with Hyacinth Chang in the lounge, trying to calm her and help her push her anger aside. For what I was going to ask her to do she had to have her wits about her. There was no room for mistakes, and anger causes mistakes. I asked if there was any chance of reconciliation with her mother. All she did was shake her head no. "How will you be able to continue in Chang Industries after all that has happened?" "I don't know and I am not sure that I care to."

"Wait a minute," I said, "You have a commanding position in the company and you said the company is doing well. I can't believe that there isn't some way to reconcile this thing with your mother." "It's not my mother who will step in to stop me; it will be my three adopted brothers. They have been waiting for this day. They sit on the board and do nothing and say nothing. All they do is watch, take notes and wait. They vote however my mother wants them to vote. They are in complete lockstep with my mother. It wouldn't surprise me if they have already had my mother's ear and have cut me out of the picture. That is how ruthless they are, very much like my twin sister Juniper was before she was killed."

Hyacinth surprised me with what she said next. "I have imagined this day would come. I have started planning to form a competitive company under my name and direction. I will compete with my mother for the same business. She will allow a certain degree of success but I am afraid that my stupid brothers will try to squash me. That is their weakness and if I am careful I can take advantage of their greed.

"I already have had the corporate papers drawn up and I have a reasonable amount of cash in a personal account in the Isle of Man. I am ready to go forward and I believe my idiot brothers have no idea of what I am doing." Luke Albert's 'machiavellian' kept going through my mind. I don't care who the person is, Dragon Lady or not, she can't be this farsighted. I do not think that this can be so well staged in so short a time. This story has got to be true. I decided we had to trust Hyacinth Chang and let her in on the whole plan.

It was less then twenty-four hours since we called New York and the Seal team was starting to arrive. One by one they checked in, went to their rooms and stayed in them waiting for instructions. We decided to have a meeting at 11 PM. Bob got on the phone, reached his contact and the word was passed to each of the nine-member team.

Then, I was knocked out of my socks. Doreen Parks called to say, Luke Albert would arrive in Beijing at about 10 PM. I couldn't believe it. I said something stupid like, "Are you sure?" "Robert," Doreen shouted, "Pull yourself together, of course I am sure. He feels that with all the possible political problems and logistics, the power of his office should be on the front lines." All I could think of saying was, "Thank God." This is going to take the weight off my shoulders.

"Doreen, is this with approval from Washington?" The last time Luke did something like this he did it on his own, headstrong. Fortunately we had a successful mission so there wasn't much anyone could say. "That is a good question,

Robert. Luke Albert told me it was with the Deputy's approval. I assume everything is clear and there will be no repercussions. However, you know what they say when you assume – you make an ass out of u and me. I wish I could give you a better answer."

I knew right then that there was no way Washington would approve Albert going into harm's way with his medical history. That history goes back to when he was an operative during World War II and almost died behind the lines in the bush in Japan. The Triguboffs found him and nursed him back to health. Later, during the formation of TAG Photographic, he had a run-in with the Dragon Lady, Madame Chang. He had lost a partner in Germany and blamed himself for being slow to react to the situation.

Madame Chang learned of his weakness and depression. She got him involved in an opium-induced trance with a prostitute. Then Chang tried to blackmail and embarrass him with the film with Washington. It didn't work because Albert told the Chang organization to "fuck off." He didn't care what they had on him and challenged them to do their worst to discredit him. Washington backed Albert but kept him behind the desk, not to venture out into the field. This is going to be a very interesting couple of days, I thought.

I got back into my room and there was a message from Debbie. "Oh my God," I said, "I haven't called or written, I am going to be killed. She must be frantic." You know, you get out on the road and get so involved that you are in your own time warp. People find that hard to believe but if you don't spend 100% of your consciousness involved in the kind of work I am doing you can get seriously injured.

I immediately called home even though it was very early in the morning New York time.. "Hi Deb, it's me." "Well, I am certainly happy to hear your voice. The office tells me you are gallivanting around the world and I haven't heard a word from you." "I know, I am very sorry. It has just been so hectic that I haven't had a moment to breathe."

"Marc is sick with strep throat, Rebecca was in the hospital with some sort of viral infection that we finally got under control and the only one still standing who has not been sick is Andrew. It has been a hell of a time. Thank God for your mother. She has been with me for a couple of days to help out. When do you think you will be coming home?"

The hundred-dollar question, I thought. "I have no idea," I said, knowing that wasn't the reply she wanted to hear. "Well, how are you anyhow?" "I'm keeping up with it; it isn't easy. Luke Albert is arriving this evening so I think you can imagine how important this trip is." That drew a silent moment on the phone. Debbie knew Luke's background and realized that there was something ultra-important going on. "OK," she said, "I can deal with this a while longer. Will you promise to take care of yourself?"

"I always do, my dear. I promise we will get away without the kids when I get home and I will try to make it back as soon as I can." "All right, Rob, I love you." "I love you, too, Deb," and we hung up. I thought to myself, it is amazing how real life brings you down to earth. I love my work but I love my family as well. That was a wakeup call and it reminded me that I really love my family more.

There was a knock at the door and Bob opened it and one by one the Seal team arrived. It was a bunch of good-looking young men in their prime. Everyone was dressed in street clothes and carried a small leather binder to take notes. They found a chair or a piece of the floor and made themselves as comfortable as possible.

One of the team members put as finger to his mouth for silence. He took out a sensor or meter about the size of his hand. He also had a handful of small boxes, each about the size of a half dollar. He walked around the room and wherever he found a listening device he put one of the boxes next to it. The little box was a white-noise device and served to jam the listening device. He finished his search after he visited our bedroom and bathrooms.

I mentioned that we were waiting for Luke Albert and Hyacinth Chang to join us. I filled the men in on who they were and gave them an overall description of what the mission was all about.

There was a pounding on the door and one of the Seal members got up and opened the door. In walked a six foot three, well built black man with a strong military bearing. I immediately recognized him and shouted, "By God, its Andrew Hardwick. What the hell are you doing here?" Before he could answer, Bob then I gave Andrew bear hugs. He caught his breath and said, "I'm responsible for these guys, so I decided to be the tenth man. Besides, when you two guys are together I knew I didn't want to miss all the fun."

As we were about to close the door Luke Albert with Hyacinth Chang entered. She was in a black pants outfit that showed off her many attributes and she was still wearing her black-rimmed large dark sunglasses. As she walked across the room every man in the room stopped talking and visually undressed her. By the time she sat down she must have felt naked.

She was in a plush armchair and took out a pack of cigarettes. There must have been four lighters at the ready as soon as she got a cigarette out of the pack. I smiled and turned my attention to Luke. We warmly shook hands, hugged and I said, "Welcome to Beijing." Luke smiled and responded, "Happy to be at your show." I said to myself, that is a clear message that he wants me to continue the management of the operation.

Bob Claypool and I started the briefing at the very beginning with the abduction of Howard Lovering. When we got to the Harry Collins part, Albert interrupted and said, "The crushed vehicle in the Vancouver junkyard had Collins' remains in it. They were positively identified. We can assume that the people we are going after did this. This has now become personal for some of us. Please continue, Robert." I did and the meeting went into the early morning hours.

At one point, I explained that Hyacinth Chang would visit Tianjin and hoped that her family hadn't changed her access to the facility. "Miss Chang has volunteered to do this and collect as much information as she can," I said, "She will be completely exposed in this mission with no backup. If she is captured or stopped we only hope she will be kept there so that she can be part of the rescue plan."

Bob and I had drawn a map and a couple of pictures of what we saw during our visit to the Tianjin facility. We could only imagine what was inside. We hoped Hyacinth would clear up that part of the picture. We asked the Seal team to take as much time as needed to plan the attack.

The aircraft carrier Enterprise was in the Bohai Gulf and would be our support and evacuation route. Once we had the scientific group in hand and secured a landing area, the choppers would come and get us, hugging the coast and the treetops. Hopefully, the pickup would be accomplished before anyone noticed.

Hardwick and his Seal team were huddled in deep conversation. All of the members were participating as equals. That is the beauty of the team. They work together and listen to everyone regardless of rank. As they were conferencing, I told Hyacinth, "You better get to your room and get some rest. You have a long day ahead of you. You have got to be on your toes tomorrow. Let's have breakfast at 8 AM and go over last-minute details. If anything comes out of this meeting that will affect you I will tell you about it then." She nodded and said, "Goodnight" to everyone and kissed me on the cheek.

I don't think an eyeball in the room missed the kiss. That was a good shot in the arm for my ego. The meeting continued and we stayed huddled up until about 4 AM. Then everyone stretched, had a smoke and went to their rooms to rest and get ready. We thought our plan would go into motion about 7 PM. That would be just after sundown.

Luke came over to me and said, "It looks like everything is under control. I will coordinate with the Enterprise. If all goes well I will be on one of the choppers to pick you up. Robby, I hope we can depend on Miss Chang. She is the key to success in this plan." I reiterated, "I am confident she is with us." "OK then, I will join you for breakfast with Miss Chang in a few hours. See you then." Luke shook a couple of hands and left the room. As the meeting was breaking up I went over to Andrew and thanked him for joining us. He said, "It is more than my pleasure to get these scientists back home. I am happy you invited me."

CHAPTER 34
THE TEST WAS PAINFUL

Rabinovich claimed that he needed more time to make some of the equipment fit better. The electronics was a mess of wires that had to be harnessed once they were all hooked up. While Rabinovich and his team pressed on, the others headed for bed, to resume at 6 AM.

After a restless sleep the next day couldn't come quickly enough. Lovering's words and the realization of what they were doing had left the others uneasy and conscience stricken. The only thing the group wanted to do now was finish the test and go home – if REC, Ltd. would live up to their agreement and let them go home. The commissary was busy at 4 AM and people started drifting into the lab as soon as they had some hot food and coffee in their stomachs.

Lovering was set up in the conference part of the lab making notes on a white flip chart on an easel. The key scientists were present, as was Tsung. Lovering set the stage for testing the PTHEL. "The first experiment," he said, "Will be set at 25 meters. At 25 meters we will flash the PTHEL in the face of a couple of white mice. The lab technicians will film the action with their Bolex 16mm movie camera and record their observations into a tape-recording machine. Thermal and brightness meter recordings will be taken at the same time. If we are satisfied with the initial results we will then go on to a one hundred meter flash. The only clear path indoors for the

100 meters set up is the driveway between the laboratory and our sleeping quarters. We have a small monkey for that experiment. If we are satisfied with our results we then will open the back doors of the hangar and organize a 200-meter flashing. It will not be necessary to use a live animal. We will take readings of thermal capacity and brightness by electronic meters. If they reach our calculated results then we can assume the flashing was successful.

Tsung spoke up, "Why not use a live subject for the 200-meter test?" Lovering answered, "I don't think that is necessary. We will have proven the results after we flash the mice and the monkey. If we get the same power results at different distances then we have proven out what the PTHEL can do. Quite frankly, it is not necessary to use any livestock if we get the right power levels. There is no need to have blinded animals running around in pain. The actual blinding of a few animals is only to satisfy the uninformed."

Tsung was not happy with that answer. He thought Lovering was talking down to him – he was the "uninformed." Tsung also knew it would be fruitless to argue the point at the conference table. He would take this matter into his own hands and have the "proper" results he felt REC, Ltd. would want to see.

Rabinovich was putting on the finishing touches as the entire lab staff stood behind the weapon waiting to see the results. Rabinovitch had one of his assistants shoulder the weapon to get a good feel of it before he hooked up the electronics. The PTHEL weighed about forty-five pounds and the sculptured shoulder position in combination with the hand grips made it feel comfortably balanced without any pitching or yawing. The assistant nodded that he was ready. Rabinovitch hooked up the electrical wiring and turned on the weapon and it came alive. The screen for the laser measuring site worked like a weapons controller in a jet fighter plane. It turned red and beeped when it locked onto a target.

Twenty-five meters away was an X marked on a white board with a number of probes on it. The assistant locked on the board and fired the PTHEL. There was a ruby-colored flash and two assistants got busy reading the output of their meters. They looked back with smiles and gave thumbs-up. A cheer rose from the crowd.

Rabinovich told his assistant to flash the PTHEL five more times in rapid sequence. Five flashes on the X appeared. Again, the team reading the probe information gave thumbs-up. Everyone seemed to start talking at once. They were ecstatic with the results. Imagine, a breadboard working right out of the box with no problems. In putting this together Rabinovitch and his team had done a remarkable job.

Rabinovich took the weapon off his assistant's shoulder and settled it on his own. He gave a signal to the meter reading team and they put a cage in the place of the X. The cage held two white mice. Rabinovitch aimed at the cage with his LASER measuring eyepiece. When it turned red and beeped he fired. Just then one of the mice turned away from the front of the cage. The ruby colored flash hit the mouse on its rump and it jumped from the heat of the flash.

The other mouse was facing the PTHEL directly. One of the assistants was talking into a tape recorder while the other was taking readings. The mouse that was hit head on suddenly was banging against the cage wall with its nose. The assistant then changed the mouse's direction to the side. It ran full force into the sidewall. The mouse was most definitely blind. The other mouse showed no ill effects from being hit in the rump. It still had its eyesight.

The measuring team came back to where Rabinovitch was standing and reported. Rabinovitch smiled and proudly said to all, "The initial indication is that the PTHEL test at 25 meters is a complete success." There was a loud cheer, "Hip, hip, hooray – hip, hip, hooray." "It will take us about a half an hour to set up for the 100-meter test. If I can use a couple of the lab specialists to assist we will be able to move right along. Everyone moved forward to help. No one wanted to be left out.

Lovering sat to one side of the group and was observing. He noticed Tsung sitting and staring as well with a smile on his face. Lovering thought, I wonder if that smile is of accomplishing something or is it a sly smile indicating that we should be very careful. I am worried about this guy. I trust him as far as I can throw him.

Everyone was now in the driveway. To make the 100-meter distance the back doors had to be opened. The crowd was too large at the other end and took some of the space away – about 20 meters. The same procedure that was done for the 25-meter test was now being repeated for the 100-meter test. The assistant who originally shouldered the weapon was again handling it. His screen went red, beeped and he fired. The test team at the other end gave, thumbs-down signal and shook their heads. Everyone seemed to stop breathing until they could figure out what was wrong. The team walked solemnly to the firing position and reported.

Lovering was called over to Rabinovich and was told, "The brightness had considerably fallen off. The heat level was as expected." Lovering said, "This is an unforgiving weapon. It has a limited depth of field in the optical path. In the future we will have to add a scale and move the elements of the illuminator to be able to adjust to the distance or range. In the meantime I will make a temporary adjustment that should do the job." Everyone waited patiently as Lovering and Kawakami opened the rear of the PTHEL and made an adjustment.

The measuring team went back to the other end of the 100-meter course. The weapon was shouldered again and flashed again. This time the measuring team gave thumbs-up. In fact, one of the team members ran back and said, "The brightness recorded had more lumens then the original 25-meter test. The sequential test was now performed and they received the thumbs-up signal from the measuring team.

Everyone hushed as a cute monkey, the kind you would see with an organ grinder on the street, was now being put in position. The attendant gave the monkey a banana to demonstrate that he would reach for it, take it out of the attendant's hand and eat it. If you reached in again to attempt to take it away he would scream. He even nipped at the hand in the cage.

Rabinovitch had again shouldered the weapon. He aimed the measuring device and the screen turned red and beeped. He fired the weapon. The monkey yelped and dropped the half-eaten banana and sat motionless. The attendant put his hand in the cage with no reaction from the monkey. He snapped his fingers and brought his hand close to the monkey's face with no reaction. He then brought another banana into the cage and then tried a piece of sugar – no reaction.

The monkey was blind. This time the crowd watching was quiet. The mice were laboratory animals that they worked with all the time. A monkey on the other hand is closer to a house pet or a person. The blinding of the monkey had a somber effect on the group. A number of the assistants left the area to go to the community sitting area or their sleeping quarters. There was no discussion, just unnatural silence. The scientists were in deep thought when someone shouted that the 200-meter test was ready.

Lovering had worked his magic with the PHTEL this time before the flashing. He knew what to expect and made the necessary adjustments. Much to everyone's surprise the weapon worked almost exactly to the calculated specifications. The test was declared a complete success. Rabinovich was about to take the PTHEL off his shoulder when Tsung asked to try the weapon. Rabinovich saw nothing wrong with that and gave him a rundown on how to fire the weapon. Tsung then said he would like the electronics turned on so he could get the full feeling and understanding of how the weapon worked.

The measuring team went to their position to record the results. Tsung captured the target, the screen turned red, beeped and he fired. He didn't quite hit the X but a corner of the target recorded the flash. The team signaled thumbs-up. Just at that point the security guards dragged a man wearing handcuffs to the target area. They sat the man down in a chair in the place where the target had been.

Tsung started up the laser measuring system and Rabinovitch pushed the PTHEL aside and shouted, "Imbecile, are you out of your mind, you will blind the man." "That is exactly what I am trying to do, doctor. That piece of dung raped a young girl and was given a sentence of death. I thought we would first use him as a guinea pig to see if this weapon works on humans." Tsung said this without taking the PTHEL off his shoulder and had a mischievous smile plastered on his face.

Rabinovich stammered, "I, I assure you it works." "I know that it works, Doctor Rabinovich but our benefactors would like to see results including a human test." Before anyone could say anything Tsung saw the screen turn red and beep. He quickly fired and almost instantly there was a shout from the subject and a gasp from the crowd of observers.

The man immediately put his hands to his face and shouted in Chinese, "I can't see, it hurts, I can't see." The guards dragged the shouting and weeping man away from the target area to a secure location so the scientists couldn't see nor hear him. Tsung intended to have a medical team confirm the results. That, he thought, would be his victory over Howard Lovering.

Howard was in the lounge area still upset about the monkey, when he heard a commotion. He saw what was going on and started running to try to stop Tsung. He wasn't even close. After the blinding of the man Howard fell to the floor on one knee and upchucked. He realized the little bastard had planned this from the very beginning. Voss and Kawakami came to Lovering, helped him up and got him to his room.

CHAPTER 35
THE PLAN GOES INTO ACTION

It was 8 o'clock in the morning and Albert, Hyacinth and I were having an animated discussion over breakfast. Hyacinth seemed to have gotten out of her depression and anger. She appeared resigned to taking the course of action we had discussed. She was still wearing her sunglasses, not so much for the bruises, she said, but any bright light hurt her eyes.

Albert briefed her on what she was to look for during her visit. "We need to know how many people are involved to be rescued. We understand that there are a number of assistants and lab technicians involved. We need to know how many guards are in the area and if they are armed. Is everyone on radio or is there a central point that controls the area where the guards report to?

"Any indication of how the space is being used will be most helpful. Where are the sleeping areas and the laboratory areas? Understanding the layout will take away any surprises for our Seal team. Is there an arsenal in the area? What kinds of weapons are guards carrying? Finally, we need to know how far along they are with the weapon they are designing. If you can see the weapon and learn of its location, that would be wonderful. If they only have it in pieces, where in the building are they being stored so we can destroy them.

"Miss Chang, I know this is a lot of information to throw at you. I don't want you to be overwhelmed by it. Anything you can get for us is more then we have at this moment. Just be yourself and be a good observer. I am sure if you do your information will be accurate and will help us immeasurably. Our goal is to remove the science team in one group, capture or destroy the weapon and get in and out of the area before we raise all kinds of alarms."

It was approaching 9 AM and Hyacinth stood up, which brought us to our feet, and she shook hands with Luke Albert and kissed me on the check. She said, "When I get back I will have the information you require. If I am detained, for any reason, you will not hear from me. I will try to stay in the area so I can be part of your capture but if there is little hope for that, Robert, I do not expect you to send an army after me. The last thing I want is to start a war or have people killed because of me." She turned and walked out without looking back. Luke said, "You are right, Robert, I now feel she is with us. I hope she can make it back to us."

Hyacinth had a Mercedes 500 and a driver waiting for her. She was dressed in a white linen pants suit and had black touches that were accentuated by a beautiful black pearl necklace. She looked like she was a fashion model by the way she carried herself and the way she wore her clothing. On one arm she carried her jacket and in the other hand she was holding a black leather briefcase that also served as her pocketbook.

As Hyacinth's driver pulled out, one of the Seal team members pulled out his Chevrolet and kept pace about three cars behind. Another team member accompanied the Seal driver. This idea was to track Hyacinth Chang and her schedule. The team members had specific instructions not to expose their cover under any circumstances. They were to be just observers. Hyacinth arrived at the gated front entrance. The Seal team drove off the road behind some scrub pines and had a straight-on view of the airfield's landing strip and the entrances of a few of the buildings. Hyacinth's car was kept waiting at the gate as a security guard called for clearance. Finally the guard walked over to the Mercedes and pointed to the control tower building. The Mercedes took off and parked in front of one of the doors. Hyacinth got out, looked around and went into the building.

About twenty minutes later she emerged with two people talking to her and pointing the way to one of the hangars. They were walking at a brisk pace and the two men seem to be running to keep up with Hyacinth's long strides. They entered the hangar across the landing strip that the Seal team recognized as the most likely target to house the scientists. The razor wire must have been double what it was on the other buildings. The team started to locate the television cameras and the guards. They carefully watched where the guards patrolled and how long it took them to walk their posts.

Hyacinth was led into the alcove of the entrance to the hangar. A guard stopped them and asked to see identification from everyone. The two Chinese men showed their work passes and Hyacinth showed her passport. The guard indicated for them to wait and went inside to make a telephone call. His call was to Tsung, who soon arrived at the front door. He said to the Chinese men that they didn't have the clearance to enter the building. They bowed and said, "Miss Chang, if you wish, please visit us before you leave," and walked back to the control tower.

Hyacinth Chang introduced herself and saw she had captivated Tsung. He's a lech, she thought. He can't take his eyes off of my breasts. This will work out fine with this little prick. Tsung said, "To what do we owe a visit to our humble facility by the daughter of Madame Chang?" He's done his homework, she thought - she never declared whom she worked for or with. Maybe he is not so stupid.

"Mr. Tsung, you obviously know that I am the president of Chang Industries. We started and support Mei Cao Lin, the broker of record with REC, Ltd. My mother and I were curious to find out what level of progress was being made on the project because we are in the middle of our budgetary planning. We would like to know if we will be able to list any income this year from the project or will we still have to carry this on our books as a future investment. The income from this project can have an abnormal effect on our budget planning and that is why we decided to take a first-hand look."

"Miss Chang, I was not informed of your visit so I will have to check it out before I can let you inside. None of our benefactors has visited the project in person. I have been sending reports on a weekly basis and that seems to have satisfied everyone regarding progress." "The reports are quite adequate," she lied. She had never seen a report on the project. "However, if we are going to have something like one hundred million dollars to contend with in our P&L then we felt it was important to actually see what is going on. Are we dealing with reality or are we just doing research?"

Tsung smiled, "Oh, we are dealing with reality. My next report will show that we tested the weapon successfully. In fact, I wish to show you the results. I am sure no one will have any difficulty with that. If you don't mind me asking, how long are you planning to remain in Beijing?" "Today and tomorrow, then I have to get back in Hong Kong for a board meeting." "I will talk to my contacts at REC, Ltd. and maybe you can come again tomorrow. By then I am sure we will clear everything up for your visit. In the meantime please come with me and I will show you something to tell you that your trip was not wasted."

They entered the hangar and Hyacinth realized that they were walking along a driveway that ran the length of the 100-meter structure. The driveway was at least 16 meters wide, big enough for trucks to drive through, she thought. There was a wall on each side of the driveway, front hangar door to back hangar door. Tsung couldn't take his eyes off of Hyacinth. He could see that his guest was puzzled.

He was confident everything was going to be approved and felt it was right to give her some information. "On the left is the laboratory and machine shop. On the right is where we house everyone on the project for sleeping and entertainment, and at the front end there is a complete twenty-four hour commissary." "It is a very large area for such a small number of men." Tsung answered "We have a working crew of about seventeen people but when you consider the lab equipment, machinery, storage and security this facility is just the right size."

They were halfway through the hangar, when suddenly a door on the right opened and three lab-coated men in deep conversation walked across to the laboratory doors. When the scientists made their unexpected entrance, the guards at the doors holding AK-47 machine pistols stepped into the driveway and asked Hyacinth to turn around. Tsung said, "Just a precaution, Miss Chang." In the meantime it gave Tsung an opportunity to study her figure. As soon as the white-coated men closed the laboratory door Chang and Tsung continued their walk.

When they reached the other end of the hangar they walked into a security office that had one man seated at a desk. Tsung walked over to a man who was sitting on a bench and handcuffed to it. The man had obviously been crying and was in pain. Because of the way his hands were manacled he couldn't bring them to touch his face. The man was distraught.

Tsung turned to Hyacinth and whispered, "Watch carefully." He lit a cigarette and put the flame of the match in front of the man and got no reaction. Then he took the cigarette with the man starring straight ahead, and brought the cigarette to within a quarter of an inch of the man's eye. There was still no reaction. The eye kept staring; it did not follow the cigarette as Tsung moved it from side to side.

Tsung turned away from the man and faced Hyacinth, "The man is completely blind. We tested the PTHEL weapon this morning and he was used as a guinea pig. He is the first human to prove that our weapon was completely successful. He was blinded at 200 meters. It happened so fast I almost didn't recognize that I shot the PTHEL"

Hyacinth turned away, not wanting to say anything but blurted out, "How awful." Tsung put his arm around her and said, "Make no mind of him. He is scum. He was sentenced to death because of raping a fourteen-year-old girl. He is getting what he deserves. Maybe we will let him die in a couple of days." Hyacinth stepped away and out of Tsung grasp.

She had seen enough. All she wanted to do was get out of the building and away from this insane lecher. She said, "I think I will take my leave now and thank you Mr. Tsung for your hospitality and assistance." "Where shall I contact you, what hotel are you staying at?" "I am staying with friends," she lied. "Here is my business card; it has the telephone number of my Beijing office. If I am not in they know how to reach me. Again, thank you for a most enlightening tour."

They walked the length of the driveway back to the front doors in silence. Tsung became wary because she seemed not to have any interest in seeing anything more and he had a desire to see her. He rationalized that he had proven that the weapon existed and that was enough to satisfy her curiosity to explain her bookkeeping budgetary problems. Tsung asked, "Will I see you tomorrow assuming I will get the clearances from REC, Ltd?" "I think I have seen enough. I will tell my mother that we should plan on additional revenue at the end of this fiscal year. I am sure that will make her very happy."

I was right, Tsung thought. However, I just can't let her leave. I have to entice her to go to dinner with me or at least have a drink. I have never seen a figure like this woman's. She is magnificent. Small waist, beautiful hips, great ass and breasts that you could die in. He ventured further, "Is there any chance that I can take you to dinner?" "I'm sorry I am having dinner with friends."

Hyacinth realized she had to play along to some degree in order to delay him from checking her out. "However," she said, "I come to Beijing at least once and sometimes twice a month. Maybe we can have a drink one of those times." Tsung smiled, "Here is my card and I have written my direct number on it. I will await your call." Hyacinth smiled, and walked out of the hangar to her car and driver.

She ordered the driver to take his time exiting the facility. Tsung was watching and was hoping Hyacinth Chang would look out the back window. She didn't. The Seal team watched her get into her car then jumped into theirs. This time they stayed far back to see if anyone was following her. Everything seemed to be moving right along and the Seal team relaxed, but kept a sharp eye on the road and the Mercedes of Hyacinth Chang.

CHAPTER 36
A FINAL DIAGNOSIS

Tsung was to check in with REC, Ltd. in a couple of hours. He was so sure of Miss Chang and Chang Industries that he figured he could wait to report her visit at that time. He had stars in his eyes concerning Hyacinth Chang. By not reporting on Hyacinth Chang immediately he had made a mistake that would cost him his life. He had broken a cardinal rule of the organization. "All security issues are to be reported immediately and the course of action will be decided by REC, Ltd. There will be no deviation from this rule."

Tsung was anxiously waiting for the medical team to arrive and evaluate the prisoner blinded by the PTHEL. He wanted to be able to make a complete report of unquestionable success to REC, Ltd. He wanted to have this ready before he was to officially report in. Tsung was pacing in the hangar when the doctor arrived. He was an eye specialist from a nearby hospital.

The doctor was immediately taken to the security room to perform his examination. The doctor looked into the prisoner's eyes not once but several times. It was as if he couldn't believe what he was seeing. He looked up and said, "When and how did this happen? There is so much blood in this man's eyes that he will never see again. There is no way to correct what has happened to his eyes. He is completely and irrevocably blind."

Tsung was almost gleeful. He was smiling when he said to the doctor, "Thank you for coming on such short notice. You will be very well rewarded when you turn in your written report. Please do it as quickly as possible. Thank you again, doctor." The doctor was confused, "Shouldn't we be attending to this patient? I would like to get him to my hospital to ease his pain." "No, that will not be necessary. We will make him comfortable here. We have a complete medical facility for our employees," Tsung lied. The doctor was uncertain but was guided back to his vehicle and left the facility.

Hyacinth made it back to the Beijing Hotel by 2 PM, pulled up in the driveway and quickly walked over to the bank of telephones to call my room. "I have returned and I must report to you what I learned." There was urgency in her voice and I said, "Let's meet in the lounge on the top floor. I will bring Albert, Claypool and Hardwick." All four had been together all morning planning the raid. They decided it was better to be seen publicly as if they had no special plans afoot.

We found a quiet corner of the lounge. The area was relatively empty; it was early in the afternoon and most of the hotel guests were with their business contacts outside the building. Hyacinth related what she had observed from the moment she entered the security gate to the REC, Ltd. facility. Hardwick was taking copious notes, which he would later pass on to his team. Hyacinth had a keen eye for detail. She went from describing the entrance to the driveway to the white lab coats to the weapons the guards carried and to the security room where the blinded prisoner was kept. She said, "Tsung used the letters PTHEL for the weapon. I have no idea what that means but that was the name of the weapon that blinded the poor man." I said, "L obviously stands for laser." Andrew Hardwick whistled and said, "Personal Tactical High Energy Laser – PTHEL. That is Buck Rodgers stuff. Our research people have been working unsuccessfully on something like that for years. I can't believe that they actually built one. That is one hell of an accomplishment."

Hyacinth said, "Believe it. The man was completely blind, even when Tsung put a cigarette almost in his eye. There was no recognition. He was a small man. Tsung said he was a guinea pig and that he was a rapist and was sentenced to die. My mother had me hit in the eyes because she knew what she was building. She gave me a warning that scared me out of my wits. My mother will blind me when she learns that I have worked against her and the family's interest."

"Hold on," I said. "No one is doing anything to anyone yet. First she has to find you and Luke will take care of that. You will go aboard the Enterprise with him for safekeeping. Let's take it moment by moment. We will deal with your mother after we have successfully brought the scientists to the aircraft carrier. Trust me, we will make a proper reconciliation or make it impossible for her to reach you."

Luke calmly said, "Miss Chang, listen to Robert. My contacts and forces will stand behind you after we are successful this evening. Your information has been invaluable. It is just what we needed." "But, I never got inside of the laboratory. I have failed you. You are still going in without knowing what is in there. I am afraid your people will get hurt."

"Don't worry, Miss Chang; because of you we now know we need transportation for fifteen to eighteen scientists plus our twelve men. Each scientist will be recognizable by his white coat. The guards do not have radios they go to a centralized area where they most likely keep their weapons stored. We can easily deal with the weapons they are carrying. They probably only have one clip of ammunition. We can also assume that there might be one or two guards inside the laboratory besides the two at each door.

"The same should hold true for the sleeping quarters. The commissary will not have a posted guard because it is close to the front door and that would be unnecessary double coverage. We know where the laboratory is and where the sleeping quarters are. We can estimate what type of machinery is in the lab from what we know of the scientists who have been abducted. We will guess at the rest.

"Finally, we now know that they have built at least one prototype of the PTHEL weapon. The weapon will be in the laboratory and the scientists can point it out to us. So you see Miss Chang, you were a great help to us. This mission now has a chance of success because of you. Now, all we have to do is pull it together and execute the plan properly."

Tsung was sitting in his office dreaming about his chances with Hyacinth Chang when the telephone rang. He picked it up after one ring. It was his REC control contact. Tsung excitedly reported in Chinese on the test of the PTHEL. He ended his test report explaining the results of the human test. His control sounded impressed but Tsung couldn't tell for sure.

Control asked, "What are the scientists currently doing?" "They are writing their reports, analyzing their results and making changes for the weapon to be more efficient and easier to use. They then might choose to build another one to show the results of the upgrade. Then I would imagine they would start the manufacturing drawings for a small machine shop run."

"After these weapons were thoroughly tested they would look to prepare the paperwork for larger manufacturing runs. Special equipment will have to be built on a larger scale." Control sounded bored, "How much longer do you estimate?"

203

"I'm not sure, but, it probably can be accomplished in and another three weeks." Control said, "That will take them over the length of their contract. This might cause a problem." Tsung confidently said, "Do not to fear, I am very friendly with the scientists and there is nothing they wouldn't do for me." "How charming," control said. "I would like your report on how you would go about this. I am sure the board of directors will be happy to see the reports."

The conversation was about to end when Tsung requested the floor to tell about a visitor who showed up seeking to view what progress was being made. She was in the planning stages of her annual budget and wanted to know how reliable her information was. Her name was Hyacinth Chang, the daughter of Madame Chang. "What did you show her?" He explained and control blurted out "Idiot. Stupid idiot! You were supposed to call immediately, what is the matter with you - you fool."

Tsung protested, "But Sir, she is Madame Chang's daughter and one of the benefactors of the project. How could it be wrong to visit the project?" Control, patient but agitated; asked Tsung if any of the benefactors have ever showed up at the facility unannounced. Tsung could only meekly reply "No."

"I also mention that Madame Chang is a member of the board but the daughter has never attended a meeting nor has been copied on any of the progress reports through my office. Officially, we have no idea who she is. Finally, our association is with Mei Cao Lin, Ltd., not Chang Industries. You have made a terrible mistake and the board will decide what to do with you." "Yes sir; I await your decision. I hope the board will remember how active and successful the project is." "Stop being a house lawyer, Tsung. There is no need to politicize your participation in the project. I am sure the board will consider what you have accomplished. Now I have to call Madame Chang to see if she has authorized this visit." Control hung up and Tsung sat in his desk chair staring into space. He was angry that Hyacinth Chang had played him for a fool. It was a terrible loss of face. "I'll get even with that bitch," he said out loud. "She will know who Inouye Tsung is when I get through with her."

CHAPTER 37
THE RAID

Luke and Hyacinth left for Beijing Airport to pick up a carrier helicopter to take them to the Enterprise. Bob, Andrew and I met with the Seal team again and reviewed the plan. Three rented automobiles would transport the team and our gear to the site. Each man carried his own weapons in a black duffle bag.

The team's equipment and clothing were set up for a nighttime raid. It was now 6 PM, and our three rented cars were in a loose convoy on the highway from Beijing to Tianjin. We were not closely following one another, just trying to keep each other in sight. We arrived about an hour and three quarters later at the overlook where the Seal team observed Hyacinth Chang's entrance to the REC facility.

The first course of business was to let a helium balloon go up about 250 feet. This assured that our communications was operational among the twelve-man team and the Enterprise. The balloon worked like a base similar to the new wireless telephones that we were seeing for the first time in AT&T stores. We all checked our headsets and I checked in with the Enterprise. "We're receiving - five-by-five," I was happy to hear.

We started our deployment plan. It was getting dark and I felt we were already behind schedule. One car went around to the back of the hangar we were going to hit. This was the spot where Bob and I made our original observations. We were confident that none of the other buildings was guarded or concerned with security. The security concentration was on the one hangar with a guard at the main gate. There were unarmed security guards in the control tower for aircraft landings. We didn't feel that they posed any kind of threat.

The back hangar team - four Seals - had to take out the observer in the peak of the building, using a sniper rifle that had a scope and a silencer attached. The other three Seals were to quietly take out the two guards using silencers on their weapons, and then make a path through the razor wire. The team would then signal they were ready. Bob, Andrew and I were to go up to the front gate, hit the security guard and drive to the front of the hangar and take out the two guards.

The back team's main assignment was to neutralize the security office with its television cameras and weapon storage. The third car would follow us in after the gate was secured and the two front guards were down. Six Seals would crash the front doors and take out the two inside guards. Andrew and I, plus three Seals would then go into the laboratory. Bob, with two Seals, would check out the commissary and sleeping quarters.

Timing was important. The back team had to get to the security office the same time we were barging through the front of the hangar. After the back hangar guards were down, cutting through all of that razor wire would be a bear. Earlier in the day, on our buying spree on the streets in Beijing, we had purchased old gym mats from a used equipment and clothing dealer. These mats would be useful – we'd lay them over the wire and scamper over it.

Everyone was in position and it was time to go. I drove the car to the security gate and as we had observed there was only one guard. He came over to the car and Andrew summarily shot him twice in the chest with his silencer-equipped 9mm Beretta. We drove to the front of the hangar where two guards were standing and smoking. As they saw us approaching they threw away their cigarettes and grabbed their weapons and came to attention. They had no idea who we were but assumed we were friendly - after all, we drove in after stopping at the front gate. Bob and Andrew stepped out of the car and shot them both. They never knew what hit them.

The backup car with the remainder of the Seals drove up and unloaded. We positioned ourselves to crash in the front doors. We were waiting for the signal from the back hangar team. A few minutes passed and we were getting antsy. Finally we got the green light. We started to make a move when the front door suddenly opened and one of the inside guards started walking out; he never made a second step. The other inside guard saw his comrade go down and hit the alarm. Bright lights flashed and a loud horn sounded. A Seal rushed inside, killed the guard and cut the alarm wires. The alarm went dead and the emergency lights went to standby. But it had done its damage, warning everyone inside.

The commissary employees ducked behind the counters and hit the floor. There were two people in white lab coats eating and they were staring, stunned, at the black-clothed men with guns. A Seal directed the two lab assistants to the front door. The commissary was secured. The back door team had quietly walked in the open rear door killed the one man on duty and secured the office.

The driveway through the hangar was empty - just a few bicycles against the walls. We clung to the walls and advanced to the doors in the middle of the hangar. Bob's team opened the doors to the sleeping quarters and was met with a burst of bullets over their heads. We opened the doors to the lab and crawled in. There was no firing. Walter Voss saw us and stood up, a shot rang out and Voss went down. The shot came from the machine shop area in the back of the hangar. A couple of Seals attempted to go forward after the shooter by crawling against the wall but were fired upon from another position and were stopped.

We seemed to be stalemated. I could hear firing across the hallway. Bob was obviously hot and heavy in a fight. We had a couple of clever guards in good positions and had to either throw a grenade or make some advance with covering fire. The Seals and I decided on the covering fire rather than blowing something up, which might cause a chain reaction.

While we were tied down, Rabinovich saw he had a clear view of the guard who had fired at Voss. At the time of the break-in, he was adjusting the illumination system for the PTHEL with Lovering. Rabinovitch shouldered the PTHEL and targeted his prey and when the screen turned red and beeped he fired, hitting the guard between his eyes. The guard stood up screaming with his hands over his eyes and was immediately shot and killed. At that very moment, Lovering stood up to see the results and I saw him standing. I made a mad dash toward him with bullets flying all around me and tackled him. We landed with a hard thud.

Lovering looked at me and said, "Robert?" "Yes, now stay down so I don't have to bring you back in a body bag to Helen, you old fool." "I don't think I can get up because I think I broke something when you tackled me." Lovering was one of the most un-athletic men I knew. He was kind of pear shaped and not very well coordinated. It didn't surprise me that he might be hurt. In the meantime the shooting heated up. I could tell that there were at least two other shooters in the room.

The Seal team advanced machine-to-machine and table-to-table. They were moving toward a guard who was making our lives miserable with an AK 47 machine pistol. There was still crossfire from the other shooter. It was very slow going when suddenly two Seals started a heavy barrage of covering fire for one of the team to make a running advance on the guard. He was firing from the hip and stitched a few bullets across the guard's chest. Everyone hit the ground.

There was one shooter left. I yelled out "Put your gun down and surrender and you will not be hurt." I had no idea if the person would understand me much less speak English. I thought we did enough killing tonight and wanted to end it. In perfect English the man replied, "I am Inouye Tsung, I represent REC, Ltd. How dare you come here and attack us. What grounds do you have to do this?" I was stunned that a well-spoken man was responding. "Cut the shit, put your hands up, drop your weapon and come out. Then we can talk about who attacked whom and on what grounds." "I am going to come out but will do so only if you show yourself first." "Not a problem. I will stand up but I want to see you immediately or you will face the consequences." There was no response.

I looked over to Andrew and said, "Get ready." I carefully started to stand up. My pistol was at the ready, a shot rang out and it felt like someone had punched me in the right shoulder. I went down and realized I was hit. Andrew and the rest of the team opened a heavy stream of fire with Andrew running toward Tsung.

Rabinovich was watching and could see the side of Tsung's face. He shouldered the PTHEL acquired the target and shot Tsung on the side of his face. Tsung's head jerked back in obvious pain and he wildly fired in the direction of Rabinovitch. A stray bullet from Tsung's pistol hit the center and lower cylinder of the PTHEL. The bullet smashed into the chemical exciter and it blew up on Rabinovich's shoulder. He was killed instantly. With the distraction of the explosion Andrew advanced quickly on Tsung's position and shot him dead. There was no more resistance.

Everybody in the lab who was hugging the floor cautiously stood up. A couple of men ran over to Voss who had taken a bullet in the right cheek. He would survive but he was bleeding profusely. One of the Seal team started a plasma bag and was cleaning the wound. I sat up leaning against a table leg while another Seal attended to my wound. My shirt was cut to expose the bullet hole, which was dressed with a sulfur powder, then bandaged. Howard struggled to his feet with the help of Kawakami and came over to me.

Kawakami looked at me in amazement and said, "Robert Schein?" He had no knowledge of my government association was astonished to see me. Howard was more concerned about my wound than his leg. The Seal who checked him out said he probably cracked his kneecap. His knee was already very swollen. We took stock of everyone and the Seal team had no losses but one man from Bob's team was wounded in the thigh.

With the building secured we called in the CH-47 Chinook helicopters. Two of them would be able to carry the entire group. The team went to the runway to light up a couple of smoke flares. People were standing outside of the control tower afraid to cross the runway to see what was going on. The control tower personnel called their managers and then the police when the smoke flares were set out. Until then they had no idea what was going on.

Howard Lovering was helped over to where Tsung was dying. Lovering, normally very compassionate, said something that was totally out of character. "I wish you could live and experience your blindness by this terrible weapon we have constructed. May you rot in hell, you miserable bastard." Tsung smiled, was about to say something and ended up staring into space, dead.

Bob came over to me, "You always have to steal the show and get the most attention. What the hell is the matter with you?" "I am fine and I love you too." Bob rubbed my head, "We were in a firefight for a couple of minutes in the other rooms but we were able to put it down quickly. None of the guards are alive. The only people left are the attendants and commissary workers." "Get everyone out of the building. All of the attendants and workers should be let go and told to get far away from the building before the choppers get here." Bob left me and started yelling for everyone to get out.

Within a couple of minutes the Chinook helicopters were landing. The team started to load the scientists and the wounded while a couple of Seals were unloading a number of knapsacks holding explosives. All fourteen scientists were loaded into the large choppers. The blinded man being held in the security area was led onboard. I was being helped out of the hangar when Luke, who had arrived on one of the choppers, came up to me with the concerned look of a father and asked Andrew how I was. I replied, "Just a shoulder wound. I'm fine." Luke grabbed my other arm and he and Andrew carried me to the helicopter.

The big Chinooks started to shudder, then slowly rose. We got up to about 200 feet and about 300 yards away when Andrew signaled his team to start the fireworks show. Pressing a button on each remote control armed them, and then the handles were pulled into position and quickly turned. With each turn an explosion occurred. A shock wave hit the helicopters as if we were flying through heavy air. We all stared in awe at the explosions.

212

The hangar was engulfed in flames that lit up the area for miles. From then on we could be targets, and the pilots hustled us to the Enterprise. When we were over water a couple of Phantom fighter jets joined us for protection. By the time we were on the Enterprise the fire trucks would be standing by helplessly watching the airplane hangar burn to the ground.

The police started to round up people in the area for questioning. They had bits and pieces of a story but the police ended the evening still not knowing what had happened. As far as they were able to determine a renegade group of Caucasian men attacked the hangar and none of the witnesses had any idea why or what the hangar's importance was.

CHAPTER 38
A QUICK RECOVERY

There are two sterile operating rooms aboard the aircraft carrier Enterprise. The Seal with the thigh wound was in one and Walter Voss was in the other. None of the wounds, including mine, was life-threatening. While I was waiting in pre-op, Howard Lovering was reviewing his 29 days in captivity. I was amazed at how everything proceeded and they were able to finish a product once they all put their heads together.

There were so many diverse backgrounds that it is a credit to everyone that they were able to focus from the very first meeting. After listening to Howard I realized he was the fulcrum and everyone depended on his leadership. "I guess everything went up in flames, drawings, experimental equipment, and the test results. If we were to try to build the PTHEL again it would be starting from scratch."

I was surprised when Howard said, "That is not quite true. Several of us were able to save our laboratory notebooks where a lot of the information is recorded. I'm not saying we would be as advanced as we were but we have the foundation to continue the work *if* we so desire. Robert, I saw the results of this weapon. We have a person in custody that was blinded by the PTHEL. I am not so sure I want to be a part of building another one." But, I mused, Lovering's scientific quest for knowledge kept him from destroying even the evil knowledge in those laboratory notebooks.

A couple of seamen medics dressed in green scrubs came into the holding area and started to wheel me into the operating room. Howard and I made eye contact and I could see that he was visibly shaken by his experience and the results of the PTHEL weapon. We smiled and he shouted, "I will be here when you wake up."

The surgeon came to my gurney and said, "I'm Commander Michael DeAngelis. My colleagues call me Doctor 'D'. I looked at the x-rays and checked your vitals. I'm sure you will come through this with no problem and should have no loss of movement of your shoulder. The bullet is lodged in the fleshy part of your shoulder just below the bone structure and did not hit any major vessels. You are very lucky. We should be able to get in and out in a matter of minutes. So if you have no questions we would like to start."

"Thank you Doc, let's get on with it." An ether mask was put over my face and I was told to count backwards from at 100. "100, 99, 98, 97, 9-" and I was out. The only thing I remember was a buzzing in my head that got louder and louder as the ether was poured on the mask.

I heard voices passing the time of day. I had a terrible headache; otherwise I didn't feel any pain. I struggled to open my eyes and the beautiful Hyacinth Chang was looking at me with a concerned expression. "I see your eyes are healed, no sunglasses." "They are on my head" and she showed me where they were. "How long was I under?" "About 45 minutes." "Yes," another voice said and I realized it was Howard's. "Here is the prize." Howard was holding a bullet that he shoved into my left hand. I picked up my arm and tried to focus on it but it was too difficult to see. I put my arm down and said, "I am very tired," closed my eyes and fell into a deep sleep.

Eighteen hours passed and I was attempting to take a shower while keeping my shoulder dressing dry. Doing this on a naval vessel is anything but easy. I got dressed and found my way to the officer's mess. I walked in and was warmly greeted by several of the scientists we had rescued, Luke Albert, Bob Claypool and Hyacinth Chang. Andrew Hardwick and his Seal team had orders elsewhere in the Pacific and had already left the Enterprise.

The four of us sat together and Luke spoke: "Each of the scientists has been debriefed and we have copies of the laboratory log books that were brought with them. Dr. Voss is progressing slowly. He will require at least two more surgeries to repair his teeth and some plastic surgery to restore a part of his check. Dr. Lovering is wearing a brace that immobilizes his knee and with a little rest and therapy he should regain his mobility. The Seal who was hurt had some difficulty because the bullet went completely through his thigh and hit a number of blood vessels that required work by the surgeons. He will also make a complete recovery. Finally, Robby, you are expected to make a full recovery. How do you feel?" "No problem. I am ready to go to work." "Can't keep a good man down," Bob needled me with a smile.

Luke continued, "The mission is considered to be a success even though we were unable to save Dr. Rabinovitch and bring out the PTHEL weapon. All in all, we disposed of fifteen security guards and a Mr. Inouye Tsung. We have had a number of conversations with the man who was blinded by the PTHEL during the test and believe he is completely innocent of the trumped-up rape charges. The man actually was a security guard who opposed a ruling of Tsung's. That Tsung guy was a piece of work.

"Keeping the scientists on the Enterprise will work for a short time. They are all itching to go home. Our problem is letting then back into society. I am not sure that the REC organization won't seek some retribution by either abducting them again or killing them. They now have some very special information that I could see REC going after. It might be dangerous to just let them back on the street.

"This brings us to Miss Chang. Do you have any opinion regarding your mother and Chang industries?" This had been weighing heavily on Hyacinth's mind for several days. She paused before responding and finally said, "My mother didn't hurt me because she loved me. She ordered the beating I took because of her greed. She watched it and stopped it when she thought it had served her purposes. I don't think we can have any reconciliation. I think I have to go my own way."

"Hyacinth," I said. "I am afraid then you will not be able to compete in the market you know best. You certainly cannot go back to Hong Kong. I believe that your adopted brothers or your mother will make sure you fail or might even eliminate you. Are you sure you don't want to make the pretense of some type of reconciliation with your family?"

"No matter how you look at it, it would be a strained and difficult relationship. No one would trust anyone. I would have to be looking over my shoulder any time I went for a walk on the street. I don't even think I want to buy any time with the pretense of reconciliation. It would be a limited timeframe and a very dangerous one."

Luke then said, "Miss Chang you have been a great help to us. Without your help we might not have been able to bring the scientists out alive. I am authorized to offer you a witness protection program where I do not think your family will be able to reach you." She adamantly said, "No. I will be out in the open and I will compete with my family. I have enough money put away that I can buy my own protection and safety. This is the only way."

"I'm not sure you are doing the right thing or know what is best. But, I admire your courage. We will be going to Japan for a few days and you are welcome to join us. I do know Chief Ichiro Hiro of the Domestic Crime Agency might not like the idea of you returning to Japan but I am willing to talk to him to see if something can be arranged." (Ten years earlier Chief Hiro caught Hyacinth Chang on film assassinating a member of the Cao family.)

Hyacinth brightened at the idea, "I think that can be very useful. I can set up my company and come back to Hong Kong with a large press and public relations presentation where it would be embarrassing to Chang Industries if they took any action against me." Difficult but clever, I thought.

"One of the ship's Goony Birds [similar to a DC-3] will take us to Tokyo tomorrow at 0800. We will land at Yokosuka Naval Airbase about three hours later. We will get Robby to the base hospital for a final check out – I started to object but Luke held up his hand for me to shut up - then we are planning to check into the Okura Hotel." The meeting was over.

Bob looked at me and I said, "You are very quiet, what's up?" "I'm amazed the way you work with Luke. Everything is up front with nothing under the table. Pretty damn good for a kid." "Hey, I'm not so much younger then you." "That is true, but you *are* younger. Also, I think Miss Chang is a dead person walking. I don't see how Madame Chang can allow her to continue." "Maybe so, but you have to admire her. She has guts." "Sure, but for how long?"

CHAPTER 39
JAPAN AND A REUNION

We endured a bumpy three-hour ride in the small Goony Bird flying at about 10,000 feet from the Enterprise to Yokosuka, Japan. We couldn't easily hear one another and it was cold. We arrived at 11:30 AM and I was dropped off at the base hospital. Everyone else, Lovering, Claypool, Chang, Kawakami, Little, Kleiber and Albert was taken to Tokyo. Lovering, Little, Albert, Kleiber and I had accommodations at the Okura Hotel and the rest of our group either went home or stayed with friends.

I was out of the hospital wearing a sling on my right arm within the hour, a record I thought, and on my way to Tokyo. I couldn't wait to get to the Okura because to a regular traveler it feels like home. I needed a bath in one of their oversized tubs and some shuteye.

When I got to my room my spare bag of clothing was unpacked, neatly put in drawers and carefully hung up in the closet. I went over to the window and poured myself a tall Chivas and water over a little ice. I took a long pull of Chivas, a deep breath and exhaled. I was finally starting to relax.

No one was bothering me and there were no messages, so I decided, now was the best time for an extended hot bath. After about fifteen minutes I could feel my muscles letting go, and I almost feel asleep in the tub. When I got out I used one of the plush Okura bath towels and then decided not to get dressed but to wear the hotel's lightweight robe. I was in heaven lying on top of the bedding.

I dozed off and had a weird dream. I was watching the beautiful Hyacinth Chang undressing. It was like watching a striptease show. The music was in my head and she was slowly disrobing. Somehow there were feathers in the dream and now she was down to her garters, scant panties, and bra and high stockings. It was all happening in slow motion. I was surprised when I noticed my member starting to get interested. The dream was progressing slowly and I was entranced by watching Hyacinth Chang. I heard a knocking, I thought it was the drummer in the band, then a bell sounded and that startled me and I awoke. I sat up and realized someone was ringing the bell to my room.

I walked to door barefooted and opened it. I was shocked and speechless with what I saw. "Don't just stand their dummy, aren't you going to invite me in?" It was my wife, Debbie. "Where did you come from?" "When you got yourself shot Luke thought it would be a good idea to bring me and Helen Lovering to Japan. We arrived a few minutes ago." I put my arms out and she ran into them. Oh, she felt and smelled so good. I really missed her. This couldn't have happened at a better time.

As she was holding me Debbie realized that I was undressed under the yukata. Her hands started to stroke my back and backside as I was finding hers. The door swung shut by itself with a click, and at that very moment Deb had found my manhood. I didn't need too much encouragement. Everything started to happen faster. I pulled up her skirt and found her panties. I worked my hands under her panties and felt her wet warmth. I backed her onto the bed, pulled off her panties and mounted her. We made passionate, uninhibited love as if it were the first time we had seen each other. I didn't realize how much I missed her.

We were lying in bed with my left arm around her under the blankets and said, "I am so happy you came to Japan." "Thank Luke for that, he made it possible but, I have always wanted to go with you when you started visiting Japan." "We are going to have to make this a very special few days for you." We stated talking about the children when I stretched across her with my right arm and felt a sharp stabbing pain in my shoulder that took my breath away.

I had forgotten about my gunshot wound and it decided to remind me. Debbie became very solicitous. She jumped up and asked, "What can I do?" "Nothing, nothing," I whispered, "I just moved too quickly in the wrong direction. Normally I hardly feel that the wound is there. I forgot."

We called for Debbie's bag, she had told the bellhop to hold it until she called so that we could have an uninterrupted reunion. My wife is a smart lady, I thought. She unpacked and we got dressed for dinner talking about Marc, Rebecca and Andrew. I was wearing a dark blue sports jacket, gray slacks, red tie and cream-colored sling for my right arm. Debbie wore a form fitting black dress with a white pearl necklace and pearl broach. I had brought the pearls home on a previous trip. She looked lovely.

We went to the Starlight Lounge and were greeted by Helen and Howard Lovering, Alasdair Little, Horst Kleiber and Luke Albert. We were in a corner of the lounge looking out of the all-glass wall of windows. Debbie pointed out several of buildings that had large electric numbers on them. I explained, "I am told that a wealthy Japanese surgeon owns those buildings and the electric numbers was his way of enjoying his prestige and community recognition."

Kleiber and Little said that they would be going home the next day and wanted to thank Luke and me for rescuing them. They had hoped to treat us to dinner in the famous teppan yaki style restaurant downstairs. We agreed and Little added, "One more guest will be arriving and then we will go to the restaurant." I made no special note of who the guest was and continued to participate in the conversation.

The beautiful Hyacinth Chang stepped off the elevator wearing a red satin Susie Wong dress with a high slit that showed off her long creamy, perfectly shaped legs. She was wearing red roses in her hair, pink pearls and red stiletto heels. My back was to her and I noticed everyone in our group looking up. I turned to see what had caught their attention and a kiss was planted on my cheek. I quickly stood up as everyone in the group stood. They were shaking or kissing Hyacinth's hand when she turned to me, I introduced Debbie.

There was a moment of silence. Debbie squeezed my arm in a death grip. The two ladies were sizing each other up before speaking. Finally, Hyacinth said, "How do you do, I am Hyacinth Chang; your husband has spoken of you many times. I am so happy to finally meet you." "Robert has mentioned you a number of times as well and I am happy to meet you."

The awkward moment had passed and we sat down. The tension between the two women was felt by all. It was like the two ladies were in our collective subconscious and were fighting to break out. Debbie whispered in my ear, "You never mentioned she was this beautiful. You always said pretty, but she is an incredible beauty." "She is no match to you, my dear. You are my one and only." I put my arm around her shoulder and gave her a reassuring squeeze.

As we were making pleasantries and the women were getting more into the conversation they started to test one another. If one liked something the other would take the other side. It wasn't because of any reason; it was just for the sake of trying to push the other's buttons. To some degree I was amused at what was going on. I felt it was harmless and didn't say anything. I was sure my wife could hold her own with anyone.

While this was going on I spied a short young man, with a very muscular build, who continually took glances at us while trying to be unobtrusive. The thing that disturbed me about him was that I saw he was packing a weapon by the bulge under his right arm. I caught Luke's eye and he had already noticed the man. I started to get up with Luke right after me when Hyacinth grabbed my arm and said, "He is with me, he is my bodyguard. I have hired a number of experienced young men, former military specialists, to serve as escorts and bodyguards. You might consider them the start of my private army," she smiled. This had a sobering effect on our conversation. The cutting remarks and argument, whatever it was, immediately stopped.

Alasdair Little announced "It's time for supper." We all enjoyed the steak that the chef prepared on a hot plate in front of us with the flair of a showman. We sat around the hot plate talking about the last month and the challenges each of us overcame. Helen Lovering sat next to Debbie and the two women never took their eyes off of Hyacinth Chang, who was at the other end of the table beside Luke. When Hyacinth mentioned her "private army" I think she earned the attention and respect of the ladies.

The evening ended with a lot of Suntory scotch and sake. Everyone was feeling happy and safe. All, except Hyacinth; she didn't drink very much and she kept checking to see where her guard was. She was being a gracious guest but you could

223

feel that she was like a cat ready to spring.

We all got to the lobby of the hotel. Hyacinth's Mercedes was waiting and her bodyguard was in front of the doorman in a strategic position. She said her goodbyes, came over to Debbie and me, and shook hands with Debbie saying, "We should get together for a coffee or lunch. It might prove to be interesting." I grabbed her hand, kissed it and said, "No you don't. I don't need two beautiful women discussing me. That can prove to be very embarrassing." The three of us chuckled and Hyacinth turned and left as her bodyguard preceded her.

CHAPTER 40
A MEETING ARRANGEMENT

This night at the Okura was one of the most memorable. I had my wife with me in bed and we had a romantic night not having to worry about the children or relatives hearing us. It was a freedom we haven't experienced for some time. We have got to get away more in the future.

On the way down to breakfast we met Luke and he said he had organized a meeting with Shirahama, president of NK, could I make myself available for it. "Of course I am available." "The meeting is at 11 this morning; a car will pick us up at about 10:30." "Fine, I will give Debbie some instructions where to shop and she most likely will go with Helen. No problem at all."

We enjoyed a full American breakfast. I thought it was a good precaution for Debbie to eat food she was familiar with for breakfast then she could be experimental the rest of the day. The breakfast was ample and much more then she was used to dealing with. She picked at it but I insisted that she have enough so that she need not worry the rest of the day.

Hyacinth Chang borrowed the house of a friend she had known since college at Wharton. It was a traditional spacious house with many shoji screened rooms. Since her friend, Tomoko was in the United States, married to an American businessman, she wasn't expected to visit Japan for some time. This was an ideal arrangement for Hyacinth to set up her business, organize it the way she believed it should operate before bringing it to Hong Kong.

Among her many attributes Hyacinth was a black belt, Shotokan Karate master. Karate was one of the key items in her life that gave her the confidence to stand up to her mother and other people in business like her beastly adopted brothers. To choose her private army of security guards she would question them on their abilities in martial arts. If they had experience she might even spar with them to see how accomplished they were.

She selected twelve men who would work out a schedule to protect her twenty-four hours a day. Those who she felt she trusted the most were retained to stay in one of the rooms of the house. Her protection was the most important item to take care of so that she would have a free mind to do the work she wanted to do. Her ultimate goal was to compete directly with Chang Industries, in particular with her brothers.

Hyacinth was moving along at a hectic pace when the phone rang, one of her assistants handed it to her. In Chinese the caller said "Hello, Hyacinth, this is Pi." Pi Chang was the youngest of her three brothers and the only one she had any kind of a relationship with. He was the most stable and she felt that there was some trust in him. "Well, it didn't take you long to find me. Now that you did, what do you want?"

"Calm down, sister. All I want to do is talk with you. Mother is obviously very angry over the events of the last few days and she has been asking for you." "I'll bet. What part of me would she like?" "She is sorry about your last meeting with her and would like to reconcile with you." "I'm reconciled, I am fine with it." "No, seriously, she is very unhappy with what happened." "Listen brother, she ordered her guard to hit me and he did until she stopped it. She didn't turn away; she stayed in the room until she felt I had enough. When she left, I was lying on the floor, she never sent in anyone to help me. No thank you Pi, I am reconciled."

"We need to talk. Will you meet with me? If anything do it for the sake of the company and its employees. You have a good relationship with the staff. If you have no feeling for your family, I hope you will consider them." "Wow, you are really pulling out all stops as the messenger. I have feelings for my family. They were terribly wounded with the actions of Mother. I don't have a whole lot of time, Pi. I am very busy."

"Yes, I know, you are setting up a company to compete against us." This was the first comment that really disturbed her. How in the world did they get this information so quickly? I have hardly made any telephone calls or talked to anyone about it. "All right, Pi, I'll agree to meet with you. It must be a public place, I expect you to come alone and I assume you will be unarmed." "Have you ever known me to carry a weapon?" Pi Chang was also a karate master.

There was silence on the line while Hyacinth was thinking of where to meet. Finally she said, "I will meet you under the first torii of the entrance to the Meiji Shrine. We will walk to the shrine and back and that is all the time I can spare." "Fine, what time and when?" "4:00 o'clock today, oh, and I will not come unattended. A couple of my people will be with me." "That is fine, sister. I look forward to later this afternoon." Hyacinth hung up her phone and wondered if she had made and error in arranging this meeting.

She decided it was time to go forward with her plan. She made a call to a young member of a Tong (secret society) she had met and developed a friendship with in Hong Kong. Then she placed a call to a former lover whose specialty was the Russian black market. Finally, she contacted a former member of the Japanese Yakuza who had broken away from the group and started his own Robin Hood-styled mafia. All of the people she called had no relationship with Chang Industries, her mother or Mama Cherry.

CHAPTER 41
A NEW PRODUCT LINE

Debbie and Helen went off for a day of shopping on the Ginza. Their plans were to first visit the American Arcade behind the Imperial Hilton Hotel. Then they were going to Matsuya department store to get the feel of what a Japanese family has available for their home and their wardrobe. The ladies didn't know it but Luke Albert had called upon his friend Ichiro Hiro to have his people shadow them just in case anyone from the Dragon Lady's organizations or REC, Ltd. got vindictive. It was a precaution that Chief Hiro was happy to be involved with. An American tourist killed in Japan would not do anyone any good.

The ladies were enjoying themselves going from china stalls to print stalls to jewelry stalls. The Yen (¥) was about 360 to one U.S. dollar so their money could go a long way. They visited the Hiyashi Used Kimono Shop where I purchased a wedding kimono to bring home on my first trip to Japan. She handed the owner my maichi (business card); it was immediately recognized and she received a warm greeting. The ladies were in heaven being treated to tea and good service.

Luke and I got into the black Mitsubishi and were driven to the Nippon Kogaku head office across from the Imperial Place. As we entered the building Miyahara, director of export sales, greeted us. We were taken to the fifth floor to visit with president Shirahama. Shirahama's office was large and tastefully fitted out with western-style furniture. He met us at the couch and coffee table, we all shook hands and made our usual greetings.

He was like a happy kid who wanted to tell us something and couldn't hold back. After tea and cookies we turned to business. Business for the Nikon 'F' system of photography was very good in 1962. We explained we had been trying to sell at list prices, Fair Trade, with exclusive dealerships when we were sued by a Texas photographic dealer.

Believe it or not, we happily lost the law suit. The reason was simple. Now we were able to become very competitive, open up our market without a loss of face to our current photo dealers. The loss of the suit allowed the product line to become available to any dealer who could afford to stock it. The exclusivity in our franchise was limiting our growth and now we were expanding at a rate that delighted us. We were selling a million dollars of product per month at wholesale pricing.

Shirahama was pleased as punch. Our success had made him a very successful president in the eyes of the holding company, Mitsubishi. Shirahama was allowed a seat on Mitsubishi's board of directors. Shirahama enjoyed this position because it made him a very strong leader in Nippon Kogaku. Perception of leadership is very important, particularly in Japan. I never considered him to be a strong leader. I was starting to learn that window dressing is everything, even without substance.

Shirahama picked up the telephone and said in Japanese "We are ready for the other people to join us." In walked Wakimoto and Nakano. They were carrying a tray that was covered. We all happily greeted each other and made ourselves comfortable around the coffee table that now had the covered tray on it.

Miyahara started the presentation, "Gentlemen, when Schien-san visited us, a short time ago, he brought an interesting camera with him for our people to look at. The Calypso is a self-contained underwater camera that eliminates plastic underwater housings and external unwieldy controls. We were fascinated with this camera because of its operation and the depth it could go to. It is a beautifully compact camera and we thought it would fit into our product line very nicely."

Nakano continued, "We made a complete facelift of the Calypso and corrected what we thought would be mechanical problems inside the unit's operation. Wakimoto then designed a wide-angle 28 mm lens for it that was sharper then what Calypso originally had on it. We think the new camera, now called the Nikonos, is an ideal fit for our product line and will be desirable to our customers."

They uncovered the Calypso then the new Nikonos. The Calypso was slightly smaller with a two-tone, dark gray-to-silver finish. The Nikonos was all jet black. The Nikonos looked like you wanted to grab it and start shooting. The camera could be used above and under the water. Without touching it Luke and I knew this was a winner.

Luke asked "What were the arrangements with the Cousteau organization to exclusively handle the Calypso." Miyahara said, "We made a very good donation to the Cousteau Foundation that gives us all rights and ownership of the Calypso product, all except for using the Calypso name. We now own the Nikonos and the patents involved with it. We have an obligation to supply Cousteau with the latest Nikonos equipment, free-of-charge for the foundation's research work. This is now an exclusive NK product."

I picked up the prototype and worked it. It was as smooth as silk. It felt good in my hands and had no vibration. I could see that a diver working it with gloves would have no difficulty. From my first look at the prototype my feeling was that this camera is a winner. Luke spoke and felt the same way I did. We were told it would be in production within six months and the production would not interfere with any production of Nikon system products.

Shirahama thanked us, me in particular, for bringing the Calypso to them and thanked us for our business. "May our business relationship continue for many years to come." We all stood up and shook hands on that thought. The meeting was over and we were on our way for a sushi/sashimi lunch in the busy arcade beneath the building.

CHAPTER 42
THE SCENE IS SET

At about 3 in the afternoon the ladies were shopped out and Luke and I had returned to the Okura. We all met in the Starlight lounge and decided to take it easy and relax before packing and confirming our plans to go home. Hopefully, we were all going back to a normal, quieter existence.

We all felt lucky we were able to think this way now that the events of the last month appeared to have been put to rest. Howard Lovering was still hobbling around on his bum leg but was mastering the use of his cane. He seemed to enjoy wielding his cane because he felt it gave him some sort of protection. He pretended to use it like a sword when walking on a crowded street.

He said, "My sword is my soul and clears my path to walk." I said, "Howard, please don't get too attached to the cane. Someone just might take you on and turn it against you." Very grandly he said, stabbing his cane in the air, "You need not worry; I am very fair with how I employ my sword. It is not done in anger." We all looked at him and Helen slapped him on his shoulder, "Don't worry, as soon as his kneecap is healed I will take his toy away." Everyone smiled.

Hyacinth, dressed in a black pants suit, arrived at the Meiji Shrine with two of her bodyguards. She walked to the first torii and waited under the large wooden gateway. Her adopted brother, Pi Chang, arrived about five minutes later. He was in a gray stylish suit, and appeared to have come alone. There was no special greeting or hug or kiss. There was only a slight bow with Pi smiling and pointing the way for their walk to start.

The winding path from the torii to the shrine was about 200 yards. During their walk they would pass through another torii before they were finished. At first there was little conversation. Hyacinth noticed the Japanese garden behind the gate on the left as they were walking. "Well, brother, I am here. What do you have to say?" "Sister, I plead with you to come back to Hong Kong and sit with your mother for a few minutes. I am confident that everything can be taken into account and we can continue together."

"Who is running Chang Industries?" "Mother." "Why not one of our brothers or why not you?" "Mother does not trust us as she has trusted you. She is paranoid about the leadership of Chang Industries since you have turned your back on the family." "I have not turned my back on the family. I disagreed with our involvement to build a dangerous weapon. I have not compromised any of Chang Industries' interests. I have involved myself against Mei Cao Lin and mother's decision to continue to pursue this dangerous weapon. It was a wrong decision by mother, but, when she makes up her mind there is no turning her around. I had no choice but to take matters into my own hands." "You said it yourself, Mother may be mad at you, but, Chang Industries must go on. For the good of the company you must come back."

They arrived in the courtyard area of the shrine. They walked to the watering station and took a sip of water from a wooden cup with a long handle. They clapped their hands twice and bowed, then turned toward the shrine and went inside.

After climbing the steps they saw three weddings being performed simultaneously by the brown-robed bald monks. The three brides were dressed in white kimonos with a traditional white made-up face and large white hats. The men were in black kimonos. It was very quiet while one of the monks in a rhythmic chant said the blessings. There was a small crowd of people, who made up the wedding parties, watching and praying.

Hyacinth and Pi clapped their hands together twice more, bowed and turned to walk back to the first torii. All along, as unobtrusive as possible, Hyacinth's bodyguards were close by. "I can never go back if I value my life. Mother is a very vindictive person. I do not believe she will let this go as you are trying to tell me. In fact, I don't believe you at all. I believe that you were sent here to try to bring me back anyway you could."

"Please, sister, come back with me. I will protect you." For the first time during the conversation Hyacinth lost her temper. "Foolishness, you are stupid to think you could protect me or that I would go back with you or anyone from our family. You really don't know what I have in mind and what I have to do to stay alive after going against our mother."

They were just passing the Japanese garden as Hyacinth stopped in her tracks and her brother took a few steps before he realized that she had stopped. He turned to her as a loud zipping sound, an arrow, pierced Pi Chang's chest all the way through to his back. He looked at Hyacinth with wide eyed amazement. Before he could fall one of the bodyguards caught him and held him up.

She walked up to him and put her hand on his cheek as he was saying "Why." He tried to say something else as a rivulet of blood trickled from his mouth, but Hyacinth interrupted. "You should not talk. I have given you a Samurai warrior's death. This is done only because you had the courage to come and talk to me." Pi Chang was trying to say something else but the life ran out of him in a long exhaled breath.

Hyacinth's bodyguards carried Pi Chang to the waiting car. Before Hyacinth left the spot she looked toward the Japanese garden and acknowledged the archer with a bow of her head. The archer appeared, bowed, and then quickly disappeared.

At about 3:45 PM Russian time a young man was interviewing Gregori Malenkov of the Mashpriborintorg organization regarding the trade deficit with the United States. The interview for a local university newspaper was lengthy but everything in Russia is lengthy. Malenkov thought the questions to be challenging and gave more thought to his answers then he normally would have. He didn't want to look foolish to this bright young student. In fact, he thought he might offer him a job when he graduated. The interview was over and the young man had left his office. Unbeknownst to Malenkov the student left a brown leather briefcase under the table that he used as his desk. At 4:30 PM there was an explosion in Malenkov's office that blew out the windows of the building. Malenkov, who was a director in REC, Ltd. could not be found. His body was never recovered.

At 4:15 PM China time, a young man visited the only working building in the REC, Ltd. complex in Tianjin, the control tower. He was part of the cleaning team. At 4:30 PM he walked out of the building and got as far away as he could without drawing attention to himself. At 4:40 PM there was a terrific explosion and the control tower, with about eight people inside, was leveled.

At 4 PM Japan time Mama Cherry was on the balcony of her apartment wondering if Hyacinth Chang would be foolish enough to go back to Hong Kong to see her mother. Cherry knew Madame Chang as if they were sisters. She knew Hyacinth's life was not worth much at this moment.

No one goes against Madame Lin Chang without paying the price, she thought. Mama Mei Cherry was having a cigar and enjoying the afternoon breeze on her apartment balcony, eight floors above her famous restaurant, the Copa. It would be her last smoke. From a few hundred yards away a sniper had Cherry in his sights and fired. Mama Cherry was hit in the head with a 30/30 rifle bullet, which would leave her unrecognizable to her closest friends.

At 4 PM Hong Kong time Cao was in his office, standing behind his desk and talking on the telephone. He always felt better when he was talking on his feet. A slight sound from the window caught his attention, and as he turned a 30/30 sniper's bullet went though his neck and landed in the opposite wall. Cao dropped like a rock.

At 4 PM Hong Kong time there was a board of directors meeting in the conference room of Chang Industries. Tea was brought into the room for the nine directors present. Madame Chang as chairwoman and her two adopted sons represented three votes of the assemblage. They would never vote again.

The serving team left the conference room and the meeting continued. At 4:15 a massive explosion blew out the windows of the conference room and a number of bodies were taken along the same path. The Changs' body parts would be found amid the rubble that the fire department rummaged through for two days.

By 6 PM Hyacinth Chang was dressing after taking a shower in the house that had been lent to her. He brother's body would be taken to Hong Kong in two days to be buried in the family plot. Hyacinth Chang realized that there now was no need to start a new company.

All she had to do was claim her rightful position as heir to the Chang fortune. In the short time she turned her back on the family there was no effort by the family to change any of the important documents required to take over the Chang Empire.

There was a rap at the door. The shoji screen was pulled aside and one of her maids asked if she would honor her by going into the living room area of the house. Hyacinth was puzzled. She didn't say anything but followed the maid. In the large living room, her entire staff and private army had assembled.

As she walked in everyone in the room shouted, Banzai, Banzai, Banzai! They then all sank to their knees and bowed to the floor honoring her. Her lead bodyguard stood up and said, "Madame Chang, we are here to follow you wherever you go. We commit our loyalty to you. Your direction is our direction."

Hyacinth was overwhelmed. She had never experienced anything like this. Most of the people present were Japanese. When she needed an independent staff that had no ties to her mother she hired Japanese people whom she thought she could trust. She was now very happy she did. With as steady a voice as she could muster she said, "Domo, Domo Arigato Gozaimas. (Thanks, Thank You Very Much)

They all stood and applauded. Hyacinth, with tears running down her cheeks, stepped before each of her employees and bowed, as they bowed, slightly lower, to her.

ΩPILOGUΩ

ebbie and I were back home in Glen Cove, New York. It had been a quick trip for Debbie and a very long one for me. The tedious flight home aboard our Pan American 707 jet only made the anticipation of getting home and seeing the children more exciting.

Passing the time, I thought about my last private meeting with Hyacinth Chang. When we met I looked at her and was surprised to see the changes that had taken place. Out of respect for her family she was dressed in a simple black dress, black hat and black low-heeled shoes. She had a few touches of pearls and she looked older and sad.

Hyacinth was now CEO, president and chairwoman of Chang Industries. Almost 7,000 employees worldwide awaited her every word. That responsibility weighed heavily on her. She was reserved in her conversation and seemed to have matured beyond her years overnight.

She wanted me to know that I was one of the reasons she turned and opposed her family. It didn't have anything to do with physical attraction, though she did say, "We certainly made a good-looking couple." It had to do with my intensity in looking for my friend Howard Lovering. When I visited her in Hong Kong it reaffirmed her conviction that it was wrong to continue to build the laser weapon.

She reviewed the events that had catapulted her to the

239

leadership of the company and her remaining family of one sister, aunts, uncles, cousins and hangers-on. She recounted each episode unemotionally and as factually as it was told to her. "All of the events took place within the hour of 4:00 PM, she said." In Japanese and Chinese cultures the number four is a sign of death.

Hyacinth further stated that she decided to continue to retain her personal army for fear of repercussions in Hong Kong or from China. She felt her mother had long arms that might reach her from the grave.

Finally, she said that any time I visited Hong Kong I always had a place to stay and a friend to say hello to. She got up from her side of the table and planted a firm kiss on my lips and without another word walked away without turning back.

Debbie and I were packing for yet another trip. We would be representing the TAG office at the memorial service for Harry Collins in Westminster Abbey. Harry was a famous pilot and World War II hero in England, and a grateful nation wanted to pay its respects. It was my understanding that a representative of the Queen would be present. It would be a grand sendoff in a manner the English are famous for.

After the ceremony we would spend a few days with Alasdair Little in Scotland. I was looking forward to the quiet time and to do a little fly fishing that Alasdair continually talked about.

Walter Voss had four surgeries and was expected to finally recover to the point that no one could tell what he'd gone through. Howard Lovering's knee was giving him trouble and he was resisting going to rehab sessions. He was warned that arthritis would set in and he would be able to tell the changes in the weather with a lot of pain if he didn't take care of himself. I doubted Helen would be successful in urging Howard to exercise.

Luke Albert was considering retirement. Our last mission was very successful and the deputy director was having none of the retirement nonsense. Besides, Nikon was making a lot of money and the CIA didn't want to lose its cash cow. Luke was persuaded to continue but the deputy had to give him more control. All that sounded pretty good to me. It meant that a raise was coming and I would have more freedom to launch many of the marketing programs I wanted to do.

The Nikonos camera was brought to market on schedule and was received by the diving community with open arms. It still is one of the most successful underwater cameras to be sold to the amateur.

Finally, taken from an article by the International Committee of the Red Cross November 16, 1994 Human Rights Watch Arms Project – United States – U.S. Blinding Laser Weapons - the author presents two key paragraphs:

"Can eyes be protected against lasers? Experts have tried for years to develop protective goggles, but without success. The problem is that goggles can only shield against lasers beams of known wavelengths. ..."

"Can a ban on blinding be achieved? In August 1994 thirteen countries from four continents expressed support for the prohibition on blinding as a method of warfare, with a number of other States informally backing the proposal. This support emerged within the group of government experts preparing amendments for the 1980 United Nations Convention. In September1995 a Review Conference of States Parties to the 1980 U.N. Convention was convened to consider amendments, which included a new protocol banning blinding as a method of war."

To this date, the author is not convinced that all blinding weapons have been prohibited. In a May 18, 2006 article in the *Los Angeles Times* by James Rainey the headline stated, "A Safer Weapon, With Risks." The sub-headline continued, "A laser device used in Iraq to temporarily blind drivers who get too close to troops is meant to reduce death, but also raises worries."

The story goes on to say, "The pilot project would equip thousands of M-4 rifles with the 10 1/2-inch-long weapon, which projects an intense beam of green light to "dazzle" the vision of drivers."

Further in the article it comments, "A decade ago, the experimental use of tactical laser devices by U.S. Marines in Somalia was curtailed at the last minute for 'humane reasons,' according to the New York-based Human Rights Watch, which called their use 'repugnant to the public conscience' in a 1995 report. The pentagon has canceled several programs for the stronger 'blinding' lasers, in adherence to the Geneva protocol, according to Human Rights Watch. But the group has said that even less powerful 'dazzling' lasers, similar to the one to be deployed in Iraq, can cause permanent damage."

As per the International Committee of the Red Cross – 11/16/94 statement, the author agrees - "What is essential is an informed and insistent public which deems attacks on the eyesight to be particularly cruel and unacceptable form of warfare."

ALSO BY Stuart Held

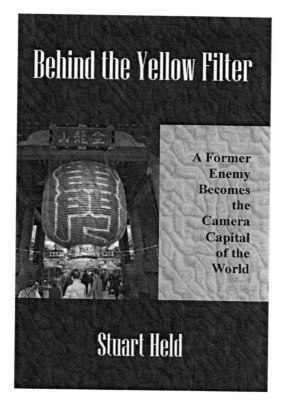

Behind the Yellow Filter

How the business of photographic equipment was accomplished in the early 1950's. The story is wrapped around the intrigue of a part stolen by the Yakuza (Japanese Mafia) from a newly developed Navy submarine periscope camera system. A young CIA agent, Robert Schein, is thrown into an international bidding war involving Red China, Russia and East Germany. Schein's 'cover' is that of a photographic distributor who imports the now popular Nikon camera system of photography. The action takes place in Japan and gives an intimate look into Japanese traditions, business methods and its people. If the reader has ever used a 35mm camera or wondered how business is accomplished in Japan then Behind The Yellow Filter is a must read for you. The author has made 27 trips to Japan and was involved in the photographic industry for over forty years. This book is an individual's look into the business and social morays of Japan.

Learn more at: www.outskirtspress.com/stuartheld

Printed in the United States
75304LV00007B/137